FALLING IN LOVE

The Sisters of Rosefield Book 4

EMMA EASTER

Falling in Love
by Emma Easter

Paperback Edition

CKN Christian Publishing
An Imprint of Wolfpack Publishing

6032 Wheat Penny Avenue
Las Vegas, NV 89122

This book is a work of fiction. Any references to historical events, real people or real places are used fictitiously. Other names, characters, places and events are products of the author's imagination, and any resemblance to actual events, places or persons, living or dead, is entirely coincidental.

Paperback ISBN: 978-1-64734-018-6
Ebook ISBN: 978-1-64119-883-7
Library of Congress Control Number: 2020933751

FALLING IN LOVE

To my parents, Joanne & Jim –
thanks for showing me a wonderful example of
true love

ONE

Zainah nervously entered the wedding reception venue, hand in hand with Faizan. She'd just arrived from the airport for her second visit to the United States. The last one, which was arranged by Faizan's friends in the government, had been an impromptu visit. It had lasted only a few hours before she'd had to get back on the private plane and return to the women's camp. Her K-1 visa had taken a few months to process, but she was finally here again. She and Faizan had just three months to get married or she would have to leave the country. It wasn't a problem as they planned to tie the knot in just a month.

She looked up at the beautiful coral and peach decorations, admiring the place. Since she and Faizan's wedding would be in just a few weeks, she doubted they would have the time to plan such an elaborate wedding. She stared at the well-dressed wedding guests and then self-consciously looked down at her plain black skirt and ruffled purple top. Faizan had picked her up at the airport, and she'd quickly changed at his house before coming here, to his sister Trisha's wedding. She felt even more self-conscious as a beautiful brunette, probably one of the ushers, came to lead them to their seats right in front of the hall.

She turned and whispered worriedly to Faizan, "I feel so underdressed." She'd worn her best outfit, but amongst these guests, it looked more like she was wearing her day dress.

He turned to her as they sat down at a table that seemed to be reserved for just the two of them. He squeezed her hand and then kissed her on the lips. "You look beautiful," he said, looking admiringly at her.

She smiled at him, feeling a little better. "Thank you for coming to pick me up at the airport even though it's your sister's wedding today." She turned away and her eyes searched for the bride. She immediately saw her, a beautiful vision in white, a few seats away. At her right side was the handsome groom. At her left was a delicate-looking blonde beauty Zainah guessed was Sienna, Faizan's other sister. She was probably Trisha's maid of honor. Sienna was dressed in a peach off-shoulder dress and she was smiling at another young man beside her.

"I'm a little nervous to meet all your sisters and their husbands," she said to Faizan.

He opened his mouth to answer but was interrupted by a booming voice asking everyone to listen. She turned and saw the groom on his feet with a microphone. He looked around the hall, waiting for everyone to quiet down. When the place was totally quiet, he began to thank everyone who'd planned the wedding and made the day a success.

He thanked all the guests for coming and then began a moving tribute to his bride that left Zainah tearful. A few other guests also had tears in their eyes.

"I still can't believe that Trisha is now my wife," he said, looking down at her, his eyes shimmering with tears. Everybody clapped as he bent to kiss her. He sat down after that and the hall immediately began to buzz again.

Zainah turned to Faizan, "That was beautiful. He really loves her."

Faizan nodded. "Frank has been in love with Trisha since they were teenagers. She only realized that she loved him some months ago. He wanted to marry her immediately, but Audrey and Sienna wouldn't hear of it. And Trisha agreed with them. If not for my sisters, they would have just done a small wedding or maybe eloped."

Zainah looked longingly at Faizan. "I wish we could also elope, but I want your sisters to share in our joy. Since they have been so kind and taken charge of most of the planning because I wasn't here, I want them to be happy and do whatever they want to do. I don't even know anything about planning a wedding, so I'll trust them to…"

Her eyes widened as a pretty blonde-haired lady who was also dressed in a peach dress and looked like Trisha, came bounding toward her, her arms wide open. Zainah had only spoken to Faizan's sisters once, but she guessed this was Audrey.

Zainah stood just as Audrey reached and embraced her tightly.

"You must be the beautiful Zainah that Faizan cannot stop talking about!" Audrey exclaimed. She pulled back from Zainah and looked her over. "My brother is crazy about you, but you know that already."

Zainah smiled. She liked Audrey already. "I love him very much too," she said. "I'm so glad to meet you, Audrey. I've also heard a lot about you and your sisters from Faizan."

"Good things, I hope," Audrey grinned and looked down at Faizan.

Zainah nodded. "Very good things." She grinned as well. "But he also said you are crazy."

Audrey laughed out loud and then shook her head as she looked at Faizan. "So, I am crazy." She turned back to Zainah. "He also has a crazy streak himself."

Faizan grinned. "No, I don't! You and Trisha are a tad insane, but that's one of the reasons I love you both." He looked at Zainah. "Sienna is the angel of the family." He looked up and chuckled. "Talk about the saint, here she comes."

Zainah turned away from Audrey and saw Sienna daintily approaching with a smile on her face. She cradled her huge belly with one hand and clutched a beaded silver purse in her other. She reached them and looked at Zainah.

"You must be Zainah," Sienna said in a silken voice that totally charmed Zainah.

"Yes, and you must be Sienna."

Sienna nodded and reached out to hug her. She drew back, and Zainah looked down at her belly. "You're almost due?"

Sienna smiled. "Yes, the doctor told me the baby will probably come by the end of this month. I am super excited about that." She shook her head and said, "But enough about me. How was your trip?"

Zainah told her it was good but tiring, and Sienna asked if Zainah had taken her things to Trisha's yet. When Zainah told her she had not yet done that, but would after the wedding, Sienna nodded. "I can't wait for all of us to go wedding dress shopping. Unfortunately, Trisha will still be on her honeymoon, so she won't be able to join us."

"But we will still have a great time," Audrey said.

"I love your accent," Sienna said.

Zainah thanked her, and Audrey asked what languages they spoke at the women's camp.

"We speak different languages there but mostly Arabic, French, and English," Zainah answered.

"Faizan told me a little about that women's camp in North Africa you lived in for years. I can't wait for you to tell us all about it. It sounds so mysterious." Audrey pulled out a chair from the next table, dragged it to Zainah and Faizan's, and sat down. Zainah sat as well.

Faizan shook his head as he sat beside Zainah. "Let her be for today, Audrey. She can tell you about it tomorrow."

Audrey waved her hand dismissively and looked quizzically at Zainah, obviously waiting for her to start.

Zainah chuckled at the look on Faizan's face.

Sienna said she wanted to hear about the camp as well and pulled another chair to their table. She sat and looked expectantly at Zainah.

Zainah looked at Sienna and then at Audrey. She asked, "What exactly do you want to know about the camp?"

"Everything. Faizan has told me a little bit about

it, but I want to hear about your camp from you. A Christian women's refugee camp in the middle of the Arabian Desert fascinates me."

Zainah thought briefly about the camp. Fascinating would not be what she would describe the camp as now. But she guessed it was kind of fascinating to her when she'd first arrived there, and definitely mysterious. She understood, though, how it would be fascinating to women like Audrey and Sienna. They were so sophisticated and delicate looking. They would probably not be able to live there as she had done for years. But then again, Faizan had told her Audrey was a tough police officer. Maybe she could live there.

She began to tell them all about the camp; how she had been taken there when her family had driven her out because of her faith. In the middle of her narrative, the groom's best man rose to give his own toast and she stopped talking.

After the toast, Audrey urged her to continue. She went on and told them about the daily life at the camp. "Everyone has chores." She told them about the daily chores. It probably all sounded like drudgery to them compared to their lives here, she thought.

"It sounds so strange," Audrey said. "But kinda exciting. You are telling me that when you aren't doing chores, you are all in the prayer tent, praying collectively?"

"Well, mostly. But we also chat and play with the children when we can."

Sienna looked up with a thoughtful expression. "It sounds a little like my first year at Beulah. All I did was pray and study."

Zainah lifted her brows and looked quizzically at her. "Where is Beulah?"

"The Bible College I attend. I'm in my final year but since my husband and I moved to Peru, I've been taking my classes online."

Zainah nodded. Faizan had told her about his sister's move to another country and how sad it was to see her go.

"Go on," Audrey told her.

Faizan smiled at her and took her hand on the table. She smiled back and continued. She gave them a brief account of how she and Faizan had met, knowing he would have told them a lot about it. She told them a little about her vow and the dream God had given her about it. She told them about leaving the camp to search for Faizan, her kidnap by her father, and then finally coming to America after being rescued. She paused and stared at the center of the hall. It was filled with people dancing to the booming music, but she hadn't even noticed as she had been completely engrossed with the story she was telling. She looked at Sienna and Audrey. Their gazes were fixed on her and they looked enraptured. Even Faizan, who already knew most of her story, was looking intently at her.

She finally told them about Faizan's proposal and how ecstatic she was when she finally knew she would be his wife soon. When she finished, she leaned back on her chair and sighed.

"What a story, Zainah!" Audrey said. "And you told it so well."

Sienna smiled. "I think you and Faizan should write a book about your stories together. It would make for a fascinating read."

"There you all are!" a voice cried from behind. Zainah turned.

Trisha was walking toward them with a huge smile on her face. Frank was beside her, their fingers threaded together. They stopped at the table and Trisha held out her arms to Zainah. "I'm so glad to finally meet you," she said as Zainah stood up. She hugged Zainah tightly and then turned to Frank. "This is the famous Zainah, Frank. Faizan's fiancée." She looked at Zainah again and said, "You are truly beautiful. Faizan told me you were but knowing how much he loves you, I thought he was exaggerating. I know now he wasn't."

Zainah smiled widely and thanked her. She stole a glance at Faizan, gave him a sweet smile and then turned back to Trisha. "Congratulations on your wedding." She looked at Frank who hadn't taken his eyes off his bride since they'd come to the table. "You are both a lovely couple."

"Thank you," Frank and Trisha said at the same time.

Audrey chuckled and waved at them. "They have me to thank for bringing them together, isn't that right, Frank?"

"Yes, Audrey," Trisha said, smiling and shaking her head. "You've said that a million times already."

Audrey stood and said to Zainah, "It was nice meeting you. I have to go find my husband now. Knowing him, he'll probably be considering how to escape the wedding and go home. I have to make sure he doesn't."

Everyone laughed as she left. Sienna stood and told Zainah she also had to go to her husband. Trisha and Frank soon wandered away.

"I love your sisters," Zainah said, grinning at Faizan.

"They are very lovable." Faizan smiled back at her. He took her hand on the table and kissed it. "I know they love you too. Everyone who meets you falls in love with you."

Her heart soared at the love in his eyes. She couldn't help herself as she shifted her chair close to his and kissed him briefly on the lips. When she drew back, he looked into her eyes and sighed heavily.

"I wish I could kiss you now the way I've been wanting to for months, but we are still not alone."

She nodded. She was dying to kiss him passionately too after months of being apart. When he'd picked her up at the airport, they'd had to hurry back to his house so she could change and go with him to the wedding. After a while, she chuckled to break the intense desire she was feeling.

"I would have said we should go back to your house as I want to kiss you so badly, but I know it would probably not be a good idea."

He nodded. "It would be a very bad idea, especially as Ken and Audrey are not there now." He grinned at her and a mischievous look crept into his face. He leaned forward and whispered, "We could go outside. There is a huge tree at the back of this building where we can kiss as much as we want without anyone disturbing us. It's private, but not too private that we will go too far and get into trouble."

Zainah's heart pounded with excitement as he grabbed her hand and pulled her up. He wrapped his arm around her waist as they walked out of the noisy reception hall.

She giggled and kissed his cheek as he led her to the back of the building. They were acting like two infatuated schoolchildren, but she didn't care.

Faizan pulled her to the back of the tree and wrapped his arms tightly around her. She trembled with anticipation as he kissed her hair, her nose, her chin. Just as their lips met, someone coughed loudly. Faizan groaned and pulled back slightly and Zainah shut her eyes, frustrated.

Zainah opened her eyes and saw a gorgeous blonde dressed in a red, figure-hugging dress approaching them. Something twisted inside of her as the blonde smiled at Faizan. Her smile was too familiar.

"I'm sorry for intruding, Faizan," the beauty said. "Trisha is looking for you. She and Frank are leaving for their honeymoon tonight. She wants to say goodbye to everyone before they do." She looked from Faizan to Zainah and then pressed her red painted lips together. "Umm... this must be Zainah."

Zainah blinked. The blonde even knew her name. That meant that she and Faizan knew each other quite well. Her stomach churned and she knew she was jealous. Involuntarily so, but still, jealous.

Faizan gave the blonde a small smile and said, "Yes, this is Zainah, my fiancée." He looked at Zainah and pointed at Lauren. "This is Lauren. She is Trisha's friend and Ken's as well."

Lauren smiled up at him. "I thought I was your friend too, Faizan." She shook her head and smiled at Zainah. "Faizan has told me so much about you,

Zainah. It's so nice to meet you."

Zainah tried to push away her jealousy and forced a smile. "It's nice to meet you as well." She wanted to add that Faizan had told her nothing about Lauren, but she held back. It would definitely sound petty. When Lauren went away, she would ask Faizan about her. She trusted Faizan completely, but there was a look in Lauren's eye. A look that clearly said she was attracted to Faizan. He probably didn't know she was.

Stop obsessing over it, she scolded herself. Surely other women would be attracted to him. He was a handsome man. There was no way she could stop that from happening.

But other women don't talk to him with such familiarity. She'd always been a perceptive person and her heart told her that Lauren and Faizan were more than acquaintances.

"Zainah!" Faizan said, looking curiously at her. "Did you hear what I just said?"

Her eyes widened and she shook her head. "Sorry. What did you say?"

"I said we have to go back in."

"Okay." Zainah turned and saw Lauren was staring at her. Why is she still here?

Faizan's eyes studied her face and then he said to Lauren. "Go ahead, Lauren. We'll be there in a minute."

Lauren nodded and walked away.

Zainah watched Faizan's face to see if he would look at Lauren as she walked away, but he didn't. He took her hands and said, "What's wrong, beloved?" She shook her head, but his gaze pierced hers. He said, "There is something wrong. Tell me what it is."

"It's really nothing," she answered.

He kept looking at her and then said, "It's about Lauren, isn't it?"

Zainah's heart thudded. How come he knew her so well? It was as if he could read her thoughts. She pressed her lips tightly together and refused to speak. Her jealousy was wrong. Even though Lauren was clearly attracted to him, she was certain he didn't feel the same about her. Still, she couldn't help her jealousy.

He smiled and chucked her chin. "Are you jealous, Zainah? You know there is nothing to be jealous about, don't you?"

"I'm not jealous," she lied.

"Yes, yes you are jealous. Well, I will tell you everything that happened between us."

A terrible dread came over her at his words. She blurted out, "Something happened between you two?"

"Nothing for you to be jealous about. However, you need to know what happened. I would have told you some time in the future, but I may as well tell you now."

"What about Trisha...?"

"I'll go visit her and Frank before they leave for Paris." He took Zainah's hand. "I went out on a date with Lauren."

Zainah gasped and her mouth flew open.

"I was pining constantly for you. Everyone told me I needed to move on, but I just couldn't. Even though I knew you and I could never be together because of your vow, I couldn't let you go in my heart."

Zainah's heart raced as he told her about Lauren's attraction to him and his constant resistance. At last, after Sienna and her husband had left for

South America, he'd decided life was too short to waste away alone. He'd asked Lauren out and they'd gone on a date.

"Lauren is a great girl, but as much as I tried, I couldn't get myself to be interested in her. After our date, she wanted to kiss me."

Zainah shut her eyes as images of him kissing the beautiful Lauren crossed her mind. Faizan put his hands on her cheeks and continued, "I backed away. I just couldn't do it. I couldn't kiss her. I kept thinking of you, and though I knew it was hopeless, it felt as though I would be cheating on you." He caressed her cheeks. "I love you with all my heart, Zainah. I hope you know you can always trust me. Lauren is probably the one jealous of you!"

Zainah opened her eyes and looked at him. Because of her vow, she completely understood why he'd given in and gone on a date with Lauren. But it didn't stop the jealousy tearing at her. She looked into his eyes and saw again his intense love for her reflected in them. She stepped toward him and said, "I trust you completely, Faizan. And I apologize. You were right. I was a little jealous."

He smiled, teasing her. "Only a little?"

"Okay, very jealous. But I was wrong to be. You are a handsome man. Of course women will want you. But you belong to me, and that is what matters."

He pulled her close. "And you belong to me, Zainah. Nothing and no one will ever separate us. Do you hear me?"

She nodded.

As he claimed her lips and kissed her the way she had dreamed of being kissed for months, her emotions churned with a mixture of pleasure and worry.

TWO

The steward opened the door and Karim Keita walked into Jibril Mohamed's house. The steward led him through a wide foyer into a living room that was tastefully furnished. He opened a door that led into Jibril's now familiar study and Karim walked in.

Jibril looked up as he came in, held out his hand, and then pointed to the seat in front of his desk. Karim sat and turned to greet Dauda who was sitting on the chair beside his. He turned back to Jibril again and then asked why he had been summoned to the man's house. Jibril said to him, "You know why I asked you to come to my house. Stop pretending like you don't."

Karim said nothing. He knew exactly why, especially since Dauda was here as well, but he was not willingly going to say he did. Dauda and Jibril kept staring at him and he sighed wearily. "Okay," he said, looking at Dauda first and then facing Jibril. "You sent for me because of your wives. I asked you some days ago when you and Dauda brought this up to give me some time. I'll find a way to get my daughter and her friend back to both of you."

Dauda said, "You've been saying the same thing for months. We want our wives right now. When your debts came due and we made that agreement not to destroy you financially and cancel your debts on the condition that I would marry your daughter while Dauda married her friend, you agreed wholeheartedly. But now you want to back out of our agreement. You can't. As you well know, the wedding rites were already said, and we are legally married to those women according to our custom. And since we are married to them, they belong to us now."

"I am not trying to back out of our agreement, and I know they are both yours now." Karim shook his head and stared at the brothers. They both looked alike, with the same bushy beards and eyebrows, though Dauda's complexion was darker than Jibril's. "I'm just asking to be given some time to find them and bring them to you again. You know what happened at the wedding was not my fault. How was I supposed to know that my daughter has armed men as friends?"

Jibril laughed harshly and then glowered at him. "You are asking me how you were supposed to know that your daughter, Zainah, is involved with dangerous men." He looked at his brother and said, "We were thoroughly humiliated on our own wedding day."

"I know, I know," Karim said exasperatedly.

"That is why we called you here," Dauda said. "We were robbed when those men took our wives. We don't care how you get them back. Just give us our wives now."

Karim sighed loudly as he looked at both men for a long while. He finally said, "I'm working on it." He muttered under his breath, "It's not as if both of you don't have harems full of wives already."

Dauda glared at him and said, "What's it to you? All we are saying is that you give us what rightfully belongs to us. How many wives we both have already is none of your business. You made an agreement with us and we are holding you accountable to keep that agreement."

Karim said, "I am simply asking both of you for more time. I am still trying to figure out a way to lure Zainah and her friend, Leila, back to Nira. I am sure I'll be able to do that in no time."

Jibril stared him down and said, "We are giving you only one month. If you have not produced our wives within one month, we will destroy your business." He glared at Karim. "Everything you own will burn to ashes."

Karim trembled with fear on the inside, but did not allow the men to see that he was afraid. The brothers had lived in Saudi Arabia for half their lives and had only returned to Nira, their hometown, last year, after their parents died. They had come with their wives, their children, and their copious amount of wealth that they had gathered abroad. They had built magnificent mansions for themselves in Nira and settled in them with their large families.

He had been so impressed by their wealth that he had quickly made friends with them, seeing the potential their friendship held for his business. If only he had not borrowed so much money from them. But he had needed the money at the time to grow his farms. When the time to pay had come, he'd found he didn't have the money to repay the brothers, and the threats had begun.

The men had seen Zainah and Leila when the two came to Nira months ago and had immediately wanted them as wives. They had instantly approached him and told him they wanted to marry the girls. And then they'd promised to cancel his debt if he would give them Zainah and Leila's hands in marriage. At the time, he had thought he was very lucky. Not only would his debt be cancelled and the threat of financial ruin be lifted off of him, but he would have a rich in-law. If only he'd known how things would turn out. But then again, it wasn't as if he had the money to pay them now or any way of ever getting it in the near future. Perhaps he'd been destined to be bound to these men.

The brothers were staring at him as though he had gone insane.

"Are you going to say anything, or will you just keep staring at us like an idiot?" Jibril said.

Karim thinned his lips and then reiterated his promise to bring Zainah and her friend, Leila, back to Nira in no time.

"You had better do it quickly," Jibril said. "We will be very watchful this time. Once you bring them to us, we will move back to Saudi Arabia with them and our entire family immediately if there is any sign of trouble. What happened last time will not happen again."

Karim nodded. "Of course," he said.

Five minutes later, he left Jibril's house. Once he was outside, he quickly made his way to his own house. He sat on the sofa and sent one of his men to call Malik. When the men went to do his bidding, he called out to his daughter, Khadija.

She appeared in the living room almost immediately and walked up to him. She looked at him quizzically. "Yes, Papa. What is it?"

He stared at her and said, "What do you mean, 'what is it?' When did you start speaking to me like that?"

She sighed loudly and said, "I'm sorry." But she did not look sorry at all.

He shoved aside his anger and asked, "Do you know your sister's new phone number? I have been trying to call her with the one she gave me when she was here, but it's not going through."

Khadija stared at him as though he had gone mad, and he barked at her, "Why are you looking at me like that?" She was the second person who had looked at him as though something was wrong with him within just a few minutes. That was not right.

"But, Papa, I don't have a cell phone, so why would I know Zainah's number?"

He felt as though steam was coming out of his ears as he glowered at her. He almost stood up to hit her but held himself in check. He needed her help at this time. Sighing wearily, he leaned back in his seat and said to her, "So you don't have her phone number. Are you sure of that?"

"I don't," Khadija answered.

"And do you know if your mother has Zainah's new number?" he asked. Zainah and Khadija's mother was away on a visit in the next town to see her own aged mother and would be gone for some time. It was unlikely that she knew Zainah's new number though, as she would have told him if she did.

Khadija said, "I don't think Mama has it either. You know she doesn't even know how to use her cell phone. It just lies around her bedroom. She calls no one and no one calls her except Grandmother."

Malik walked in and Karim turned to face him. As usual, he was sour-faced. He had been the same way for months now. Thankfully, Karim didn't have to deal with Malik's brooding all the time. He had sent him to work on his farm in shifts. Karim wasn't sure whether to be amiable to try to get the information he wanted from Malik or whether to threaten him. Almost immediately, he chose the former and smiled. "Malik, I'm glad to see you back after your weeks away."

Malik glared at him. His animosity was clear and palpable. Karim struggled to control his anger. Both his children were treating him with such disdain. He had to find a way to put a stop to it all. But for now, he would let it go.

Malik said, "Please, Father, do not pretend that you are happy to see me. What do you want from me?"

Karim stared at him for a long moment and then stood up. "I am very sure you have Zainah's number, or at least that Leila girl's. I need you to tell me what it is."

Malik rolled his eyes and shook his head. "I don't have Zainah's new number and Leila does not have a cell phone. But even if I had their numbers, I would not tell you what they were. Not after you showed me clearly that you do not have their best interests... or mine, at heart." He turned around and left the house before Karim could say anything else.

Karim stared at the door for a long moment and ground his teeth in anger. He turned around to face his daughter, but she had also left the living room. He wanted to go after her and Malik, grab them by the ears, and scold them for their insolence, but he reined his anger in and sat down on the sofa again.

How will I get Zainah and her friend Leila back to Nira? he thought to himself. How was he going to get Zainah and her friend to come back here when he didn't even know where they were? He had to find a way to get them to come back now, before the one month Jibril and Dauda had given him ended. If he could not get them back here by then, he would have to kiss his farms and everything he had goodbye.

*****

Just before the break of dawn, Leila left the prayer tent after the general morning prayers. She removed the shawl covering her hair as she walked to her tent. The other women milled around her. Some were in groups of three or four, chatting, while others yelled at their children, ordering them to stay still. Leila barely noticed any of the women or children. In fact, throughout the prayers, she'd struggled to concentrate. Her mind refused to remain on anything but her misery. She longed for Malik with all her heart and she missed Zainah terribly.

She was confused by Malik's absence during her

and Zainah's almost forced marriage and conversion months ago. He'd been the one to help them escape the shack Zainah's father had locked them in. And he was the one who had hired the driver who was supposed to take them out of Nira, Zainah's tiny hometown. But the driver had not taken them out of Nira. Instead, he had waited on the roadside for them to be captured again by Zainah's father's men. They had been locked up again. Thankfully, Faizan's armed friends had rescued them.

Zainah had insisted then that Malik was the one who'd betrayed them. But Leila didn't believe that then nor did she really believe it now. However, it was all so strange. How had the driver gotten in touch with the men who'd recaptured her and Zainah if he didn't know beforehand who the occupants of his taxi would be? They had not seen him make any calls while he drove them almost to the outskirts of town. Worst of all, Malik had been nowhere in sight after they were captured again nor had he tried to find her since then.

"He promised we would be together," Leila whispered to herself as she entered her tent.

"Who did?"

Leila turned and saw Halima, one of the women she shared the tent with, staring at her. She'd thought she'd spoken in a whisper. Apparently not. "No one," Leila said impatiently to the petite young woman.

Halima shook her head, sympathy clearly written on her face. She put her hand on Leila's shoulder and said softly in Arabic, "Since Zainah left for America, you have been so sad and very quiet. I know she was your best friend, but you have other friends here as well. You can't keep isolating your-self from everyone."

Leila gave her a small smile. "I do miss Zainah, but I am so happy for her. She's with the love of her life now."

Halima shook her head. "But you don't look hap-py at all."

Leila sighed. She'd tried so hard to be happy for Zainah, but envy tore at her constantly. Zainah was now with the man she loved and they would soon get married, while she was left aching after Malik, wondering if she would ever see him again. Zainah's absence had only made her misery worse. She would have liked to have her closest confidant to talk to. Zainah always knew what to say even if Leila sometimes didn't listen to her.

She sighed and sat down on her sleeping mat, sadness weighing her down. Halima sat beside her and put her arm around her shoulders. "Will you be able to go to Zainah's wedding?"

Leila turned. "And how do you suggest I go to America even if she invites me?" she snapped at her. "Should I fly there like a witch? Are you too dense to know that I need a visa and money that you have never even seen in your life in order to get there?"

Halima's eyes widened and her jaw dropped. She stared at Leila in obvious shock.

Leila shut her eyes, deeply regretting her out-burst. "I'm sorry," she said to Halima. She opened her eyes and looked at Halima. "I don't know what came over me. Please forgive me."

Halima smiled thinly. "It's okay. I understand your concern." She stood up and quickly left Leila alone.

Leila sighed again. Halima was right. She was isolating herself and not talking to the other campers. But Zainah was the only one that really understood her.

She smiled in self-mockery. Zainah understood her except when it came to men and relationships. While Zainah believed that Christians were supposed to leave finding their life partners to God, Leila believed Christians played an active role in it. They had quarreled a lot in the last few months because of that. She knew what Zainah would tell her now if she shared her deep yearning for Malik. Zainah would tell her the same thing she had said when they were in Mali. She would say her brother didn't share Leila's faith and therefore they couldn't have a relationship.

And Leila had believed the same thing for years until she'd fallen for a Muslim man. She knew she couldn't marry Malik because he was not a Christian, but it didn't stop her from falling in love with him and vice versa. She pursed her lips. It was another thing she had to worry about. If she ever saw Malik again, how would she convert him? Because, in spite of how in love she was with him, Zainah was right. She couldn't marry someone who didn't share her love for Jesus.

She lay on her sleeping mat and closed her eyes. The sun would soon be up. She was supposed to fetch water at the well for the women whose turn it was to cook breakfast for the camp, but she didn't feel up to it at all. Depression had sucked up all her strength. She would tell them to replace her with someone else today because she wasn't feeling well.

How long will you continue like this? she thought.

She couldn't go on like this for much longer. She had to do something. If Malik wasn't going to do what he promised and find her, then she would go looking for him. And when she found him, she would not rest until he became a Christian. Then they could get married.

*****

Zainah smiled at Audrey and Sienna as she went with the consultant to try her wedding dress on. Entering the dressing room, she stood still while the consultant handed her the wedding dress Faizan's sisters had chosen for her.

She had fully agreed when Faizan had told her his sisters wanted to choose her wedding dress and buy it for her, as she didn't have the faintest idea what an American wedding dress looked like.

The consultant buttoned up the back of the dress, straightened it, and then turned Zainah around so she could look at her reflection in the mirror.

"You look great! What do you think?" the consultant asked, smiling.

Zainah stared at herself in the mirror with a mixture of worry and admiration, but more worry. The wedding gown was a beautiful white satin dress, but it was strapless, had a low neckline, and was fitted to her body. She'd never worn anything as revealing as this. Not even close.

"What's wrong?" the consultant asked. "You don't like it?"

Zainah forced a smile. "I do. It's beautiful... but I have never worn anything like this before. I feel so exposed."

The consultant laughed. "You are wearing this for your special day. You are not supposed to have worn anything like this before. I think you look spectacular in it."

Zainah thanked the consultant and then told her she was ready to show the dress to her sisters-in-law. The consultant lifted the dress from behind while Zainah daintily walked out of the dressing room.

The girls gasped as Zainah approached them. She smiled a little shyly as she came to stand in front of them. "What do you girls think?" she asked, looking at the duo. They both had huge smiles on their faces.

"You look amazing!" Audrey said. "Faizan will probably cry when he sees you."

Zainah laughed. "I doubt that. He is sweet, but he's not really a crier."

Sienna had tears in her eyes as she said, "My brother is blessed to have you, Zainah. He loves you so much. I'm really glad you are here because he was a wreck for so long without you."

Zainah held back a sob. When Sienna got up, Zainah hugged her tightly. Audrey also got up and wrapped her arms around her. The three of them laughed and wept together for a few minutes and then Sienna and Audrey sat down again.

"You are now officially one of us," Audrey said to Zainah.

"Thanks," Zainah said. "You ladies have been so kind to me since I came to America. And I am so glad you helped me pick out this dress because I would not have had the guts to pick it out for myself."

The consultant led Zainah back to the dressing room. She slipped out of the wedding dress and put on her shift navy blue dress. She walked out of the room and went to meet Sienna and Audrey. They all left the bridal store together and got into Audrey's car. Sienna sat in front with Audrey, while Zainah got into the backseat.

As they talked, Zainah felt herself becoming a little sad. Soon, Sienna and Audrey would go back to Peru and Miami, respectively. She would have to start taking up a lot of the planning herself. Yes, Faizan would help her out and Audrey would be here on some weekends, but a lot of the planning would fall on her.

Suddenly, she felt her heart twist as she thought of Leila. How she missed her best friend. If Leila were here, she would not have any cause for concern. Even without her sisters-in-law, she and Leila would plan the wedding together. Even though both of them didn't really know much about planning an American wedding, they would figure it out together as they went along. They always did.

"Zainah, what's wrong?" Sienna asked, looking back at her. "You suddenly went quiet."

Zainah sighed softly. "It's just that I miss my best friend, Leila."

"Is she at the camp now?" Audrey asked, looking at her in the rearview mirror.

"Yes," Zainah answered. She looked out the window at the cars zooming past and the big buildings and then thought about the camp, how small the tents were. How simple the life there had been. She wondered what Leila was doing now.

"Is there no way she can come to America for the

wedding?" Sienna asked.

"No." Zainah shook her head. "She doesn't have any money now to make the trip here or to get a visa, and I don't have any to give her."

Sienna looked back at Zainah. "That's no problem. Any of us can easily sponsor her trip here."

Zainah shook her head. "I couldn't ask you to do that. Besides, even if you give her money for the trip, she has no chance to get a visit visa. When I was processing my visa, I researched her chances of getting one because I really wanted her to come to the US for my wedding. I found out that the chances of her getting a visa were almost nil."

"But we could at least try," Audrey said. "We are family now, Zainah. If you need something, we are here to make it happen. If we act as your friend's invitees and sponsors, maybe she would be given a visa. There is no harm in trying."

Hope began to stir in Zainah's heart. Maybe Sienna and Audrey were right. When she married Faizan, his sisters would be her family as well. Maybe she should just let them pay for Leila's trip here. As much as she didn't want to impose, she really wanted Leila here. A huge grin broke out on her face and she nodded. She leaned forward and said to Sienna and Audrey, "Okay, thank you both so much. I'll tell Faizan about it."

"And how will you contact your friend?" Sienna asked.

"I'll have to try to contact Miriam first. She's like the leader of our camp and the only one with a phone."

"But how does your leader charge her phone if there is no electricity?" Audrey asked in a curious voice.

"That is the problem and why I am unable to speak with Leila a lot of times. Miriam tries to conserve the battery power because she only goes to town once or twice a month, so the phone is almost always off. I will keep trying until I get through to her. I'll ask Leila to leave the camp. We have a friend called Fatima who leaves in a town some distance from the camp. She can stay there while her visa is being processed and it will be easy to contact her from there."

Sienna turned around and took her hand. "We'll try everything we can to make sure your friend is here. Don't worry about it."

Zainah smiled appreciatively at her.

As soon as they got to Audrey's house, Audrey went to the room she shared with her husband while Sienna sat on the couch in the living room beside her husband, Bryan. She put her feet up on the coffee table and exhaled loudly. Bryan grinned at her and drew her close.

Zainah smiled at how cute they looked together. Bryan's hand was on Sienna's swollen belly, while Sienna ran her fingers through his blond wavy hair. Zainah left them and went to look for Faizan. The house was huge; not quite as huge as the Rahmanis' mansion, the house she'd worked as a maid last year, but huge all the same. She didn't find him downstairs, so she climbed up the stairs to search for him.

A few minutes later, she found him on the patio overlooking the courtyard. He was leaning on the balustrade with his back to her, looking into the distance. He turned when she began walking toward him and a huge smile spread across his face.

Holding his arms wide open, he enfolded her in as she went to him.

"How did your dress fitting go?" Faizan asked, squeezing her tightly.

"It went great," she said, her head buried in his chest. When he drew back slightly, she realized her words had been muffled and he hadn't heard what she'd said. She said again, "The dress fitting went well. It doesn't need any adjustments as it's perfect the way it is."

Faizan smiled, kissed her cheek, and then let her go. "I can't wait to see you in it," he said, leaning on the concrete balustrade again.

She nodded and stood beside him.

For a long moment, they stayed in comfortable silence, gazing at the courtyard below with the swimming pool surrounded by palm trees. After some minutes, he turned and said to her, "I think I've found a few places that we might be able to move in to once we are married. We can go see all of them sometime this week, and then we'll both decide which place we like best. It definitely won't be as big as this one, but it will be nice."

"I would like that very much," she said, smiling. She liked this house where he lived with his sister and her husband, but it wasn't theirs. As big as the house was, she wanted them to start their married lives together in total privacy. A shiver of anticipation ran through her and she said to him, "I can't wait for us to get married and start living together."

When he turned to wink at her, she smiled from embarrassment and pleasure. "I can't wait either," he said. He took her hand, kissed it, and threaded their fingers together.

For about an hour, they talked about their hopes for their future together.

"I want a lot of children," he said to her. "That's if you want that as well."

She nodded, her heart beating with excitement at the thought of having his children. She couldn't believe she was standing beside the man she loved with everything in her, talking about marrying him and having his kids. "As you know, I grew up in a large family. I want that as well." She grinned. "But unlike my father, I'll be the only woman having those kids for you."

He looked into her eyes and then put his palm on her cheek. "You are the only woman I want and will ever need as the mother of my children."

She leaned in to kiss him briefly and then said, "About the wedding, Audrey and Sienna promised to be Leila's sponsors so she can have a better chance of getting a visa. They also promised to pay for her trip here."

He shook his head and looked at her. "I asked if I could help with her trip, Zainah, but you said you didn't want to impose."

"I told your sisters the same thing, but they insisted. Besides, I didn't want to burden you financially, knowing your high school income isn't that much."

A strange expression crossed his face and she frowned. She tilted her head and searched his eyes. "What is the matter?" she asked.

"Nothing," he said and smiled. "Umm... it's not something I can discuss right now. I'll tell you when we are married."

She studied his face, looking for clues to what he

wasn't saying, but he looked away and stared into the distance again. For a moment, she wondered what he wasn't telling her, and then she let it go. Just as he said, he would tell her when they were married. She trusted him fully and she was totally safe with him.

She sidled up to him, and he held her again. He kissed her hair and her cheek.

As she stood with her arm around his waist and his around hers, her heart overflowed with love for him until she couldn't hold it in anymore. She said softly, "I love you so much, Faizan."

He beamed at her. "I love you, Zainah. Know that I will always love you."

THREE

Faizan held Zainah's hand as they walked into the third house they were to view for the day. The realtor had shown them the first two already—an Edwardian-style house that Zainah liked, and a two-bedroom single-story home that she was also enthusiastic about. Faizan also liked the houses, but not enough to choose either of them. He had his suspicions that Zainah would like all the houses they were going to see today. Hopefully, there would be one that she liked more than the others, and that he would also like that one as well. If it went that way, they would choose the home they were going to live in for a long time and raise their children in. He couldn't contain his excitement.

This particular house was a modern three-bedroom home and furnished. Zainah's eyes widened as they entered the plush living room.

"It's beautiful, Faizan!" she exclaimed. "But won't it be expensive if it's furnished?"

"The furniture is just to make the house look interesting to buyers," Faizan said to her. He looked around the living room, decorated in white furniture with gold accents. "You need to envision the house without this furniture."

Zainah looked disappointed and Faizan added, "But sometimes, it can be sold to buyers if they like the furniture."

Zainah nodded. "I like it."

Faizan smiled at her. "Okay... but maybe we should look at the whole house first before you decide. And we still have two more houses to look at."

The realtor, a man in his late thirties with bleached blond hair, led them to the kitchen. It was bigger than Faizan thought it would be. As usual, Zainah loved it. She especially loved the marble island and polished wooden cabinets. The realtor walked out of the kitchen and led them to the guest bedroom.

They walked from one room to the other. When they went upstairs, the first room the realtor led them into was the master bedroom. It was a well-appointed room, with a large bed and en-suite bathroom. Zainah gasped beside him and he turned.

"I love this bed," she said to him. She went to sit on the bed and Faizan smiled. It did look very inviting. He couldn't resist going to sit beside her. She caressed the blue and white duvet and then looked up at him with a dreamy expression on her face. "Can you imagine it, Faizan?"

"What?" he asked, smiling with amusement.

"Can you imagine waking up here," she looked deep into his eyes, "with me?"

His heart jumped at the sultry expression on her face. It was the first time he'd seen this look on her face and it set his body on fire. He was glad the realtor was in the room because he didn't trust himself to hold back if the man wasn't.

"Let me give both of you some privacy to take this place in," the realtor said, and walked out of the bedroom before Faizan could protest.

Faizan's pulse raced wildly as Zainah shifted closer to him, the sultry look still on her face. She put her arms around his neck, pulled him to her, and kissed him.

His heart beating, he drew her even closer, and kissed her with every yearning he felt for her. As they kissed, he pulled her down on the bed and dug his fingers in her hair. Suddenly, as he realized that they were both straining to get closer even though they were already wrapped around each other, alarm bells rang in his mind. He told himself to pull back, but he couldn't. He whispered a prayer for help. His cellphone began ringing in his pocket and he jumped. Zainah pulled away, and he took a deep breath.

His body shook as he fumbled to get his phone out of his pocket. He finally dug it out, cleared his throat and answered. "Hello," he said, avoiding looking in Zainah's direction. He felt slightly guilty for his lack of control. Thankfully, the Lord had delivered them using this phone call.

Jake's voice on the other end of the line said, "Faizan, it's Jake. Listen, I have a job for you." Faizan's eyes widened in surprise. After he'd been recruited by the CIA to act as an informer and helped them get Hassan and the members of the terrorist groups he had formerly belonged to, he had been told to lie low in Rosefield for now. That had been quite a while back. He'd lived a fairly ordinary life since then, though at the back of his mind, he knew he would one day be called upon again to work for the CIA. He'd dreaded this call. And it couldn't come at a worse time.

He looked self-consciously at Zainah. She was staring quizzically at him. He'd told her he had made some friends in the government and that was why he wasn't indicted when he confessed his terrorist past. She didn't know that he worked for the CIA and he couldn't really tell her until they were married.

He stood up from the bed, quickly told her to excuse him, and left the room. "I'm planning my wedding now," he whispered into the phone as he went into another room furnished with a shaggy white rug, pink and white bedding, and fuscia pink curtains. He smiled in spite of himself. It seemed so strange and a little funny to have the kind of militant conversation he knew he was about to have with his handler in such a soft, girly room.

"I don't really care, Faizan," Jake said. "I told you I was going to collect soon when you asked me to help you get your friend out of Mali. Do you remember?"

Faizan sighed. "Yes, I remember, and I'm not saying I won't do what you want. It's just that the timing isn't right because…"

"You are planning your wedding," Jake finished his sentence for him. "Unfortunately, what we want you to do cannot wait. You have no choice, and frankly, neither do I. The powers that be want this done now, and you are the best person to do it."

"And when do I have to leave for this 'job'?"

"First thing tomorrow."

Faizan laughed harshly. "You can't be serious."

"I am dead serious."

Faizan's heart began to pound. He asked, "Is there no way it can be postponed? My wedding is in less than a month…"

"No!" Jake said. "It can't be postponed."

Faizan shut his eyes as he tried to keep his frustration in check. He asked, "And how long will this 'job' last?"

"Anywhere from a week to several months. I can't really tell right now."

"What?" Faizan's eyes widened. "Several months! No, Jake. If Zainah and I don't get married in three months, she will have to leave the United States."

Jake said, "I'm sorry, Faizan. There is nothing I can do about that."

For the first time in a long time, Faizan felt like swearing. He pressed his lips tightly together and raked his fingers through his hair. This could not be happening. He had to marry Zainah now. But they couldn't even elope with Jake saying he had to leave first thing tomorrow.

Jake said again, "You haven't even asked what your assignment is to be. You might enjoy this one."

"The only assignment I want now is to marry the love of my life!" Faizan spat out.

Jake continued as though Faizan hadn't spoken. "You'll be flown into Washington tomorrow and briefed on your assignment. I'll meet you at the airport." Jake ended the call before Faizan could protest again.

For a full minute, Faizan stood looking at his phone. He suddenly let out an angry roar and almost threw the phone across the room. He sighed when Zainah rushed in, followed by the realtor.

"Is everything okay?" the realtor asked, looking at Faizan.

Faizan nodded and looked at Zainah who had come up to him and placed her hand on his shoulder. She had a worried look on her face as she stared at him.

"What's the matter?" she whispered.

He forced a smile and shook his head. "It's nothing, really." He looked at the realtor and said, "Let's continue the house tour."

The man hesitated for a few seconds and then moved to the door. "Okay, let's go on to the other bedrooms."

Faizan took Zainah's hand and they followed the realtor.

The house viewing was over half an hour later. The realtor asked Faizan if he wanted to see the remaining two houses now, but Faizan declined. He told Zainah that he was slightly tired and therefore was not in the right frame of mind to look at any more homes.

"We will continue another day," he said to her.

On the way to Trisha's where she was staying, Zainah kept asking him what was wrong, and he kept insisting there was nothing. He felt terrible for lying to her, but he didn't know what he was supposed to tell her. Worse, he couldn't think of a plausible excuse to give her when it came time to travel to Washington. He would have to tell her more lies. The thought tormented his mind as he drove.

Faizan parked in Trisha's driveway and waited

for Zainah to unlock the door. He followed her in, thought better of staying, and then began to back away. If he stayed here with her, she would probably get the truth out of him, and he couldn't let that happen. At least, not yet. Worst of all, they might end up kissing passionately again and then things would start to get out of hand the way it had back at the house they had just viewed. If that happened, he wasn't sure the Lord would send any more interruptions to deliver them.

Zainah caught his wrist as he turned toward the door. "Where are you going?" she asked. "I thought we were supposed to spend the rest of today together."

He shook his head. "Remember what happened back at the house we went to see. The realtor was in the house and we couldn't keep our hands to ourselves. I don't think we can risk being alone for now."

She sighed and let go of his hand. He went to open the door and she followed him out of the house.

He turned back and stared curiously at her, and then frowned. "Where are you going?"

"I'm going back to Audrey's house with you."

"Why?" he asked, confused.

She shrugged. "Well… we can't stay here alone, but Audrey and Ken are at home, aren't they? We are supposed to spend the day together and we will." She shook her head. "And don't look at me like that, Faizan. I know there is something you are hiding from me and you are trying to avoid telling me about it. But it's not going to work. I want to know what exactly is bothering you."

He sighed wearily and turned away from her.

"Tell me what it is," she said.

He turned back to her and looked her in the eye. He said softly, "I can't tell you right now, but I will soon."

She studied his eyes. "Why can't you tell me now, Faizan? What are you hiding?"

He took her hand and asked, "Do you trust me, Zainah?"

"Completely," she replied.

"Then please trust me when I say it's nothing for you to worry about. I promise I'll tell you what it is very soon. All I can tell you right now is that I have to go out of town tomorrow."

She gasped and then asked, "For how long?"

"I'm not yet sure."

She shook her head. "Do you really have to go?"

"I have to. I have no choice, Zainah."

She cried out, "What about our wedding planning? What about our wedding? It's in less than a month."

"I know. I promise I'll try to be back way before then. It's just that I have to go now."

She stared at him for a long moment and then said, "It has something to do with your past, doesn't it?"

"Umm… kind of."

Her eyes searched his again. She thinned her lips. "You aren't going to tell me what it is, are you?"

"I can't tell you now," Faizan said. "Please trust me, Zainah. I will tell you in due time."

She smiled sadly. "You mean you are not allowed to tell me now."

He nodded.

She looked at him for another minute and then her shoulders sagged. "Okay. I'll let it go. But I am coming with you to Audrey's. I want to spend every waking moment with you until you leave tomorrow." She grinned. "And I want to play with Ruby as well."

He smiled and cupped her cheeks. "I want to spend every moment with you too."

They stared at each other for a long moment and then Faizan took her hand in his. "Let's go then."

She followed him to his car and got in the front seat beside him. All through the short drive to Audrey's, Faizan had one hand on the steering wheel and the other grasping Zainah's. His emotions roiled as he kept thinking of leaving her tomorrow. He didn't want to. If only they could elope and get married this evening. But it wasn't possible. Besides, his sisters would kill him if he did.

She lifted their joined hands and kissed the back of his. "It's okay, Faizan. I'll be alright."

His stomach twisted with worry. "Audrey and Ken will soon leave for Miami and Sienna and Bryan will go back to Peru. You will be alone in Rosefield."

"Like I said, I'll be fine. I have been taking care of myself for a long time."

"But you are not used to being alone."

"I'll find something to occupy me while you are gone. Trisha and Frank will be back soon anyway."

He wanted to tell her he would ask Lauren to look in on her, but he remembered how insecure she had been when she'd met Lauren at the wedding and changed his mind. He had to trust that she would be fine without him. But it wasn't that he didn't believe it, it was just that he would miss her terribly. Anger against Jake and the CIA as a whole stirred in his heart, but he pushed it away. There was no point getting angry. Besides, he owed them. He would be in jail if not for their leniency. This was the agreement he had with them and he had no choice but to fulfill it.

They reached Audrey and Ken's and then discovered to their chagrin that the couple were not at home. Faizan rubbed his face with his hand and then laughed harshly. "No one is at home. This was what we were trying to avoid."

Zainah didn't seem too troubled. She laughed and said, "I'll just sit on this couch. You can sit at the other end."

He shook his head. "No, let me sit on a different sofa." He went and sat on the sofa facing her.

Zainah stared longingly at him. "I wish we could get married now," she said.

Faizan raked his fingers through his hair and shook his head slowly. "Stop gazing at me like that, Zainah. Do you want me to come over there and kiss you?"

She groaned. "This is so hard. All I want to do is kiss you and hold you, especially as you'll be leaving tomorrow."

He gazed at her for a long moment, struggling with himself. Everything in him wanted to go to her, kiss and hold her, and never let go of her. But he knew that would be the wrong thing to do. He stood and went to turn on the TV. "Let's watch a movie," he said. "It will take our minds off everything."

She shook her head. "I don't want to watch a

movie. I just want to talk to you."

He looked up thoughtfully and then went to sit back down. "Okay, let's talk," he said to her.

They sat facing each other and talking about everything. They talked about their deepest longings and fears, their childhood dreams, their future hopes. They talked about both the things they had already shared with each other and the things they hadn't yet shared. About two hours later, Audrey and Ken came back. They all had dinner together, and then Faizan told them he had to leave town the next day. Because of Zainah, he didn't tell them exactly where he was going or why.

They all sat in the living room, chatting and laughing. Every time Faizan remembered he had to leave Rosefield tomorrow, he began to feel gloomy. Each time, he pushed the feeling away and focused on the conversation going on again.

It was almost midnight when he finally drove Zainah back to Trisha's. He tried to prolong his stay by chatting with her in front of the house. But after an hour, he knew he had to leave. She clung to him when he told her he had to go and cried softly.

He wiped the tears from her eyes and then promised he would try to call her as often as possible. "By God's grace, I'll be back before you know it," he said.

"I wish you could spend the night here," she said. "I can't wait for when we get married so we don't have to say these goodbyes. It's always so painful."

"I know." He pulled back and looked at her. "I'll miss you. But hopefully, I won't be gone for too long."

"Please hurry back to me," she said, wiping the

tears on her cheeks with her fingers.

"I will."

After he kissed her, he backed away quickly. If he stayed any longer, he might go into the house with her and never leave. He got into his car, waved to her, and drove away.

All the way home, he couldn't stop picturing her face as tears ran down her cheeks and the sadness in her voice when she told him to hurry back home to her.

FOUR

Zainah paced her room in her nightgown. Waves of worry coursed through her as she thought about Faizan. She didn't even know where he was now or if he was in trouble. All she knew was that she wanted to scream. She sighed and sat on the bed. Lifting her voice to the Lord, she said, "Please help me. I miss him so much and I'm so worried about him."

She sighed again and then decided to stop worrying. It wasn't like her worry was going to accomplish anything like bring him back to her. She picked up the cellphone Faizan had bought her and decided it was time to start trying Miriam's number so she could speak with Leila. She dialed Miriam's satellite phone number not expecting it to ring and then gasped when it did.

Miriam's voice came on the line. "Hello, who is this?"

"Miriam! It's me, Zainah!"

"Zainah! How are you?"

"I'm fine, Miriam. Please, I need to speak to Leila. It's urgent!"

"Okay. Let me get her for you."

Zainah waited, her heart beating with excitement. She hadn't spoken to Leila in a while now and she couldn't wait to do it. Most of all, she couldn't wait to tell her that there might be some hope of her attending the wedding. Seconds later, Leila's voice came on the line. She sounded breathless.

"Zainah! Oh, my Lord. I've missed you so!"

Zainah grinned, thrilled to hear her best friend's voice after so long. "I've missed you, Leila. How are you?"

"I'm good. I was washing."

"Oh, that is definitely one of the things about the camp that I do not miss," Zainah said, chuckling. "How is everyone? Halima, Amina, the children?"

"They all miss you, Zainah."

Zainah smiled, thinking about the women and the children at the camp. She said, "Leila, I have good news for you. My sisters-in-law told me they could act as your sponsors and help with your visa and airfare here. That means you might actually be able to attend my wedding. It will be such a relief if you are given the visa. You will need to go to Fatima's and apply…"

Leila cut her off. "I'm not going."

Zainah's eyes widened in astonishment. She shook her head and said, "I'm sorry. Did you just say you were not going to come for my wedding?"

"Yes."

"Even if you got the visa?"

"Yes. In fact, I am not going to apply for a visa. Not unless you are postponing your wedding."

Zainah's insides twisted. "Why don't you want to come to my wedding, Leila? And why on earth would I postpone the wedding?"

"I'm certainly not asking you to postpone your wedding. I'm just saying I won't be able to make it."

"Why?"

Leila didn't say anything for a few seconds and then she said, "I need to find my own groom, Zainah. I need to find Malik."

Zainah's mouth dropped open. She finally found her voice and said, "Your groom? Did you and Malik get secretly married?"

"No!" Leila sounded exasperated. "But we will be married… if I can just find him."

"And how do you plan to find him?"

"I'll have to go back to your hometown, Zainah."

Zainah's heart jumped and she gasped. "You cannot be serious! You want to go back to the town where you were imprisoned and almost forced to marry someone you don't even know?"

"Yes. I'll do anything to find Malik."

"You are crazy, Leila! You are not going back to Nira, have you heard me? In case you've forgotten, we were threatened and asked to convert or lose our lives by marrying cruel men. How can you even think about going back there?"

"Listen, Zainah, I know you are worried, but I will be careful. I just need to find him."

"It's madness!" Zainah exclaimed. "You don't even know if he still loves you. You remember he didn't even show his face when we were recaptured. If he really cared, he would have found another way to free us. Most of all, he would have found a way to contact you by now. I still believe he was the one who told my father we were planning to escape."

"Zainah, how can you still believe that? That

doesn't even make sense. Why would he go through all that trouble to help us escape if he was just going to get your father to imprison us again?"

"Like I said before, I don't know. One thing I do know is that he hasn't bothered to reach out to you or me."

Leila sighed loudly. "Malik is a good man, and I know he loves me. I can't explain his absence when we were recaptured, but it's one of the reasons why I must go back. I need answers."

"But what about my wedding, Leila? I don't like this. What you are about to do is dangerous and frankly, futile. Please, don't go."

"Zainah, please don't try to convince me not to go anymore. You have the love of your life with you. Let me find mine."

Zainah sighed softly. "Actually, I don't."

"What?"

"Faizan was called away to some mission yesterday… I don't fully understand it all. He doesn't know when he will be back. He called this morning to tell me he is safe, but I am so afraid for him."

"What kind of mission?" Leila sounded curious.

"I don't know. But I already really miss him. I just hope we don't end up postponing this wedding. I hope he comes back soon. I will have to leave America if we don't get married before my three-month visa ends." Zainah shut her eyes, feeling overwhelmed. "All I want to do is marry that man now."

"Then you should understand my desire to find your brother. I love him very much."

"But you hardly know him," Zainah cried.

"But I still love him. I fell in love with him immediately I saw him."

Zainah felt an urgent need to talk Leila out of this crazy idea to go back to Nira and search for Malik. "You know you can't marry him, Leila. You know what the Bible says about being unequally yoked with unbelievers."

"I know," Leila said, sounding exasperated again. "I believe he'll come to Christ soon."

"He might not ever come to Christ."

"How can you say that? He is your brother!"

"Okay, I pray with all my heart that he will. But you don't know when that will be. Please, Leila, reconsider..."

"I'm sorry, Zainah. I have to follow my heart. Don't worry. I'll be careful. If I find him quickly, I promise I will go to Fatima's and start the visa process so I can come to your wedding."

"Leila, please listen to me," Zainah pleaded. An idea came to her and she said, "I will tell Miriam what you plan to do so she will stop you from going."

Leila laughed harshly. "Nothing Miriam says will convince me to not go find Malik. She would have to physically hold me down and lock me up for me not to go. I doubt she would do that."

"If I tell her your life will be in danger if you go, she just might."

"Stop it, Zainah! I'm going, and you cannot talk me out of it."

"Please, Leila, just listen to..." Zainah gasped as the line went dead. "Leila, hello?" She couldn't believe it. Her best friend had hung up on her. She blinked and pulled the phone away from her ear.

She looked at it for a full minute and then slowly stood up from the bed. Her heart raced as the worry that had settled on her since Faizan's departure yesterday doubled.

"Great!" she muttered harshly. Now she wasn't only worried about Faizan, but she had Leila to worry about as well. What is Leila even thinking, deciding to go back to Nira?

She became overwhelmed with worry and sank to her knees. "Lord, please protect Faizan and Leila. I don't know what I would do if anything bad happened to either of them." She shuddered as images of Faizan lying on the floor, hurt, rushed into her mind, followed closely by an image of Leila's face streaked with blood.

"Get yourself together," she scolded, and closed her eyes tightly. She began to intercede for Faizan and Leila, asking the Lord to protect them.

"Lord, I know you can do it," she said. "Please, don't let Leila go to Nira. Most of all, please protect my Faizan and bring him safely back to me."

*****

Leila stood up from her sleeping mat and looked around the tent. All the women and the two little children she shared the tent with were still asleep.

Good. She could sneak off without anyone knowing. She put her hand behind the box where she'd hidden the few clothes she would take with her, and pulled out a bundle. She had tied up five outfits in a scarf. They would have to do for this trip. Hopefully, it would not be a very long one. She planned to find Malik, return here to let everyone know where she was and tell them she was leaving, and then go with Malik to wherever he suggested.

She took a wrapper from her bed, carried the bundle, and tiptoed out of the tent. Once outside, she ran to the spot where the truck was parked, waiting for Miriam. Leila had timed her departure to the day Miriam usually went to town. She knew Miriam went on a Friday every month. Since this was the last Friday of the month, and Miriam had not yet gone to town, Leila knew today was the day the truck would come to get her. She also knew from having observed it several times that the driver hardly ever stayed near the truck when he arrived. He usually roamed the camp until Miriam was ready to go.

It was just before dawn, light enough for Leila to see the truck, but not enough for her to be spotted by someone who was far away. She climbed into the back of the truck, covered herself with the wrapper, and then with a tarp which was always at the back of the vehicle.

Her heart raced as she listened for the driver and Miriam. If, for whatever reason, either of them checked the truck bed, they would notice a huge bundle covered with a tarp. Hopefully either of them would think the bundle belonged to the other. If both of them checked at the same time, though, she would be discovered. Without a doubt, Miriam would send her back to the camp. She whispered a prayer, asking the Lord not to let that happen. However, she wasn't sure God would answer her. She hadn't exactly asked if this quest to find Malik was His will or not. She had a niggling feeling it wasn't, but she wouldn't pay attention to that now.

She took deep breaths as she waited. It seemed like she'd waited for an eternity when suddenly she heard voices and felt the door to the truck open and then shut loudly. She held her breath and waited as the truck began to move. As it picked up speed, she became more and more exhilarated. The truck finally settled at an even speed and she breathed a sigh of relief, realizing that she was not going to be found out, at least for now. If they later discovered her here, it would be too late to send her back.

The truck drove for a long time and Leila slept on and off. She made calculations concerning what to do. Once she got into town, she would take another bus to Kazi, a town near Zainah's small community, and from there, she would get a taxi or bus to take her to Nira.

She kept sleeping while thinking about her plans to find Malik. The truth was that she had made none. Her only plan was to go to Nira to find him and make sure she wasn't seen or caught.

For a long time, she slept, dreaming about seeing Malik, holding him, kissing him. She dreamt that someone saw them together and reported to his father. They were inevitably separated and she was thrown in that terrible shack where she and Zainah had been held when they'd gone to Nira months ago.

Leila awoke groaning and then she remembered where she was. She pressed her lips together, scared that she would be discovered, and waited. But neither Miriam nor the driver lifted the tarp she was under.

She fell asleep again after some time and it seemed the dream picked up where it had stopped.

She found herself in the shack, weeping and wondering what had become of Malik, why he hadn't come to find her.

Leila awoke sometime later, more exhausted than before she'd slept. Her eyes suddenly widened as she realized she'd slept for a long time and they were still moving. What if the driver had dropped Miriam off and had turned around again? She wouldn't be able to go to Nira.

She slowly opened the wrapper and tarp and peeped. The truck suddenly came to a stop and her heart jumped. She quickly covered the tarp again.

She heard Miriam's voice thanking the driver and heard the door open. This was her chance to get out of the car. She threw off the tarp and without looking to see if the driver was watching, she jumped down. The driver drove away almost immediately and Leila sighed with relief.

She looked around her. It was nightfall. Even the usually busy Blima market had mostly emptied of people. There would be no more buses going to Kazi now. She had to find her way to Fatima's.

She began walking in the direction of Fatima's home. She felt slightly scared as the road was almost deserted. When she had first come to this town, she'd been in the company of Zainah and it hadn't been this late at night. Fatima had met them through a divine direction and had taken them to her home. Leila had gone out to this market several times when they were at Fatima's, but usually with Fatima's daughter, Safia. She felt a thread of excitement go through her at the prospect of seeing Safia again. She hadn't told Fatima she was coming, but the woman would be happy to see her.

She came to the road before Fatima's and her heart began to beat fast as she heard a deep male voice leering from behind her. Without turning, she began to walk fast. She heard footsteps behind her and turned slightly. A tall man wearing a cap was following her. She couldn't make out his face in the darkness, but his lewd words stunned her. She picked up the pace and he did as well. She began to run, her heart in her mouth. When she heard him running behind her, she ran faster.

When she came to the field of flowers before Fatima's, she stopped and turned around in fear. The man stopped too and gave a chuckle that made her tremble.

"You have nowhere to run now," the man said.

Leila turned abruptly and dashed into the field. When Fatima had led her and Zainah here the first time, she had been surprised when Fatima had parted the flowers and a small house had emerged. She raced for the house now, knowing the man was following her.

She got to the front door of Fatima's small bungalow and pounded on the door. "Lord, please let someone open before this man reaches me." The last thing she wanted to do was lead the man right into Fatima's house. The woman had two small children and two teenagers. That would not be good. But she couldn't afford to have this man catch up...

A huge hand went around her throat and she gagged.

"Shh, don't scream or I will strangle you," the man whispered.

She frantically calculated what she could do as the man began to pull her away from the house. She knew what would happen if he succeeded in getting her away. With all her might, she elbowed the man and was gratified when he yelped. He let go of her and she screamed and staggered away. She got to Fatima's just as the door opened slightly. Pushing it in with her body, she entered quickly and then closed the door. "Lock it!" She yelled and then saw Fatima staring at her with her eyes bulging.

"Someone's coming, Fatima. Lock it now!"

The door suddenly began to open and Leila and Fatima pushed against it with all their might. But the man was too strong for them. Just as it seemed he was coming in, all Fatima's children, including Safia, came out and immediately began to push the door. They shut it quickly and then Fatima locked it.

The evil stranger on the other side of the door began to pound on it, causing the two small children to jump.

"We can scare him away somehow," Samir, Fatima's thirteen-year-old son, said. "I can find a paddle or something and chase him away." He began to leave the living room but Fatima ordered him to come back.

"You don't know if he has a gun," Fatima said. "What good will your paddle do if he does?" She asked him and Safia to check the back door to make sure it was locked. The rest of them stood staring at the door. Leila felt like her heart was going to burst out of her chest as the man kept pounding on the door.

The pounding suddenly stopped and Leila blinked. Samir, who had returned to the living room, went to the window and drew back the curtain.

"Close the curtains!" Fatima immediately ordered.

"I think he has gone," Samir said, closing the curtains and coming to stand beside his siblings.

A minute later, they all sat on the couch and sofas.

"How did you come across that man?" Fatima asked Leila.

"I was coming to your house. The road was deserted. I heard someone shouting at me from behind and when I turned, I saw him. He started following me here and when I began running, he ran after me. At one time, he caught me, but I managed to escape." She took a deep breath and, in her heart, thanked God for His deliverance. She told the others she had come because she was heading somewhere and it was getting late.

Ten minutes later, the kids went to bed except for Safia. Fatima looked at Leila and asked why she had really come.

"I met a guy some months ago," Leila started. "We fell in love almost immediately… but something happened." She looked at Safia and then turned back to Fatima. "It's a long story. He promised to call me and that we would be together, but I haven't heard from him since. I've not been able to stop thinking about him and I just have to find him."

Safia shook her head. "Leila, you are still like this. But I guess it's because you stayed out of the real world for so many years. Guys say what they don't really mean all the time. If he was truly serious about being with you, he would have made the move by now. I don't think he is really interested."

Leila sighed wearily. "You sound just like Zainah."

Fatima narrowed her eyes. "Where is Zainah, anyway? Is she back at the camp?"

"No." Leila smiled widely in spite of herself. "You know that man, Faizan, that she was searching for when we came here?"

Fatima and Safia nodded eagerly.

"She found him and they are getting married soon."

Fatima gasped while Safia hollered.

"Oh… thank God! I am so happy for her!" Fatima said. She laughed. "After all that worrying, she found that guy at last and they are getting married."

"She is in America with him now."

"Wow!" Safia exclaimed. "That's so great." She looked up with a dreamy expression on her face. "I hope I meet someone I love that much someday. Someone I will search for no matter what and not give up until I find him." She smiled at Leila. "I guess that's why you are going to look for this guy. I hope you find him, too."

Leila nodded. "I hope so, too. I need to sleep now so I can leave very early tomorrow."

Safia pouted and said, "Can't you stay for one more day, Leila?"

"I wish I could, but I really need to start looking for Malik now."

Fatima nodded. "Okay. You remember the way to the room you and Zainah stayed in when you were here?"

Leila smiled. "Yes, of course." She looked at Fatima and then at Safia. "I can't thank you enough for your hospitality. I'm really sorry I brought that crook to your door."

"It's okay," Fatima said. "And I'm glad you came

here. We've missed you and Zainah so much."

Minutes later, Leila lay on the bed she'd slept in when she and Zainah had stayed here. She thanked God again for His protection. After that, she prayed that the Lord would wake her up early tomorrow. Most of all, she asked that she would find Malik once she got to Nira, and that he would still be in love with her. Because she was still madly in love with him.

*****

Malik took his three-year-old daughter, Fanta, from his mother's arms. He hastily thanked his mother for looking after her while he was at the farm and then left the house. He walked in hurried steps and didn't stop until he entered his house, a short distance from his father's.

He sat her down on the sofa and bent down to look her in the eye. "How was your day?" he asked her. He knew she would tell him the same thing as yesterday—that it was fine and that grandma had given her biscuits. And that was what she told him with a huge smile on her face.

He looked her over as he'd started to do since that awful day a few months ago. As usual, he saw no mark on her. Nothing that indicated that she'd been maltreated by his parents. He shook his head. Why should he expect anything different, though? They loved Fanta—his mother and father. They would never hurt her. It was just him they didn't mind hurting.

He was very thankful they'd never hurt Fanta, but he felt resentful for having to still depend on them to watch her whenever he went to work. His mind traveled to Leila as it had done countless times since he'd first seen her. She would be a great mother, he was sure of that. Unfortunately, she would never be a mother to his daughter.

He'd dreamed about Leila so many times since she'd left Nira that it had become strange for him if he went a night without dreaming about her. The dreams, though, were not just dreams. Many of them were nightmares.

He carried Fanta to her room. She was already nodding off by the time he entered her room. Since his mother had already fed her dinner and bathed her, he put her to bed. His mind still revolved around Leila and the faithful day when his dream of a future happy family with the woman he loved were dashed.

He had hired a driver to take Leila and Zainah out of Nira before they were forced to wed men they hardly knew. Just as he'd left them, some young men had jumped out from behind a tree and grabbed him. He struggled to free himself from their grasps but he couldn't. They took him to his father who had him locked up in the outskirts of the town for betraying his own family. Before his father left the small building where he was imprisoned, he told him Leila and Zainah had been apprehended by his men and would be married off by the end of the next day.

The pain he felt at his father's words was indescribable. Even though he'd known Leila for only a short time, he had fallen irrevocably in love with her. They'd planned to get married soon and raise a family together. He could not bear to think that she would be given to another man. He screamed and screamed throughout that night and the next day until he was hoarse. He pounded on the door and tried to find a way to escape, but he couldn't. By the third day in captivity, after he believed Leila was now married to another person, he sat on the floor, feeling completely hopeless. By the fifth day, when his father still didn't release him, he began to worry about Fanta.

His father released him two weeks later, after he'd become sick with worry about his daughter.

"Where is Fanta?" he barked at his father when he was led out of the building. He closed his eyes as the sun briefly blinded him. He opened them slowly and, shading his eyes from the sun, asked his father where his daughter was again.

"Where else would Fanta be?" his father sneered at him. "She's safe with your mother in the house. Do you really think we would hurt her?"

"I have to see her!" Malik yelled. "Right this minute, Father!" He tried to move past his father so he could go get Fanta, but two of his father's men held him back.

"Listen, Malik," his father said. "You did a very bad thing trying to sneak your sister and her friend out of Nira. You only complicated their problem. They are both married now and in purdah. That means you will never see them again. You will never get to marry that girl, Leila. She now belongs to another man."

Malik roared in anger and made to attack his father, but he couldn't escape the hands of his father's goons. He settled for sneering at the old man. "I know the man Leila is married to. I'm going to get her out somehow, no matter how long it takes me."

His father laughed and then stared at him. He said, "First of all, that is impossible. You cannot take another man's wife or you will be killed. Besides, I'm going to make sure you don't go anywhere near Dauda or Jibril, Leila and Zainah's husbands. Fanta is with us now. The only way you will be allowed to see her every day is to behave."

Malik saw red. He shouted, "If you touch my daughter..."

"As I said before, I would never harm Fanta. But you will not be allowed to take her home or see her again if you don't cooperate. Your mother will still watch Fanta while you go to work. If you behave and don't go near Zainah and Leila's husband's houses, you will get to see and take Fanta home after work. Before you go to work, someone will come and take her to my house where your mother will watch over her until you are back. If, however, you try to break Zainah and Leila out of their marital homes, you will never be allowed to see your daughter again. Is that understood?"

He had been forced to accept his father's terms.

"And one more thing. I'm transferring you to my farm in Dogon. You'll work for two weeks there and then come back here for a few days before going back again. That's punishment for your treachery."

He had raged and raged, but his father did not listen to him. He'd had no choice but to agree to everything his father had said.

He stretched out on his couch and took a deep breath. He had just returned from another two weeks of intense work at his father's farm in Dogon. Every time he came back, he tried to spend as much time as possible with Fanta, knowing he had only a few days with her. His father's men watched him closely to make sure he didn't escape out of town with her. Even now, he knew they were watching his house.

He groaned and turned on the couch as Leila's face appeared in his mind. Since his wife died, he'd been content to just be Fanta's father, and taking care of his daughter had been his only priority. Until he met Leila. He had tried to forget about her after his father's threats, but couldn't. Every day, he was tormented with the knowledge that she was married to another man. She was probably miserable and he couldn't do anything about it.

He shut his eyes as the memory of their last kiss flooded his mind. Groaning, he tried to shut her out of his mind, but he couldn't. Knowing she was in this same town but he couldn't even see her was nothing but pure torture. He sighed, got up, and went into his room to try to sleep. But sleep completely evaded him.

He sat up and tried to pray to Allah, but he changed his mind. He'd been praying for a solution since he'd found out that Leila and Zainah had been forced to wed men they didn't know, but there was no help. But why was he expecting some divine help? It wasn't like he would get that when he was asking for another man's wife to be set free so he could marry her. It didn't matter under what circumstances they'd been married, or what her present station was now. All that mattered was that she was a married woman. He had to forget about her, before he did something that would cost him his daughter.

But rather than forget about her, he did something that surprised him. He prayed that he would find a way to somehow free Leila and Zainah from their marital imprisonment so he could marry Leila. But he didn't pray to Allah, the one he'd prayed to all his life. He prayed to the God who was against forced marriages and conversions, and practices like purdah. He prayed to Leila and Zainah's God.

FIVE

Faizan shut his eyes and held the phone tightly to his ear. He sighed loudly, opened his eyes again and said, "Jake, I've done everything you said I should do. I got the names of the men planning that terrorist attack in Florida and even the name of their leader. What else do you want from me?"

Jake said, "I need you to stay there for now. We still have a lot to learn from these men."

"The longer I stay here, the more dangerous it is for me. Soon, the men will begin to suspect I am not who I say I am. One of them has ties to my old terrorist organization. I want to be far away from here before he finds out who I truly am. Besides, I need to go home to my fiancée. Like I told you before, if we don't get married before the end of her ninety days, she will have to leave America."

"I'm sorry, Faizan, but there's nothing I can do."

"I'm sure there's something you can do." When Jake said nothing, Faizan said, "Okay, can you at least tell me exactly why you still want me here?"

Faizan blinked and then groaned as the phone began to beep. He removed it from his ear and looked
at it. Jake had hung up... again. He had a way of
hanging up on him all the time. It made Faizan so
angry.

His heart twisted as he thought about Zainah.
He was as worried about her as he knew she would
be about him. He looked around the small room in
which he had resided for more than two weeks. It
was plain, with just a bed and a small dresser. He
was in the middle of nowhere, in the desert, but the
familiarity and ease with which he had settled into
this role he was playing was discomforting.

He wanted to go back to America, to his church,
to his sisters, and, most of all, to Zainah. But he
couldn't. He was stuck here in this life that brought
back so many unpleasant memories, amongst violent men who reminded him so much of his old self.

The hardest part was having to pretend to pray
with the men. He sat on the prayer mat with them
and went through all the rituals that he knew so
well, but he whispered the name of Jesus under his
breath.

"Lord, please help me. I can't stay here any longer. I need to go home to Zainah." He couldn't even
call her for fear that he would somehow get her in
trouble. He knew how unreasonable that was since
it was unlikely the men would trace his call and
find her in America. Still, he avoided calling her.
She would wonder why he hadn't called for so long.

He stared at his phone and felt an overwhelming
urge to call her. He started to dial her number, and
then jumped when someone pounded on his door.

"Faizan!" the voice of Khalid, the leader of the small terrorist group he'd infiltrated, boomed on the other side of the door.

He went and quickly opened the door. In this place where suspicions were rife, you did not delay or hesitate when the leader called for you.

Khalid, bearded with hard eyes and a constant smirk, said to him in Arabic, "I need you to come with me. I'm supposed to meet with someone who only speaks English and I need you to act as my translator."

Faizan groaned inwardly, but on the outside he smiled. This was not the first time he had acted as a translator for Khalid. It was during both times when he had done so that he had learned about the plan for an attack in America. He had promptly reported back to Jake.

Jake had promised he would be out of this place before the CIA made their move against the terrorist group, but here he was, still in their midst. At any time, he could be discovered and shot.

He followed Khalid out and put away all his complaints and concerns. For now, he had to focus on the task at hand and learn as much as he could. The earlier he did that and passed on his information to Jake, the earlier he could get back to America so he could finally marry Zainah.

He hid a smile of self-mockery as he entered the truck and sat beside Khalid. Hopefully he would make it through today and be alive to marry Zainah.

He silently prayed for protection as they drove

away from the headquarters of the terrorist group and held Zainah's image firmly in his heart, eagerly waiting for the day they would be reunited.

*****

Leila got to the bus station where she would take a bus to Kazi. She looked around in confusion. There were no buses around. She went into the bus terminal and found it was empty. She looked around her and finally saw a petite woman standing at the corner of the station terminal with a huge bowl of assorted fruit. She was probably a trader who had stopped at the station to rest before she continued selling her fruit. Leila walked up to her and asked why there were no buses around.

The woman looked up from her bowl of fruit and said, "The drivers are striking over the lack of safety on the roads and also for an increase in their wages."

Leila put her hand on her head as a flood of frustration went through her. She shut her eyes briefly and then opened them again. "Do you know when the strike will end?" she asked the woman.

The woman told her she wasn't sure. "I don't think the drivers will end the strike until their wages are increased."

With a heavy heart, Leila left the bus station and went back to Fatima's house. She told Fatima what she had discovered at the bus station.

"When will I get to see Malik again?" she asked. "The woman I saw at the bus station said the drivers would not end the strike until they got their salaries increased. Apparently, this strike could go on forever," Leila said, laughing harshly.

Fatima touched her hand and smiled sympathetically at her. "Don't worry about it, Leila. You know what the Bible says. All things work together for the good of those who love God and are called according to His purpose."

Leila sighed sadly. "I thought I would get to see Malik in just a few days' time."

Fatima looked up with a thoughtful expression, and then she looked at Leila again. "Leila, are you really sure about this journey you want to take? From what Zainah told me when you both lived here, I think it's not really safe for you to go to Nira, especially after what you told me happened to both of you there. Maybe this drivers' strike is God's way of telling you not to go."

Leila put her hand on her forehead and said, "Not you too, Fatima! Please, I'll be careful."

Fatima settled back on the sofa and shrugged. "Okay, Leila. I'll pray that the Lord will protect you when you finally go. I just wish you would take some time to think and pray about it."

That night, Leila tossed and turned in her bed. She thought about taking Fatima's advice and praying, but she immediately changed her mind. She couldn't pray and ask the Lord to help her when she was almost certain that she was not in God's will.

The next day, bleary-eyed from lack of sleep, she went back to the bus station to see if the drivers had ended their strike. She found the place still empty.

She groaned and went back to Fatima's. She went straight to her room and lay on the bed, fighting her depression. She decided she would go to the bus station every day until the strike ended. Then she could make her way to Nira and finally get to see Malik again.

*****

Faizan got up as Khalid came into his room.

"You have to go with me to another meeting to translate the man's words," Khalid said to Faizan.

Faizan couldn't hold back his curiosity and asked, "What is this meeting about?"

Khalid glared at him and then said coldly, "You don't need to concern yourself with what it's about. All you need to do is to prepare to be my translator as usual."

Faizan nodded. "I'm sorry," he said. He followed Khalid outside to the waiting truck. He got into the back of the truck while Khalid sat in front with the driver. Faizan blinked when a dozen other men—Khalid's men, fully armed with assault rifles, jumped into another truck behind them. He turned and his heart raced. This was definitely not just another meeting where he had to translate. There was something more.

The truck began to move and Faizan looked out at the desert sand as it swirled around them. Memories of his time as the leader of his own terrorist group flooded his mind. He felt ashamed at the rush of excitement and anticipation going through him now. He felt like his old self before a mission. He didn't want to feel that way. He whispered a silent prayer to the Lord, asking for God's presence to feel him. Little by little, he began to feel the presence of the Lord surround and fill his heart, until he felt completely inundated with it.

They drove for a long time with Khalid talking in hushed tones to the driver. From time to time, he made and answered calls, speaking in symbolic words so Faizan could barely pick up what he was saying.

Faizan intermittently looked back at the other truck behind them as they drove. The men were still following them. Almost an hour later, they approached a Bedouin tent. Two men, also armed, milled around the tent. They stopped what they were doing when Faizan and Khalid's truck approached.

All of a sudden, Khalid's men opened fire on the two men. They tried to fight back, but there were too many of Khalid's men. The other men were gunned down and Khalid's men jumped down from the truck and quickly surrounded the tent.

Khalid entered the tent and motioned for Faizan to come in with him. A Caucasian man wearing a turban and two Arab women sat in the tent, huddled together, cowering. Khalid screamed at him. "Where is he?" He looked at Faizan and ordered him to translate.

Faizan did, his heart beating.

The man shook his head, his eyes wild with fear. The women were clutching him, whimpering. "I don't know where he is," he said in English.

Khalid laughed humorlessly and then grabbed one of the women. She screamed, and the other screamed too. "If you don't tell me where Tariq is right now, I'll start by shooting this one."

The woman screamed again and tried to escape Khalid's grasp, but he held on tightly. He looked at Faizan and yelled, "What are you waiting for?

Translate!"

Faizan slowly translated while assessing the situation and wondering what he could do. Though he was supposed to be a covert agent and not supposed to interfere, his conscience would not let him stand by and do nothing. Khalid was going to kill these people, whether this man told him what he wanted to know or not. But he didn't know what he could do. He was just one unarmed man. There were a dozen armed men of Khalid's outside the tent and Khalid himself was armed.

The man shook his head again. "I don't know where Tariq is," he said in a shaky voice. "I am telling the truth."

"Then this one will die," Khalid said coldly. He pressed the gun to the woman's head and Faizan reacted without thinking further about it. He kicked Khalid and felled him to the ground and then he grabbed the gun from his hand and pointed it at him.

Khalid's face was full of shock at first and then he gave Faizan a wicked grin. "You traitor. You cannot get away with this. You know that. The men are all outside waiting. They will kill you and these people you are trying to protect as soon as you walk out of here."

Faizan said, "Not if I use you as my hostage to get away." He told one of the women to get him a rope or something he would use to tie Khalid up. When she got him a twine, he told the man to tie up Khalid while he kept the gun pointed at him.

"Hurry!" he ordered the man in English. Any moment now, one of Khalid's men would grow suspicious and wonder why he was still in the tent, and would come in to inquire. He would have to have Khalid tied up and on the move before then.

After Khalid's hands had been tied up behind his back, a cloth stuck in his mouth and then tied with a piece of cloth, Faizan hurled him up. He told the man and the women to follow him slowly from behind. He would use Khalid as a bargaining chip for himself, the man, and the women to get away.

He held Khalid in front of him like a shield and then told the man and women again that they had to follow close behind if they wanted to be safe. They would get into one of the trucks and drive away. He would release Khalid once they were far away from the men. The plan was slightly sketchy, he knew, but it was all he could come up with at this time.

He began to walk out of the tent with Khalid and then turned to speak to the man just before he did. "Remember—" His eyes bulged as a man hit him on the head with a gun. The last thing that went through his mind before he faded away was that he had blown his mission and his cover and now he would probably never see Zainah again.

*****

Leila walked to the bus station, her heart pounding in fear. For the past week, she had been going to the station every single day, hoping the driver's strike had ended. And every day, she came back to Fatima's house disheartened and disappointed.

Fatima had suggested leaving off going to the station for about a week, since it seemed that the drivers were determined not to start work until they got every single thing they were agitating for.

"Who knows when that will be," Fatima said.

Leila approached the bus station and heard loud shouting, yelling, and arguing. She turned a bend, and her heart leapt with joy as she saw the station was filled with drivers, passengers, and hawkers, all talking and arguing and bargaining. She smiled widely. Never had she been so happy at the sight of people quarrelling as she was right now.

"Thank you, Lord," she said as she lifted her eyes to the sky.

She went to the counter where she and Zainah had bought a bus ticket to Kazi months ago. There was a long line of people standing at the counter. She stood at the back of the line, took a deep breath, and waited for her turn.

Twenty minutes later, she got to the front of the line, and opened her purse to bring out the money she'd saved for this trip. It was money she'd been paid at the women's camp for the rugs she had woven. She didn't usually weave a lot of rugs like some of the women there, but she had this time. She knew she had to make money in order to afford the trip to see Malik and so she had woven as many rugs as she could. It wasn't a lot of money, but it would be enough to take her to Nira, and then back to the camp after she'd seen Malik.

She paid the unsmiling man behind the counter and collected her ticket. Walking out of the bus station building, she went to sit on one of the benches in front of the building. She stared at the people boarding buses some distance away while waiting for all the passengers that were traveling on the same bus as her to pay for their trip so they could finally leave.

"Lord," she said, "please lead me today. Please help me find Malik when I reach Nira. Cause that no one else from Malik's family will see me while I search for him."

Suddenly, fear descended on her. Until now, she hadn't really thought about how exactly she would accomplish that—finding Malik in Nira without being seen by anyone else from his family. She'd been so consumed with the idea of finding her one true love and being reunited with him that she hadn't actually thought about what exactly would be involved in finding him.

She took a deep breath and then forcefully pushed the fear threatening to choke her out of her mind. To distract herself, she glanced around the bus station compound. She gazed at passengers boarding buses, hawkers selling snacks and fruits to passengers, and drivers impatiently waiting beside the buses while gnawing on chewing sticks and spitting out gunk.

Half an hour later, she boarded the bus with all the other passengers going to Kazi.

On the long trip to Kazi, she prayed incessantly. She also slept a lot, trying to avoid dwelling too much on her predicament. She knew very well that she was going to Nira like a sheep knowingly walking into a den of wolves. However, she had no choice. She couldn't see herself living without Malik. Even though she'd known him for only a short time, she loved him as though she'd known him all her life.

She prayed quietly. "Lord, I know he's not a Christian, but I believe he'll soon be one. I know he loves me and will do anything for me. I'm sure he will become a Christian when I ask him to. Lord, all I ask is that you help me find him, and that you protect me so no one else from his family, or connected to the family, will see me."

Even though she was still sure she wasn't in God's perfect will, she had no choice but to keep praying and asking for God's help. She needed His help now more than ever.

When she'd first arrived at Fatima's house, and Fatima had tried to convince her not to go to Nira to look for Malik, she'd avoided praying. She knew she wasn't walking in God's will. But now, all she did was pray.

She stayed awake as they passed through tiny villages and then long stretches of road with no houses or people in sight. She slept after a while, bored with the lack of scenery.

Suddenly, she awoke with a start when she heard someone scream. Her eyes widened in shock as she saw men with flashlights surrounding the bus. It was already nightfall, but the bright lights from the flashlights illuminated the scared faces of her fellow passengers. Leila looked around. They were in the middle of nowhere. If these men decided to harm or even kill them, no one would come to help.

Leila's muscles tensed in fear as the girl in front of her was dragged out of the bus. The other men were pulling out passengers from the bus and depositing them on the ground.

Leila looked into the eyes of the man who had dragged out the girl in front of her. Brutality was etched on his face and his eyes were dead. He barked at her to get down from the bus immediately. She screamed as he grabbed her and literally threw out of the bus and onto the ground. The woman who had been seated beside her helped lift her up. She sucked in her breath as she sat up. Her back hurt from her fall.

Leila trembled with fear as the armed men with red, blazing eyes surrounded her and the other passengers, their guns pointed at them. She took hold of the woman beside her and they both clung to each other.

"Hand over all your valuables," the men said, looking at all the passengers.

The armed men began going around, snatching purses, wristwatches, earrings, and bracelets. Leila quickly removed her tiny earrings so they wouldn't tear them out of her ears when they came over. She'd heard horrible tales of armed robbers tearing out earrings from women's ears when they didn't remove them from their ears quickly. The earrings were the only jewelry she had on her.

When one of the men came to her, he pointed the gun at her head and held out his palm. "Give me everything you have," he said impatiently.

She gave him her earrings and handed over her purse. However, she sat on the money she'd planned to travel to Nira with, hiding it. She couldn't afford to hand that over to him or she would not be able to get to Nira from Kazi.

The man stared at her and said, "Is this all?"

She nodded and then shuddered as he continued to look at her. Her heart kept pounding and didn't stop until he finally moved on.

After what seemed like an eternity, the ordeal finally came to an end. The men got into a car parked some distance away and drove off. Leila took in a deep breath, relieved they were gone. Thankfully, nobody had been seriously hurt.

Everyone began to stand up to get onto the bus again.

Leila stood and then gasped in pain and almost fell.

"Is everything okay?" the woman beside her asked.

"I can't walk! My back and my leg hurt."

The woman helped her into the bus and sat her down. Leila bit her lip in agony. Her back was on fire. She fought the urge to cry out in pain as the bus began to move again. Some of the women in the bus were still whimpering, while others chanted prayers.

Leila shut her eyes, trying to shut out the pain in her back and leg, but not succeeding. *How will I be able to get to Nira and find Malik if I can't even walk without excruciating pain?*

They got to Kazi about seven o'clock in the morning. The driver parked in the bus station, and everyone began to disembark. Leila prayed, asking the Lord for help. She got up and started to get off the bus and then bit her lip as pain shot through her back and her leg. She finally managed to get down from the bus, breathing heavily and trying not to think of the pain.

She saw an empty bench in front of the station, focused on it, and moved slowly towards it, trying as best she could to ignore the pain wracking her body. Just before she got to the bench, a group of girls sat down on it. She groaned and looked around. Tears filled her eyes. She couldn't stay standing for much longer. She had to find a seat. But there were no empty seats around.

Lord, what am I going to do?

How would she be able to go into the bus station, stand in line waiting to pay for her ticket, buy the ticket, and board a bus to Nira when she was in so much pain?

One of the girls who had taken the seat she was aiming for asked if she was okay.

Leila shut her eyes, opened them again, she shook her head, and said, "No." She looked down at the girl and said, "My back and leg hurt. Our bus was attacked by robbers on our way here. They threw me to the ground. When I got up, I found I couldn't walk well. My leg and my back are aching."

The girl got up and asked her to sit down. When Leila did, the girl said, "Do you need me to do anything for you? I can buy your ticket for you if you want."

Leila looked up at her in surprise and said, "You would do that for me?"

The girl nodded.

Leila thanked her profusely and gave her the remaining money that she had hidden from the robbers. She told her she wanted a ticket to Nira and watched as the girl hurried away into the bus station.

Some minutes later, the girl came out and handed her a ticket to Nira. "Here you go," the girl said.

Leila smiled at her. She whispered a prayer of thanksgiving to the Lord. This girl's help was purely God's grace and an answer to her prayers.

Leila sat waiting with her hand on her back, praying that God would give her strength.

The other passengers on her bus did not start to board until almost an hour later. Leila boarded the bus and sat at the back.

The hour-long trip seemed much longer and at the same time shorter than she remembered. As much as she wanted to see Malik again, she feared that not only would her leg and back not be able to withstand the strain of finding him, but that she would be seen by Malik's father and maybe captured the way she and Zainah had been the last time they were in Nira.

I can't let that happen, she said to herself.

The bus driver reached the outskirts of Nira and parked at a bus station opposite the small Nira market. Leila waited until everyone disembarked from the bus before she hobbled down. She stood on her leg to test it. Thankfully, the pain in her leg and her back had subsided. It was still painful, but not as unbearable as it had been in Kazi.

She dragged her feet as she moved away from the bus. Some distance away, she stood to cross the road. Thankfully, there were hardly any cars on the narrow road. She crossed as best and as quickly as she could, her leg throbbing. On the other side of the road, she avoided the market, not knowing who might be there who might remember her and her connection to Zainah and Malik's family.

The memory of her almost-marriage months ago in this town came flooding back to her, and she winced inwardly. If anyone saw her and re-membered that she was one of the brides who was supposed to marry one of the richest men in the town but then was rescued by armed men who stormed the community, they would probably go and tell Zainah's father. That in turn would lead to a manhunt and ultimately to her being found out. Who knew what would happen to her after that?

She found an empty hut and, once again, lifted up a prayer of thanksgiving to the Lord. She entered the hut and sat on the bare floor. When it was dark, she would go out again to search for Malik. He had shown her his house some days before that sham marriage almost took place.

"Hopefully, you can come and see my house later this evening," he had said to her as they walked by it. "Right now, there are so many people around, and it would seem a little inappropriate to have a single woman enter the house with me. It'll be better when it's dark."

She had thought then that what was inappropriate was going to the house with him when it was dark, but she had not told him so. Unfortunately, she had never gotten to see the house. She and Zainah had been thrown into the horrible shack with the single window. They had been locked up for days in the shack until their "wedding day". Thankfully, Faizan's friends had rescued them.

Leila spent the rest of the time in the hut praying and sleeping. She woke up and found the hut was totally dark. She pulled a tiny flashlight out of her pocket. She had brought it along with her specifically for this purpose—to search for Malik. She turned on the flashlight and shined it around the hut. She stood and then pressed her lips together as pain shot through her legs. Sighing, she hobbled out of the hut and began to walk into Nira, the flashlight illuminating her way.

She felt slightly confused as she walked through

a narrow pathway towards what she hoped was the road leading to Malik's house. All around her were trees and tall grass. She kept praying and hoping she was going in the right direction.

She walked on, still uncertain about the direction to Malik's.

I hope I am going in the right direction. All she could do now was pray and hope that this lonely road she was working on would lead her to Malik.

Soon, she saw Zainah and Malik's father's house. The brick house was the only building that was lit up, clearly by a generator. The other houses around, most of them actually huts, were in the dark.

Leila walked on the other side of the road, completely avoiding Zainah's father's house. She jumped as two men suddenly came out. Switching off her flashlight, she hid in the shadows. She focused on the road in front of her, walking slowly while praying with all her heart that they would not see her. Even though she had switched off her flashlight, light from the house still dimly illuminated the path she was walking on.

When she had gone some distance away from the house, she sighed in relief. Neither of the men had seen her.

"Thank you, Lord," she breathed when she finally saw Malik's house. It was very similar to his father's, only much smaller.

She paused in front of the house, turned on her flashlight, took a deep breath, and then knocked on the door. "Lord, please let him be at home," she prayed. She wasn't sure exactly of the time, but it seemed like it was about nine p.m. A few people were about, but most were in their homes.

Her heart thudded as she waited for Malik to open the door. She felt excited and nervous at the same time. What would he say when he saw her? Surely, he would be ecstatic to see her.

After a few minutes, she frowned and knocked on the door again. She waited, but still no one came to the door. She shut her eyes. Where is he, Lord?

She suddenly jumped and yelped as someone touched her shoulder. Turning around, her eyes widened in shock as she looked into the eyes of Khadija, Zainah's younger sister.

"Shh!" Khadija said. "I was just passing by when I saw someone that looked like you in front of Malik's house. I didn't believe it was you. I didn't think you would ever come back here after everything you and Zainah went through the last time you were here." She shook her head and said, "What are you doing here?"

Leila looked pleadingly at her and said, "Are you going to tell your father I am here in Nira?"

Khadija shook her head again. "No. I regret even participating in that forced marriage, Leila. I'm glad you and Zainah were rescued from it. I won't tell my father. But I need to understand, Leila. Why are you here?"

"I came to find Malik," Leila answered. "Do you know where he is?"

"You must really love him to risk coming back here."

Impatiently, Leila asked again, "Malik? Do you know where he is?"

Khadija said, "He's not here. He has gone to my father's farm in Dogon."

Leila's heart sank. "When will he be back?"

"In about two weeks' time," Khadija answered.

Leila closed her eyes and sank to the floor in misery. Khadija knelt in front of her and put her hand on Leila's shoulder. "I'm so sorry."

Leila couldn't speak. All her hopes and dreams of meeting and finally being in Malik's arms were for naught. All her dreams to be with him right now melted away. What I am going to do? I don't want to leave without seeing Malik.

She looked at Khadija and said, "Where is Dogon? Can you give me directions to the place?"

Khadija shook her head. "I don't really know where it is."

Leila sighed sadly. Why was she even asking for directions when she didn't have any money to go there? Plus, her back still hurt like crazy. There was no way she would make it there in her state. She looked away from Khadija, feeling completely hopeless.

Khadija tapped her shoulder. "I have an idea!" she exclaimed, as a huge smile spread across her face.

"What is it?" Leila asked.

"You can stay in Malik's house until he comes back."

"But it's locked," Leila said. "I tried to open…"

Khadija cut her off. "My father has the key to Malik's house, but I can steal it and bring it here for you."

Leila's heart soared and she said, "That would be a good idea." It would afford her the opportunity to heal up while she waited for Malik to come back to Nira. And then she thought about something and frowned. "But how will I stay hidden here? Are you sure nobody will find me here somehow and report to your father? Besides, what will I eat?"

Khadija gave her a small smile and said, "Don't worry about that. I'll try to get food for you every day. As for somebody finding you here, you will need to remain locked in the house, of course. I'll try my best to make sure nobody comes near here."

Leila nodded. Aside from the fact that she had no choice, this was the best idea. She looked at Khadija and wrapped her arms around the girl. "Thank you so much! Thank you."

When she let go of her, Khadija smiled again and nodded. "Now wait here. I'll go get the keys. My father will not be in his room now so I can steal them and bring them here for you." She went away quickly, and Leila tried the best she could to remain quiet so no one would know she was there.

She waited for a long time, and then became worried when Khadija did not come back. She soon began to wonder if Khadija had been found out trying to steal the key to Malik's house. Or had she told on Leila so that even now one or more of her father's men were on their way here?

Leila's heart beat in fear. Maybe I should leave, she told herself. But her heart refused to listen. She would see the end of this, no matter what. She had to believe, somehow, that Khadija would come back with the keys to this house.

She waited some more, but when Khadija still didn't appear, she knew the girl had told on her. Fear overwhelmed her. At any minute, the same men who had captured her and Zainah and locked them up at Zainah's father's command would come and take her away to be locked up again.

She heard footsteps approaching and her muscles tensed up.

Khadija arrived and bent down, breathing hard.

Leila let out a huge sigh of relief and said to Khadija, "What happened?"

"My mother sent me on an errand immediately I got to the house. I had no choice but to do what she asked me to or I would have been found out. I'm sorry. I ran all the way here."

"No need to apologize," Leila said.

Khadija quickly unlocked the door and she and Leila entered the house. Leila shined the flashlight around the living room. It was small and simply furnished. She smiled and took in a deep breath. She could smell Malik's scent here. It was a pleasant mixture of the sun, earth, and musk.

Khadija left the living room and came back almost immediately holding a candle and a matchbox. She lit the candle and placed it on top of the mantel near the loveseat. "Unfortunately, there will be no light for you here as my father's generator is not connected to the house right now."

Leila chuckled. "I'm used to staying where there's no light. The camp where I live has had no light for years. In a way, I prefer it."

Khadija smiled and nodded. She looked at Leila with a somber expression and said, "What about my sister, Leila? Is she okay?"

Leila gave her a big smile. "She is better than okay, Khadija. She is in America and she will soon be married to the man she loves."

Khadija gasped and then grinned. "Oh, I am so happy. I have been so worried about her."

Before Khadija left, Leila enfolded her in her arms, hugged her tightly, and thanked her again for her help. When she left, Leila stretched out on the couch and thanked God for bringing her here safely. She still felt disappointed that Malik was not here, but she was grateful for what God had done. He had worked a miracle in Khadija's heart and sent the girl to help her.

Leila smiled and said, "Thank you, Lord, for everything." She said to herself sarcastically, "Now, all I have to do is hide out in here for two weeks. How hard can that be?"

SIX

Faizan opened his eyes and looked around him, feeling disoriented. He couldn't see anything, as everything was dark. He kept looking around until his eyes adjusted to the darkness, and then he saw that he was in a small room that was completely empty. He shut his eyes, put his hand on his forehead, and groaned. He had a splitting headache. It felt just like someone was continuously pounding on his head with a huge stick.

He licked his lips. His mouth was terribly parched.

He groaned again as images of the events that had taken place, and probably landed him here, flooded his mind. He remembered clearly being hit on the head by the man who he'd been trying to save. Confusion filled his mind and he moaned. Why had the man, who he had risked everything to save, hit him on the head? Why had he even risked exposure to save the man?

He looked up at the ceiling and said, "Please,

Lord, help me! I made a terrible mistake and because of that, I might never get to see Zainah again." Images of her came rushing back to him. Zainah making him promise that he would come back on the last day they were together; her laughing face as she told him about shopping with his sisters for her wedding dress; Zainah kissing him, hugging him, and saying 'yes' on the day he asked her to marry him. He suddenly couldn't hold back and screamed, "What have I done? I should never have interfered."

But he knew he would never have been able to live with himself if he hadn't tried to save the women and that man, even though it turned out his interfering had been a huge mistake. The people he was trying to save, at least the man, was in cohorts with the enemy.

He put his hand on his pounding head and shut his eyes again, trying to sort out the pain in his heart, which was overwhelmingly greater than the physical pain he felt in his head.

He blinked in surprise as the door to his small cell burst open. Light flooded the room as the bulb on the ceiling lit up. The man he had tried to save back at the Bedouin tent came in. He stared at Faizan as though he was studying a science experiment. Faizan glared back at him in anger.

Khalid walked into the cell and for a long moment, stared at Faizan with disdain. He finally said, "When Nazeem told me you looked like the leader of his former resistance group who turned on them, I told him it was impossible because I trusted you. But when he insisted it was you and said you had betrayed the group, and that only a few of them had escaped, as most had been apprehended and taken to jail, I decided to test you to see if it was really true. I set a trap for you. Needless to say, you failed the test." He looked at the man beside him and said, "You can imagine my anger and disappointment, Chad."

Faizan glared at him. He felt his anger growing and then forcefully pressed it away. In his former life as a terrorist, he would have tried to attack these men, and maybe he would have succeeded in overpowering them as long as they didn't have a weapon on them. But now, he was a changed man, and violence didn't come so easily for him anymore.

"So that was why you wanted me to go with you," Faizan said to Khalid.

"You fell into the trap I set for you," Khalid said.

The man Khalid called Chad shook his head and said, "What a shame. He seems like such a smart man. We would have been able to use someone like him. He would definitely have been perfect for our next mission."

Khalid said, "Unfortunately, he turned out to be a traitor." He looked down at Faizan and sneered. "Before the end of today, you will be shot."

Faizan remained silent, but his heart beat with dread. He felt no fear for himself. The pain and fear in his heart was because he knew his death would cause Zainah excruciating pain. More than that, their dreams of getting married would never materialize and he would never see her again. His sisters would mourn for a very long time for the brother they had just found and now was dead.

He shut his eyes and allowed the pain to take

over him. Images of Zainah, Trisha, Audrey, and Sienna filled his mind. His heart flooded with overwhelming grief and pain. They would never again see him and he would never again get to tell them how much he loved them. He opened his eyes, looked up at the ceiling, and asked God to let them know how much he loved them. He asked the Lord to grant them comfort when he died.

He looked at Khalid again and found that he and the other man were staring curiously at him, probably wondering why he looked so much at peace when he'd just been told he would die before the end of the day. With a voice free from fear, he made his confession of faith. "I believe in the Lord Jesus who is and will always be the master and savior of my soul."

Khalid laughed harshly and said, "So, you are a Christian. Unfortunately for you, your Jesus will not be able to save you today."

The man beside him shook his head and said, "Like I said before, it's such a shame!"

Khalid and Chad walked to the door of the cell. Before they went out, Khalid turned around and said, "Such a waste. But that's what you get for your betrayal."

Both men left the cell, leaving it in complete silence.

Faizan sat watching the cell door as a guard locked it. Soon, he felt claustrophobic, and then he gradually descended into a pit of despair. He knelt on the cold floor and began to pray. He prayed and prayed, asking the Lord for peace, until at last he felt the peace of God descend on him. Within seconds, he fell into a dreamless sleep.

*****

Zainah quickly got up from the bed when she heard the front door open. She had moved into Audrey's old house when Trisha and Frank had come back from their honeymoon in order to give the newlyweds their privacy. She had been pacing the whole house since morning, worrying about Faizan. She had finally exhausted herself half an hour ago and sat on the bed. She called Audrey, who was in town and at the police station, to know if she'd found out anything new about Faizan. He usually called her and his sisters several times a week, but she hadn't heard from him in what seemed like forever. Their wedding was supposed to be in a week's time, and yet she didn't know where he was now.

She went to the living room and saw it was Audrey who had come into the house. Walking up to Audrey, she asked, "Have you heard from him?"

Audrey shook her head and slowly sat on the sofa. She looked away from Zainah, sighed audibly, and then looked down at the floor.

Zainah's eyes widened as fear gripped her. She had seen something in Audrey's eyes before she'd looked down at the floor. Something that looked like terror. She stood staring for a full minute and then went to sit beside Audrey on the sofa. Putting her hand on Audrey's shoulder, she said in a shaky voice, "Please tell me what you have heard about Faizan."

Audrey did not look up or say anything to Zainah. Instead, her shoulders began to shake and a sob escaped her lips.

Zainah felt blood rushing up to her ears and she trembled. Without meaning to, she shook Audrey's shoulder and yelled, "Please, just tell me that Faizan is okay!"

Audrey looked up with tears flowing down her cheeks and said, "I just got a phone call from Ken before I came here. He said he got word that Faizan was kidnapped some days ago. Nobody has heard from him since."

Zainah felt like throwing up. "What do you mean, kidnapped?" she asked. "Who kidnapped him?"

Audrey looked away for a brief moment and then looked back at her. "I don't know if I should tell you this," she said, "but, I think it's probably time you knew." She began to tell Zainah that Faizan worked for the government as a covert CIA agent.

As she talked, Zainah's heart beat with fear. She had suspected Faizan worked for the government, but she had never known he was in this deep. Now, they had jeopardized his life. She felt angry and depressed. When Audrey finished, she pressed her lips together so she wouldn't cry and then said, "So, you are telling me that all this time, he has been living with violent terrorists?"

Audrey nodded and then shut her eyes as a look of agony twisted her pretty features.

Zainah shook her head slowly. Her body turned to stone and for a few minutes, she could not move at all. For a long moment, she stared at the wall in front of her, and then terror unlike anything she had ever experienced flooded her mind, followed closely by an overwhelming sadness. Suddenly, she screamed and began to say, "No, no, no! Please, Lord, not my Faizan. Please!"

*****

She turned to Audrey who was weeping silently beside her and said, "Maybe he wasn't kidnapped. Maybe he just went off the grid. I'm sure he's safe. We don't know that he was kidnapped, do we?"

Audrey said in a broken voice, "Jake, his handler, was the one who told Ken about it. He's pretty sure Faizan was kidnapped."

Zainah said desperately, "Okay, if he was kidnapped, we can find out who the kidnappers are so we can start the process of freeing him."

Audrey looked up into Zainah's eyes and said, "Zainah, Ken told me that the people who kidnapped him, the terrorist group he has been living with, are very brutal. They are known to kill even their own members at the drop of a hat. Jake feels that he was found out. People who betray the group like that are always..." She didn't finish her sentence. She covered her mouth and wept.

Zainah stood up, not wanting to hear any more. She tried to walk away, but her feet could not carry her, and she sank to her knees. Spots danced in front of her eyes, and she felt nauseated. She shut her eyes and passed out.

She opened her eyes after what seemed like a minute later. Audrey's face floated over her head. She sat up, realizing that she had been carried and laid on the couch by Audrey.

"Are you okay?" Audrey asked, placing a hand on her forehead. "You passed out all of a sudden."

Zainah shut her eyes, and then pain began to course through her as she remembered what Audrey had told her a minute ago about Faizan. She opened her eyes and began to shake her head again. All she could hear herself say continuously was, "No!"

Audrey wrapped her arms around her and tried to comfort her. She said, "Maybe you're right, Zainah. Maybe Jake and Ken are wrong. Maybe, like you said, he just went off the grid."

Zainah suddenly couldn't hold back again and began to sob loudly. And then, just as suddenly, she stopped crying.

Crying would not solve this problem. They had to pray for Faizan right now. If there was any chance that he was still alive, he needed their prayers right now. She turned to Audrey and said, "Let's pray for him right now."

Audrey dabbed the tears on her cheeks and nodded.

Zainah took her hands and shut her eyes. She said, "Lord, we are not sure where Faizan is right now, but we choose to trust that he still alive. We know he needs your protection and that is what we are praying for. Please, Lord, please protect him. Keep him safe from harm. Whatever he might be going through, please deliver him."

Zainah continued to pray, asking that the Lord would shield Faizan and that He would send His angels to watch over Faizan. She prayed that the Lord would send a miracle and deliver Faizan no matter where he was and what he was going through.

After she prayed, Audrey also prayed.

*****

After the prayer session, Zainah said, "Audrey, we have to trust the Lord. We have to trust that He will protect Faizan no matter where he is and deliver him from harm."

Audrey smiled sadly and said, "You're right. We definitely need to trust the Lord at this time."

For the rest of the day, Zainah walked around the house like a zombie. She felt completely numb. She was trying hard to believe that Faizan was still alive and that God would protect him, while continuously fending off the doubts that assailed her.

Before she went to bed, she prayed again, asking the Lord for a miracle for Faizan. "Bring him back to me, Lord," she said, lying flat on her back on her bed, and looking at the ceiling. "I cannot live without him."

She tossed and turned throughout the night. The next morning, she got out of bed, and quickly went to find Audrey. Audrey was still in her room. Zainah knocked on Audrey's room door and when she heard her say "Come in," she opened the door and entered.

She saw Audrey sitting on her bed and said to her, "Have you heard anything about Faizan's whereabouts?"

Audrey looked up. Her eyes looked red. She had probably not slept a wink, just like Zainah. "I haven't heard anything," she answered.

Zainah went and sat on the bed beside Audrey. She took her hand and said to her, "Let's pray for him."

They began to pray with all their hearts, because that was all they knew to do. They prayed again that the Lord would come through for them, and that Faizan would return to them, safe and unhurt.

SEVEN

Faizan looked up as someone entered his tiny cell. Two burly men, Khalid's men, grabbed him by the arms and hurled him up. He hadn't eaten any real food for days and he felt weak. They dragged him out of the cell, down a narrow corridor, and outside to the bright sunlight.

He squinted and shut his eyes briefly to shut out the glaring sunlight. The light from the sun hurt his eyes as he had not been outside for days. Apart from the fact that he felt weak from lack of food, he also felt sad and undefeated. He knew what was about to happen to him. He was about to be shot and he would never see Zainah or his sisters again.

His heart filled with sorrow and he whispered a prayer to God, asking for help and asking that the Lord would comfort Zainah and his sisters when they heard the news of his death.

The two men dragged him to the fence at the back of the expansive compound of the terrorist group. He took a deep breath as they left him standing there and asked that the Lord receive his soul when he died.

Another man came out of the building facing the one they had brought him out of. He was holding a rifle. He came and stood beside the two burly men and pointed his gun at Faizan.

Faizan lifted his eyes to the sky and began to pray. He was determined to die praying to the God who had saved him from a violent life.

He continued to pray and soon his prayer turned to worship. At any minute now, he knew he would feel the searing pain of a bullet piercing his chest or forehead. He kept his eyes lifted to the sky while his heart clung to the Lord.

The booming sounds of gunshots shattered the air and he squeezed his eyes closed.

So, this is it, then, he thought in his heart. He would die here, far away from all his loved ones. They would never get to see his body. He sighed sadly. Well, at least his soul would be with the Lord. That was what mattered the most.

He kept waiting to feel the pain from the gunshot, but he felt absolutely nothing. He opened his eyes and began to wonder if he had died already. He looked around and his mouth fell open in astonishment. The man called Chad was holding a gun and standing over the bodies of the man who had pointed the rifle at him just a few minutes ago and the two burly men who had dragged him out of his cell.

Faizan looked past the man and saw three trucks parked behind him. Armed men wearing fatigues trooped out of the trucks and surrounded all the buildings in the compound. Some of them entered the buildings.

*****

More gunshots sounded. Chad put his gun in the holster around his waist and walked up to Faizan. The man said, "Sorry for whacking you on the head. I had to pretend I was on Khalid's side to make sure my cover was not broken." He put his hand on Faizan's shoulder and asked, "Are you okay?"

Faizan couldn't speak. He just stared at the man.

Chad smiled at him with his hand still on Faizan's shoulder and said, "My real name is Chuck. I was sent by Jake to partly carry out another secret mission and partly to watch out for you. When Jake heard you were in trouble, he sent me to help you out. I've been working closely with Khalid for a while without him suspecting who I really am."

Faizan shook his head in astonishment, still unable to believe he had been rescued. He looked past Chuck again. The men in fatigues were dragging out Khalid's men from all the buildings. Chuck left him and walked over to his men. He said something to them that Faizan didn't hear.

Faizan walked over to him and watched as Khalid's men were bundled into the trucks. Minutes later, two men came out, dragging Khalid along with them.

Khalid turned and glared at Faizan. He suddenly broke out in an evil laugh and then turned away again, still laughing. He was dragged away and shoved into one of the trucks. The captured men were driven away, and Faizan turned his attention to Chuck again. He opened his mouth and asked the major thing that had been on his mind since he'd left Rosefield and that he wanted more than anything in the world. "Can I go home now? I'm supposed to get married in a week."

Chuck chuckled and nodded. "Yes. Yes, you can go home now."

Faizan finally couldn't hold down the relief that flooded his heart and mind. He sank to his knees, choked back a sob, and gave God praise for saving his life. He stood up and said to Chuck, "I'm ready to go now."

Chuck drove him to a small house where he could bathe. He had not bathed for days. He entered a small room with only a bed and an ensuite bathroom and shed his clothes. He went into the bathroom, and just before he got into the shower, he looked at himself in the mirror. He looked a little gaunt, had a long beard, and was wearing dirty clothes, but that didn't matter. His heart was full of joy. He was alive and he could finally marry Zainah. That was all that mattered.

"Thank you, Lord," he said for the umpteenth time since he'd been rescued.

After he finished bathing, he changed into a white t-shirt and jeans that Chuck had laid out for him on the bed. He quickly combed his hair and then went out of the house.

Chuck was waiting for him outside, beside a black SUV. Faizan entered the car and sat in the back seat beside Chuck. The driver drove them to a private airstrip, and then walking briskly, Chuck led him to a small plane.

Just before Faizan entered the plane, Chuck said to him, "You are lucky you get to go home now. I can't do that until I complete my mission."

He pounded Faizan's back and then pointed at the plane. "Home awaits," he said. "Goodbye... until we meet again."

Faizan smiled, but he hoped that would not be any time soon. He shook Chuck's hand, thanked him again for rescuing him, and entered the small plane. He was the only passenger in the plane but his mind was not on that. All that was on his mind was the fact that he could not wait to see Zainah. She would be sick with worry, having not heard from him for so long. His sisters would also be worried about him. He hoped the hours would fly by quickly, so he could get home to Zainah and his sisters.

As the plane took off, his heart also soared. He whispered a prayer of thanksgiving to the Lord again, then settled down in his seat and excitedly counted the hours before he would be reunited with his loved ones in Rosefield.

*****

Zainah was distraught.

There was still no news of Faizan. Audrey had been calling Ken for hours, trying to find out if there was any new information about Faizan's whereabouts. Ken had only bleak news for them.

Zainah paced Audrey's living room while Audrey sat on the sofa, her eyes planted on her phone on the coffee table. Trisha and Frank sat together on the loveseat. Frank held Trisha tightly while she wept softly. Unfortunately, they had come back from their honeymoon days ago to the sad news that Faizan had been kidnapped and was probably dead.

Zainah refused to believe any of the reports she heard that Faizan would not still be alive because the terrorist group that was holding him was known to be swift to execute justice on people who they perceived had betrayed the group.

Audrey's phone rang and Zainah turned sharply to her. Maybe it was Faizan calling, or at least Ken with news about the man she loved. She looked expectantly at Audrey and then sighed in disappointment when Audrey whispered that it was Sienna on the phone.

Zainah listened for a while to Audrey's phone call with Sienna. She was trying to calm Sienna down as she was heavily pregnant. Her due date was almost here and Audrey reminded her about that. "Calm down, Sienna," Audrey said. "When we hear any more news about Faizan, we will let you know. You need to stop freaking out and think about your baby."

Zainah tuned out the conversation and started to silently pray. She had been praying nonstop since she heard that Faizan had been kidnapped. She would never let go of the hope that God would perform a miracle and deliver him, no matter what anyone said.

She finally grew tired of pacing the floor and sat down on the sofa facing Audrey. She shut her eyes and gradually fell asleep. Her dreams were filled with violence. She dreamt that Faizan had been killed and his body left to rot under the sun. She awoke trembling in fear, tears streaming down her face.

She looked at the time and saw that hours had

passed since she'd fallen asleep. Looking round the living room, she found that Trisha and Frank had fallen asleep and were wrapped up in each other's arms on the loveseat, while Audrey lay asleep on her back on the couch.

Zainah stretched out on the couch, her heart growing heavier and heavier as the hours flew by. What if he doesn't come back? she asked herself. What if he's dead?

She shook her head. I refuse to think like that. But her mind would not give up the images of him dead, his body left bloating somewhere in the Arabian Desert. She stood, as she couldn't take the agony anymore. She rushed into the bathroom, sank to her knees, and began to sob bitterly.

"Lord, where is my Faizan? What has happened to him?" She wept and wept and found no relief for her grief. After a while, she finally got tired of crying and decided to pray some more. She wiped her eyes, stood up, and went upstairs. She went to the patio where she had last spoken with Faizan before he left for his secret mission. Leaning on the balustrade, she stared at the lush courtyard below. Suddenly, she couldn't stop herself from screaming. She yelled as loud as she could and then said, "Lord, why?"

She covered her eyes with her hand and then she opened her eyes again. Staring into the distance, she tried to pray, but all she did was mumble.

She narrowed her eyes as she began to hear loud noises and commotion coming from somewhere in the house. And then she nearly sank to the floor, her legs unable to carry her. She leaned on the balustrade and bit her lip. Audrey had probably got a phone call from Ken with bad news about Faizan. It was probably Audrey and Trisha weeping now.

I should go to them.

But she could not muster up the strength to go. She didn't want to hear any bad news about Faizan. She would not be able to take it.

She suddenly cried out, "Faizan, where are you? Please come back!"

"I am here!"

Her eyes widened in shock. The voice she'd just heard . . . was that Faizan, or did she just imagine it because she so wanted to hear his voice, even if it was for one last time?

"Zainah, it's me!"

Her heart skipped violently and then flooded with a mixture of fear and hope. She turned around slowly and then she gasped. Faizan was really standing before her. Her heart soared and every trace of sorrow she'd felt suddenly disappeared. She ran to him and fell into his arms. She began to weep loudly while he rubbed her back. He said, "I'm here, Zainah. There is no need to cry anymore, baby."

She continued to weep, but out of relief, and joy, excitement, and ecstasy.

He held her tightly, letting her cry on his shoulder. After a few minutes, she drew back and looked into his eyes. She studied his face, the face which, just some minutes ago, she had feared she would never see again. She said, "Oh, Faizan, thank God you're safe! I was afraid something terrible had happened to you." She caressed his cheeks and then ran her fingers through his hair. She moved back even more and said again, "Thank God you came back!"

He grinned and said to her, "Of course I came back! I wouldn't miss my own wedding."

She laughed despite herself and said to him, "There's nothing more I want now than to marry you."

She hugged him again tightly, as though she were afraid that at any time he would disappear. After a while, she pulled back and kissed him on the cheeks.

"Did you continue with the wedding planning?" he asked her.

"How could I when all I was thinking about was your safety?"

"Well, I guess we have to continue planning it now. We are still getting married in a week's time, aren't we?"

She laughed. "Of course we are. Even if we have no food, drinks, guests, or a venue, I don't care. All I need is you and the minister who will marry us."

He smiled at her and then a torturous look crossed his face. He said, "I thought I would never see you again, Zainah." He pulled her close, dug his hands into her hair, and kissed her. He pulled back slightly and said hoarsely, "I've missed you so much."

She trembled and held him tightly as he kissed her again.

He began to pull back again, but she clung to him. This time, she would never let him go, no matter what. Just half an hour ago, when she thought she had lost him, she'd known she couldn't go on living without him.

She kissed him with everything in her, letting

him know that he was everything to her. Finally, when she was sated, she drew back slightly and laid her head on his chest. He kissed her forehead and then wrapped his arms around her.

She sighed in contentment. Since he'd left, she'd dreamt every day of this—being in his arms. She felt completely safe. She could stay like this forever, in the arms of this man she loved with all her heart, who she had feared was dead. She looked up at him and said, "I can't wait to marry you, Faizan."

He grinned. "I can't wait to marry you either, Zainah."

She trembled with excitement at the thought of becoming his wife and finally getting to live with him. Soon, they would begin their life together as man and wife. She could hardly wait.

EIGHT

Leila stood up from the floor where she slept beside Malik's bed. She had been sleeping on the floor in Malik's bedroom because she was uncomfortable with the idea of sleeping in his bed. Plus, she was used to sleeping on the floor from her many years of doing so in the women's camp. She immediately went to brush her teeth. She quickly had her bath, changed into a long black and white dress, combed and braided her hair, and went into the small kitchen to fix herself some breakfast.

Since she'd come to Nira, she did the same thing every single day. She prepared carefully for the day as though it was the day Malik would finally come back. Today, as she stood at the kitchen counter making an omelet for herself from the food items Khadija had brought for her five days ago, she thought about the women's camp and what Miriam would say when she discovered Leila was gone. Miriam would be exasperated. She'd had to come to her and Zainah's rescue when they had come to Nira months ago. Miriam would be praying she had not gotten herself into another predicament. She finished making breakfast and carried it to the living room to eat.

After she had her breakfast, she walked around the house, looking at the simple furniture, imagining Malik living here with his daughter. Many times, she also imagined herself living in this house with Malik; married to him and both of them raising his daughter and the children they would have together. However, she knew that if and when by God's grace they got married, they couldn't live together in Nira. Everyone around, especially his family, would oppose their marriage. She was a Christian. That would not go down well with his family.

She'd been praying and believing that he would become a Christian soon, because she could not marry him if he wasn't. Her heart twisted at the thought that he might never convert to Christianity so they could get married, but she immediately put aside that bleak thought. She focused on what she had always drawn hope from, and that was that Malik loved her enough to do anything for her, including converting to Christianity so they could be together forever.

She slightly drew back the curtain in the living room in order to peep out the window. She was always bored. Since there was nothing else to do, every day, after she had breakfast, she stood looking out the window at people passing by. That was her only entertainment. So far, she had managed to avoid being seen by anyone except for Khadija.

In the evenings, when it began to get dark outside, she lit one of the candles that Khadija had brought her the night she came to Nira, sat on the living room sofa, and thought about Malik and Zainah.

With all her heart, she longed to attend Zainah's wedding, but she just couldn't. It wasn't only because she had no money to travel to America or any hope of getting a visa, but because she had to be here and be reunited with the love of her life. Zainah had given her a new number with which to call her and she yearned to, but she had no cellphone. She'd asked Khadija if she could use her cellphone, but Khadija had told her she didn't have one. Apparently, her strict father forbade the use of cellphones by his teenage daughter, even though Khadija was at the cusp of womanhood.

Leila kept looking out the window, imagining the lives of the people passing by the house. A boy who looked about seventeen walked slowly and kept looking back. He smiled each time he did, and then quickly turned again, only to look back a few seconds later.

Soon, a girl who looked about the same age also began to pass by, and also walking slowly. Leila smiled in pleasure. The girl was the reason why the boy kept turning and smiling. Each time he smiled at her, she shyly smiled back. The whole thing made Leila's heart smile. It was the beginnings of young love, and she was a hopeless romantic. At the same time, she also felt a little sad as she watched them, wishing Malik was here with her.

Her eyes followed them as they walked farther and farther away from Malik's house until they disappeared from sight. She sighed. They had provided great entertainment for her. Now she was left watching people hurrying past with anger or impatience etched on their faces and making up stories in her mind about them. A few were expressionless, so she had to guess what was on their minds, what they were up to, and where they were going.

Her eyes grew wide as Zainah's father and another man began to walk towards Malik's house. Her heart thudded as she realized they were actually coming to the house and would be on the front porch in no time. Panic engulfed her and she looked at the door. She felt tempted to check the doorknob just to make sure Khadija had remembered to lock it before she left the night before, but she knew it would be the wrong thing to do. Zainah's father, Karim Keita, would know someone was in the house.

Leila closed the curtain when Karim Keita and the other man were almost at the front porch. Fear and anxiety flooded her heart, and for a second, she stood frozen, not knowing what to do. She began to move her feet once she heard the door being unlocked.

Lord, please help me, she prayed silently. She quickly ran into the bedroom, snatched up her nightgown from the bed, and went to hide in the closet. She stooped down, trembling, and prayed with all her heart that they would not find her. It was only after she finished praying that she realized she had left a bottle and her half-drunk glass of water on the table in the living room. That would definitely give away the fact that someone was in the house. There were also other traces of her presence in the living room and especially in the kitchen. There was no way Karim Keita would not know someone was here, living in his son's house.

She began to hear loud voices and footsteps approaching the bedroom, and she squeezed her eyes shut, as though by doing that she could will the men to go away.

The bedroom door opened and her heart thudded as she heard Mr. Keita's voice in the room, telling the other man that someone was in the house. Leila began to frantically pray, asking the Lord to keep the men away from the closet so she would not be found. She remembered with startling clarity what had happened the last time she and Zainah were in Nira. She shuddered. It had been dangerous for them then, with the forced marriage and the threat of death hanging over them if they refused to convert to Islam. What would Karim Keita do to her if he found her hiding in his son's house? She continued to pray while her heart raced wildly. And then, she heard scrambling feet and realized Zainah's father and the other man were searching the bedroom. She kept praying and then her muscles tensed when the closet door began to open.

She prayed fervently. Malik didn't have many clothes to hide behind. She would definitely be seen.

And then she heard Khadija's voice call out, "Papa, please come! I need to show you something now!"

"What is it, Khadija?" her father called out.

"Please, just come. I want to show you something in the house. It's urgent!"

There was silence for a few seconds and then Karim shut the closet door. He said to the other man, "Let's go. We will come back later."

Leila heard the bedroom door close and continued praying earnestly until she heard the front door shut. She remained in the closet for about ten minutes more, just to make sure the men had really left the house, and then she climbed out of the closet. She trembled from fear and relief as slowly sat on the bed.

Lord, thank you!

When she felt finally ready to stand up again, she stood up slowly, took a deep breath, and left the bedroom. She went into the living room and found that it was just as she had left it. The glass of water and the bottle were still on the coffee table. The curtain was ever so slightly open.

Her heart began to race again as she realized she was not out of danger yet. Mr. Keita knew someone was living in his son's house. He would come to investigate again soon. Any day now, she would be caught, and who knew what would happen to her then? She would definitely not get to see Malik if she was discovered. She couldn't let that happen.

Now what? she thought.

She slowly sat on the sofa and began to ponder what she could do, but she came up with nothing except to leave the house. Which also meant she would have to leave Nira, as she had nowhere else to stay. She thought about staying in the hut where she had hidden before coming to Malik's house, but it wasn't a good idea. The hut had no door and it was near the market. She would easily be found there. She had only been able to stay there for a short time because it was nighttime. Plus, she would probably starve, as she knew Khadija would not be able to get her food all the way there without someone getting suspicious.

Her only option was to leave Nira.

She shook her head. There was no way she would leave Nira or even this house without seeing Malik first.

But at the same time, how could she stay here, knowing that any day now, she would be caught?

She jumped as the keyhole turned. Someone was unlocking the front door. Before she could scramble up from the sofa and out of the living room, the door opened and the person came into the house. Leila shot up the sofa and then relief unlike anything she had ever felt settled on her as she saw Khadija standing at the door, looking at her with concern on her face. Leila gave a huge sigh of relief and then settled back on her seat as Khadija locked the door again.

The urgency of the moment settled on Leila and she said to Khadija with her heart drumming, "Your father knows that someone is living in Malik's house, doesn't he?"

Khadija nodded. She came and sat beside Leila and said, "If I had not come just at the time I did, he probably would have seen you. I had to make up something in order to get him out of the house."

"What did you say to him?" Leila asked curiously.

"I told him my toilet was blocked and the bathroom had flooded. I poured some water on the bathroom floor. He will soon discover that the toilet isn't blocked and will come back here to investigate again." Khadija took Leila's hands. "You will have to leave now, Leila. If my father finds you here, and he will very soon, you know what kind of trouble you will be in."

Leila shook her head. "No. I cannot leave, Khadija. I have to wait for Malik to return. I will not leave Nira without seeing him."

Khadija looked into her eyes and said, "I don't have to tell you what kind of trouble you will be in if my father finds you here. You already know what will happen."

Khadija was right. The terror and hopelessness she had felt when she and Zainah were almost forced to marry people they didn't know came rushing back to her. She knew she had to leave, but the thought of doing so without seeing Malik was too much for her to bear. Tears pooled in her eyes.

"I can't leave, Khadija! I can't!"

"Yes, you can," Khadija said. "I love how much you care for my brother, but if you don't leave now, you'll never get to be with him or even see him again."

Leila didn't say anything for long moment. Conflicting emotions warred within her. She sighed resignedly at last. There was nothing else to do but leave. "I guess you're right, Khadija," she finally said. Tears fell down her cheeks and she quickly wiped them away. "I will have to go and come back again."

Khadija smiled sadly at her. "I wish Malik had been here when you came, but I know that you and my brother will be together somehow. Your love for each other is so strong that it will make a way for both of you."

Leila smiled at her in appreciation. "Malik will be back in a week, won't he?"

"Yes," Khadija said.

"I guess I'll go back to my friend, Fatima's. I'll

stay there for a week and then come back."

Khadija nodded and said again, "You have to leave now, Leila. Anytime now, my father will come. You and I will be in trouble if he finds us here."

Leila squeezed Khadija's hand. "Thank you so much for all you've done for me, Khadija. I will never forget how kind you were to me throughout this week. God bless you."

Khadija smiled.

Leila reached out and gathered her in a hug. And then she gasped as a loud knock sounded at the door.

"Open the door!" Karim Keita's voice boomed.

Leila shuddered, and Khadija's eyes widened in fear.

"Open the door right now, Khadija!" Mr. Keita roared again. "I know you stole the keys to Malik's house from my room. Open this door right now!"

Leila's heart raced as she looked at Khadija and whispered, "What are we going to do?"

Khadija shook her head. "You have to leave now," she said quietly. "I will handle my father."

Leila shook her head. "There is no way I will leave and let you take the blame for me. Your father is going to hurt you just like he hurt Malik. You told me he locked Malik up because he tried to help Zainah and me escape. There is no telling what he will do to you if he finds out you helped me hide here and have been bringing me food."

Khadija whispered, "My father doesn't know you're here. He won't know I helped you so I won't be in too much trouble."

"What if he insists you tell him who has been

living here?" Leila asked.

"I'll tell him I'm the one. He is hardly at home anyway." She frowned as her father banged on the door and threatened to break it down if she didn't open up for him. "You can climb out of Malik's bedroom window. Once you do, turn left and you will find a small cleared path. It will lead you to the market. From there you can go to the bus station."

Leila stood up as Khadija went to the door. Leila turned around one last time to look at Khadija and then hurried to Malik's room. She quickly climbed out of the window, praying that no one would see her do so.

Some children were playing near the back of the house. They stared curiously at her as she jumped out of the window. She smiled at them and ran past.

*****

Khadija listened carefully to make sure Leila had left the house and then she opened the door for her father. He stormed in and gave her a dirty look. Fear gripped her at the look in his eyes, but she hid her fear as carefully as she could.

She winced when her father grabbed her shoulders and shook her. He said angrily, "Khadija, what have you been doing in here? Who has been in here with you?"

She avoided looking him in the eye and said, "No one was in here with me. I've been here all by myself, Papa."

He laughed harshly and slapped her hard. "Tell me right now who was in here with you. If you had a man with you here, I will kill you."

She staggered back in pain. Cupping her cheek, her eyes widened in fear. He looked like he was about to hit her again. She shook her head vigorously. She had to convince her father that she had not been in here with any man. The penalty for that was grave. "Father," she said, "please go around this house and if you see anything that makes you think a man apart from Malik has been here, then do with me whatever you will. But I am telling you, I have had no man here with me."

He glared at her and then looked back. "Musa," he said to one of the men standing behind him, "come and take her away!"

One of her father's bodyguards, an always angry brute, came and grabbed her arms. Khadija screamed and tried to wrench her arms away, but she couldn't.

"What are you doing, Father? Tell him to let me go!"

Her father looked at Musa and said, "Lock her up in the shack behind the house until she's ready to tell me the truth!"

"You can't do that to me!" she screamed at her father.

"Yes, I can. You will stay locked up until you tell me what I want to know."

She blinked as she stared at her father. He had always been a hard man, but never this wicked. At least, not until some months ago. Suddenly, he had become an evil person who didn't care who he hurt, even if it was his own children. But maybe he had always been evil and she had never wanted to acknowledge it... until now. After all, he had chased Zainah out of their community. At that time, she had thought his actions were justified. Now, she knew better. The worst thing was that her mother saw everything he was doing and still did nothing about it. In fact, she supported his actions most of the time.

Khadija did not struggle anymore as Musa took her to the shack and locked her up. Fear ran amok in her mind, causing her to tremble. Fear of what her father planned to do if she did not tell him who had been living in Malik's house for the last week, and fear for Leila. Hopefully, by now, she would have gone far away from the house so she could escape.

Papa will probably have people looking around the community for a stranger, Khadija thought.

She sat on the floor and bit her lip until it became too painful to do so. For a long moment, she sat waiting for her father to come to the shack. When she realized he wasn't coming back, she lay down on the floor and fell asleep.

*****

A few people turned to look at her as she followed the path Khadija had told her about. She didn't look at any of them as she ran, her heart beating fast. It was nighttime when she had arrived in Nira, so nobody had really seen her. Now, it was broad daylight. People in this community probably knew everyone who lived here and would know she was a stranger. If someone who was affiliated with Karim Keita saw her now, they would definitely remember she was the girl who was supposed to get married to one of Karim's friends but had made a fool of him when armed men came to rescue her. They would go and tell him, just like that driver who was supposed to take her and Zainah out of Nira had told him they were trying to escape. Zainah's father had had them recaptured. Leila pursed her lips. She would not be safe until she was out of Nira.

She kept running until she was almost at the market. When she got to the market, she began to walk while trying to make sure she looked no one directly in the eye. A trader who sold all kinds of meat called out to her to come and purchase his meat. She ignored him and walked on.

Someone ran into her and apologized. She didn't look at the person or acknowledge their apology. She kept going, praying that no one would recognize her. When she finally got to the bus station, her eyes widened and panic overwhelmed her as she remembered that she didn't have any money to pay for her trip. The robbers had stolen almost of it.

She scolded herself harshly for not hiding the money she would need for her return trip from the robbers. She had only hidden the money she needed to go to Nira. At that time, she had believed Malik would be in town and she hadn't been bothered about her return trip.

Without a doubt, she was in trouble. She began to pray desperately, as desperately as she had prayed when she was almost forced into that sham marriage months ago.

An idea came to her, but she didn't know if it would work. However, she didn't have any choice. She had to follow the idea.

She went to the counter and stood in line. There were only two people in front of her. She prayed that the idea she had in mind would work, because if it didn't, she would be stuck in Nira without a place to go, a place to sleep, or anything to eat.

When it was her turn to pay for her ticket, she said to the woman behind the counter, "Do you have a taxi I can hire... just for myself?" She knew her plan was far-fetched. This was a bus station. And even if they had a taxi, it would be outrageously expensive to hire one to Blima, just for herself. Hiring a whole bus was definitely out of the question.

The woman looked at her as if she were insane. "This is a bus station," the woman said. "We do not have taxis." The woman looked past her and told the person behind her to come forward, dismissing Leila.

Leila sighed softly and then went out of the bus station. She stood on the road opposite the market to wait for a taxi, feeling miserable, and prayed that she would find one along this road, which would be difficult as taxis hardly ever plied here. Her plan had been to hire a taxi for herself to take her to Fatima's. There, she would borrow money from Fatima to pay the driver. But now, the bus station didn't have a taxi for her to hire.

When the plan had come to her, she had simply just hoped that Fatima would have the money to lend her, but standing here now, she admitted to herself that her plan had holes. She was taking a huge gamble. Even if she found a taxi here to hire, what if Fatima did not have the money to lend her?

She pressed the thought out of her mind. She couldn't think about that right now. At this time, she had to focus on finding a taxi.

She stood on the road, praying and hoping. A few

drove by, but they were fully occupied. She began to grow tired and desperate after about an hour of standing and waiting on the road.

After another two hours, she almost wept. Her leg and back, which had mostly healed from her fall during the robbery, were now on fire. She felt like collapsing to the ground. Her stomach was rumbling with hunger.

She decided she couldn't stay standing any longer. Her leg and back were hurting terribly. Any moment now, she would not be able to stand any longer. She had to find somewhere to sit down.

But she was slightly hesitant to do so. What if she left and an empty taxi drove by?

Like that is going to happen now after I've been waiting for so long, she said to herself.

She looked back at the bus station. It was the only place she could find a seat. She began to limp back there, wincing in pain. Every step was pure agony.

Just before she entered the station, she noticed a man standing beside a car. The car was old and rickety-looking. Hope entered her heart. Maybe the car was for hire. It might not be, but there was no harm in asking. She slowly walked up to the man, still in pain, and said to him, "Excuse me, is your car for hire?"

He nodded and asked, "Where do you want to go. Kazi?"

"Blima," she said.

The man's eyes widened in shock. "That is a two-day journey!"

"That is where I want to go," she told him. She looked at the car again and wondered if she should back away. It did not look like it could make the journey to Kazi, let alone Blima.

The man said pensively, "It will be expensive to take you there. Can you pay the money for the trip?"

"How much is it?"

He named his price and she almost choked. "That is too expensive," she said, shaking her head in shock. "Can you not go lower?"

"That is as low as I will go."

She looked at him and from the determined expression on his face, she knew he would not budge. She also knew he was her only hope out of Nira. She sighed loudly and then told him she would pay the money he had quoted. She entered the backseat of the car and he got into the driver's seat.

He drove out of the grounds of the bus station. As he drove through the community, Leila kept her head down so no one would see her. She did not raise her head or breathe easy until they were far away from Nira. The car was surprisingly fast. She had expected it to move at a snail's pace, but the car was eating up the distance and racing past several other cars on the road.

When they got to Kazi, she let out a huge sigh of relief, and then told herself not to get too comfortable. She wasn't even sure Fatima would have the money that the driver had quoted to give her. If Fatima didn't have the money to lend her, she would be in trouble. This driver would not let go until she had paid everything she owed him. And rightfully so.

As the car sped on, she kept praying and praying that Fatima would have the money to lend her.

"Lord, I need a miracle," she whispered.

As nightfall approached, fear gripped her as she suddenly remembered the robbery. If her memory served her right, they were almost at the spot where she and the other passengers had been robbed. That could not happen again. Not that she had anything that thieves could steal this time. The robbers had stolen everything.

She felt slightly relieved when they passed the spot where she and other passengers had been robbed. Still, she was too concerned and doubtful about how she was going to pay the driver to sleep. She stayed wide awake throughout the night. Just before daybreak, she finally fell asleep.

She awoke much later with her stomach rumbling. She had bought a small loaf of bread and a small bottle of water earlier with some coins she'd found in her pocket and had eaten some of it. She ate the remaining piece of bread. After that, she washed it down with the bottle of water. Sated, she settled back on her seat and fell asleep again.

She woke up some time later and found that they were in a traffic jam. The driver was complaining bitterly about the traffic. She smiled in amusement. All the complaining in the world would not free up this traffic jam. She looked out the window and shook her head at the impatient expressions on the faces of some of the people in the other cars.

Soon, she yawned. She was bored. If only she had a book to read. She had only gotten out twice since the journey started, both times to use the restroom at a restaurant and bus station. Now, not only did her leg and back ache, her behind did too. She would tell the driver to stop at the next bus station so she could use the restroom and stretch her legs.

The traffic jam did not free up until an hour later. When they began to move again, she gave God praise. The heat had been stifling. Now, as the car picked up speed, she smiled as the cool breeze blew on her.

Just before nightfall, the driver drove into a compound of a dilapidated building. He had told her they would have to stop tonight to sleep and rest before they continued the journey tomorrow. She stared at the guest house with the words PALATIAL HOUSE etched on it. It was anything but palatial. It was a dump. She was used to staying in places that were a far cry from 'luxurious', but this building just looked awful.

The driver came out of the car she also exited. She followed him into the 'guest house' and waited while he went to the check-in counter to pay. She had told him she had no money on her and that she would pay him once they got to her friend's in Blima and he had been surprisingly okay with that. More than that, he had also generously told her he would pay for her room here.

She looked around the place that was supposed to be the lobby. It was no better than the outside of the building. Men who looked like vagrants and bedraggled women and children wandered about. She hoped none of the men here were robbers. Some of them looked to her like the men who had robbed her. One of the men looked at her, and she shuddered. She sighed in relief as the driver walked up to her, clearly finished paying for their rooms. He handed her a key and told her to follow him. Apparently, he had been here more than a few times.

She followed a little reluctantly, and then began to climb a flight of stairs with him. Doubts assailed her as she climbed the stairs. What if this driver had an ulterior motive? He had been too nice, offering to pay for her room. What if she was in danger here? She kept praying in her heart as she followed him up the stairs.

At the top, he opened the first door on a long corridor and then pointed at the door next to it. He said abruptly, "That's your room," entered his without saying anything more, and then shut the door.

For a minute, she stared at the space in front of her and then said, "Well then!" She unlocked the door to her own room and entered.

The room was not what she had imagined. She had been sure it would be terrible, with old stained sheets, dirt-stained walls, an unswept floor, and barely any furniture. And definitely without a bathroom. But it was actually clean. The sheets were clean and fairly new, the walls had been freshly painted, and there was an ensuite bathroom.

She felt greatly relieved as she went into the bathroom, had a much-needed bath, and came out feeling refreshed. She stretched out on the bed after shedding her clothes, and immediately fell asleep.

The next morning, she and the driver got back in the car and continued the journey to Blima.

The rest of the trip was uneventful. Hours after they left that morning, they reached Blima. Leila's heart pounded as she gave the driver directions to Fatima's house. Her heart beat in dread. What if Fatima was not home?

They got to Fatima's house an hour later and

parked right in front of her door.

"Lord, I need your help right now," Leila muttered. She smiled scornfully at herself. It was too late now. If Fatima was not at home or did not have the kind of money she needed to pay the driver, she was in serious trouble.

She got out of the car and went to the door. Her hands were clammy as she knocked and waited.

The door opened a moment later, and Fatima came out of the house. "Leila, you are back!" she exclaimed. She grinned and gathered Leila in a hug. "I'm so glad you've come back, Leila."

Leila smiled nervously at her and looked back at the driver who was waiting patiently beside his car. She turned back to Fatima and said, "I have something to ask you, Fatima."

"What is it?" Fatima stared curiously at her.

"I need a huge favor. I was robbed . . ."

"Oh no!" Fatima exclaimed.

Leila continued quickly, "All my money was stolen and I did not even see Malik in Nira. I had to hire a taxi to come all the way from Nira to this place. I need you to lend me the money to pay the driver. I promise to give it back to you as soon as possible."

"How much is it?" Fatima asked. When Leila told her how much it was, her mouth fell open.

Leila's heart sank. Fatima does not have the money. What am I going to do? She said to Fatima, "I know it's a lot. I'm sorry for asking. I was desperate. I guess I knew you wouldn't have that sort of money to give, but I just hoped . . ."

"No," Fatima cut her off. She shook her head and said, "I mean, yes. I have exactly the amount you're asking for. It was given to me today by someone who owes me for some goods he bought from me over the past year. He just came and unexpectedly handed me the money. I was happy to get the money back, but now I know the Lord touched his heart to pay me just so I can help you out. That it is exactly the same amount is amazing and shows it's the Lord at work."

Leila felt tears swimming in her eyes. Her heart flooded with gratitude to God, but also shame. Even in her disobedience, He had blessed her with His grace. He had still come through for her, even though she didn't deserve it. She whispered, "Lord, how wonderful you are." She smiled at Fatima and thanked her even before she was handed the money.

"Let me go get it," Fatima said and went into the house.

Leila turned around to look at the driver. He was tapping his feet, watching her with an impatient glare. She turned around again as Fatima came out of the house. Fatima handed her the exact amount she needed and Leila said, "Thank you so much, Fatima. I will pay you as soon as possible." She quickly walked up to the driver and paid him the money. After that, she gave a huge sigh of relief as he drove away.

She and Fatima went into the house. She asked Fatima about the children, and Fatima told her they had all gone to visit their cousins.

"So, Malik was not around," Fatima said. "You didn't see him at all?"

Leila shook her head. "No, I did not."

"You must have been so disappointed," Fatima said.

"I was devastated, but his sister was so good

to me. Because of her, his absence was somewhat bearable."

Fatima sat down beside Leila and said, "Tell me everything that happened."

Leila sighed and began to tell Fatima everything that had taken place, from the day she left the house up until her return minutes ago.

After she finished, Fatima shook her head and stared at her with a worried look. "Wow! You went through a lot to find your Malik. It was a close shave, Leila; too dangerous for my liking. And yet, you say you will return there?"

Leila nodded. "Yes, I plan to. A week from now."

"That is true love if I have ever seen it," Fatima said. "I will keep praying that the Lord will protect you, but you might just be tempting fate. You are not even sure Malik is God's will for you as he isn't a Christian."

"He will soon become one," Leila said, trying to brush away the worry that Fatima's words caused.

But as she lay in bed that night, she couldn't get Fatima's words out of her mind. Maybe he was truly not God's will for her life. Maybe she should cancel her plans to go back to Nira. But she pushed away her concerns. There was no way she would not go back. She couldn't fathom a future without Malik. She would go back to Nira and he would propose to her. Before they got married, he would become a Christian… because of her. She was certain of that.

*****

Khadija awoke with a start as someone slapped her back. Her father was standing over her and two of his men were behind him. He looked down at her with disdain in his eyes. "Are you ready to tell me what I want to know?"

She did not say anything.

"Your silence simply means that you definitely had a man with you in my son's house. For that, you will die."

She trembled as she looked up at him and said in a shaky voice, her heart beating with fear, "I did not have a man with me. You have to believe me, Father."

He smiled wickedly at her and narrowed his eyes. He asked again, "If you did not have a man in Malik's house with you, then tell me right now who has been living there. Because I know for a fact that someone has been living there for some time now. You have been stealing the keys to the house from my room so you can visit that person. And don't try to lie to me. I will know if you are lying."

She shook her head. "No one apart from me has been there," she said. "I promise you, Father."

She gasped as he struck her. "I told you not to lie to me, you wicked girl! Tell me who has been there with you, or I will assume it was a man, and you know what the consequence is for that is, don't you?"

She rubbed her cheek in pain and then stared into his eyes. From the way he was looking at her, she was certain he was not bluffing. He would mete out the ultimate punishment if she could not convince him she hadn't been with a man in Malik's house. She had to tell him the truth, but how could she just give up Leila like that? She said to him in a small voice, "Okay, I have not been there all by myself. My friend, Binta, has been living there..."

She cried out as he hit her again. "Stop lying to me! Binta has not been in Malik's with you! I know she has been away in Bamako to see her cousins because her father told me. And she came to visit you at the house before I came here just to tell you she has returned. So I know you are not telling me the truth! Lie to me one more time, and I swear you will not live to see the end of this week."

She trembled at the evil look in his eyes, and tears began to pour down her cheeks. He would know for sure if she lied to him again. She sighed sadly and whispered, "It was Leila, Zainah's friend."

"Speak louder!" he barked.

"It was Leila," she said a little louder. Her heart drummed as her emotions roiled with a mixture of fear and guilt. She had given away her friend. Hopefully by now, Leila would be far away from Nira. But the only problem was that she was going to return in a week's time.

"Leila? Zainah's friend?"

"Yes."

"And where is she now?"

"She has left Nira already," Khadija answered.

He looked intently into her eyes and asked, "And will she be back here soon?"

Khadija looked down at the floor and did not answer.

"Tell me!" her father yelled.

She shook with fear but still did not answer him.

"Musa," he said, looking at his bodyguard, "take her away."

"No, please!"

"Then tell me if Leila will be back and when."

Shame and guilt smothered her as she told him the truth—that Leila had said she would be back in a week, when Malik was back in Nira.

He stared at her, his eyes glittering with contempt. "So, you tried to hide all this from me. You will stay here for another day as punishment and then you will be released." He snapped at his two bodyguards and walked out of the shack. The door was shut and then locked once again.

What have I done? Fear had led her actions, but she'd had no choice. Or maybe she'd had a choice. She could have found another lie. However, her father would still have known she was lying. If only she knew how to contact Leila and tell her not to come back to Nira. But she didn't. She had betrayed her friend. Who knew what fate awaited Leila when she returned?

Khadija covered her face and wept.

NINE

Faizan wrapped his arms around Zainah and kissed her on the lips. He smiled down at her and said, "I wish I could stay with you but I have to go to church for the welfare meeting. I really miss it."

Zainah groaned and then kissed him on the forehead. "Okay, I guess you have to go," she said. She let go of him and smiled. "Okay, so, remember that we have to finalize the cake tasting and decide on what flavor we want."

He smiled at her, "I'll try to come back early so we can go this evening. If not, then we will have to go tomorrow."

He left Trisha's house, got into his car, and drove off to church. As he parked in the church parking lot, he thought about the time he had spent working undercover in the terrorist group and the torture he had suffered after Khalid, the leader of the group, found out he was working for the American government. When he'd been brought out to be shot and had thought he was going to die, his greatest sorrow had been that he would not get to marry Zainah. But now, within days, his dream would finally come true. He would marry the love of his life. He couldn't help but smile.

He locked his car and walked into the church building. As he climbed the stairs to go to the vestry where the welfare meetings were usually held, he ran the future plans he had for the group through his mind. Everyone in the group and even in the church as a whole did not know the ordeal he had recently endured. They simply thought he had traveled out of the country and had just recently gotten back to town. In most ways, he preferred it that way, except for one thing: he wished he could talk to the senior pastor and get some spiritual comfort.

He woke up every night still thinking he was in that dank cell, about to be killed. The real torture he had endured had been waiting to die, away from his loved ones.

He received great comfort from Zainah and his sisters, but he would have liked to talk to the pastor and get some counseling for his mental state. He didn't want to share specific details of his time at the terrorist camp or in the holding cell where he thought he had spent his final days with Zainah. He wanted to keep her from knowing all he had suffered there.

He entered the vestry and found that most of the welfare members were already here and were on their feet praying, led by one of the members.

He frowned and looked at his watch. He was almost half an hour late and he hadn't even realized it. As the leader of the group, he was supposed to set a good example, and here he was coming in late.

For the past few days since he'd come back, he had spent all of his waking moments with Zainah at Trisha's house or a restaurant or at the park. Today, he hadn't wanted to leave her and had stayed much longer with her than he'd intended, even though he knew he was supposed to come to church.

His assistant, Sarah, walked up to him and whispered, "You are late, Faizan. I asked Gerald to lead the prayers while I waited for you to arrive. Anyway, I am glad you are here now. We've missed you."

He smiled apologetically at her. "I'm sorry. I was at... umm... an important meeting and time ran away from me."

She smiled back. "I understand. Welcome back."

"Do you have any specific activities planned for today?" he asked her, "or do you want me to take charge of the meeting?"

She said, "I think you should take charge today. I had some things planned, but since you are here, we..."

He cut in. "Don't worry about it. We will do whatever you have planned. You take charge of the meeting today."

She stood and went to pull one of the members, a girl who usually led praise and worship, aside. Faizan closed his eyes and joined in the prayers for a brief moment. When he opened his eyes again, the girl, Shirley, had taken over from the young man who had been leading the prayer session. She raised a well-known worship song and everyone joined in with their hands lifted.

Faizan worshipped, but only partly. His mind was on Zainah and their cake tasting and their wedding plans. There was still so much to do. He didn't know or understand how they could do everything in just a few days, even with Trisha and Audrey's help. But as much as he cared and wanted their wedding day to be special, he would not allow the wedding planning to stress him out. None of it really mattered in the end. All that mattered was that in a few days, he would marry Zainah.

After the praise and worship session ended, his assistant took over the meeting. She talked about the places and people they had visited while he wasn't around and then she told the group that they would visit only two places today. One would be the youth center and the other, the old people's home.

Like Faizan always did, she divided the group into two. Faizan once again fell into the group that would visit the old people's home. The welfare meeting soon ended and the first group left together. It was only as he gathered his things that he noticed that Lauren was in church. He had not thought about her for a long time.

She walked up to him and smiled brightly. "You are back, Faizan," she said. "I... umm... we missed you."

Faizan gave her a small smile and said, "I have missed the group as well. I am glad I am back." He turned away from her, picked up his Bible and notebook and then turned around again. She was still standing beside him. The other members of the welfare group had already left. She was the only one there with him. She said, "Can I ride along with you to The Fruitful Vines, as I don't have a car yet?"

His mind immediately went to Zainah and how

jealous she had been the first time she had seen Lauren and knew they were friendly. Warning bells sounded in his mind and he considered telling Lauren that it would not be a good idea to ride in the car with him. However, he thought better of it. It would be very petty to tell her she couldn't come with him to visit old people in the town.

He nodded at her and said, "Sure, you can come with me."

As he walked down the stairs with her, he couldn't stop thinking about Zainah and how she'd felt when he told her he had gone on one date with Lauren because he had thought he had no chance of ever being with her. What would she think now if she found out that Lauren had driven with him to The Fruitful Vines?

As he entered his car and Lauren got into the passenger seat, he scolded himself for being so worried about what Zainah would think. Surely she knew he would never do anything that would cause her to doubt him or their relationship. And he knew she trusted him totally. She had told him so. He had no reason to worry.

He started the car and drove to The Fruitful Vines. When they got there, he and Lauren went into the first room they saw. Two members of their group were already there with an elderly man, praying with him. Faizan backed away and quietly shut the door. He turned to Lauren and said, "Let's go to the next room."

But when they opened the door to the next room, they found members of the group there as well. He backed out and smiled at Lauren. "Well, I guess we might not have anyone to visit today."

She said, "Remember that old lady we visited the last time we came here together?"

He frowned. "The one who told us that story about her late husband?"

Lauren nodded. "Yes. That sweet old lady. You remember you promised her that we would be back?"

Faizan groaned inwardly and said nothing.

Lauren said to him, "We need to keep that promise we made and go and visit her now."

Faizan said, "Other members of our welfare group will probably be there by now."

Lauren shrugged and said, "Let's just go and see. If there are other members there, we will leave. Or better yet, we will wait for them to leave and then go in to see her. Just to say hi to her."

Faizan wanted to refuse because the old woman had thought they were a couple when they had visited her together. That had made him cringe, not because the thought of being in a relationship with Lauren repulsed him but because the idea of being with any other woman than Zainah did, even though at the time he thought he and Zainah could never be together.

Lauren kept looking at him and then said, "You shouldn't back out of a promise, Faizan. Especially one made to such a sweet elderly woman. We should go see her now. She will be very happy to see us and we will be doing a good thing."

Faizan sighed wearily and nodded. "Okay, let's go then. Do you remember the way to her room?"

"Umm, I think I do," Lauren answered.

He vaguely remembered the way to her room, but he didn't want to put in the energy required to find it. Lauren was the one who wanted them to go see the woman. He would let her lead the way.

He followed her down a long hallway with rooms on both sides of it and stopped at a door. Lauren knocked and opened the door. She stepped into the room and Faizan went in after her. None of the members of the welfare group was in the room, but the old woman seemed to be asleep. Her eyes were shut and Faizan could hear her soft breathing.

He felt relieved that they didn't have to talk to her today. Her continuous insistence that he and Lauren were a couple when they had visited her the last time had made him uncomfortable, especially knowing that Lauren liked him. He turned and said to Lauren, "She is asleep. Let's not wake her up."

He started to leave the room and then turned around when a groggy voice said, "Oh, my dears, you came back to see me! I'm so glad you both came." She beckoned to them with her hand. "Come."

Once again, Faizan groaned on the inside. He walked up to the old woman and stood by her bedside. Lauren walked up to the other side of the bed, but the woman waved her hand and told Lauren to come and stand beside Faizan.

She said to them, "So, you lovebirds, what have you been up to?"

Lauren giggled, but Faizan sighed in exasperation. He said firmly but kindly, "Ma'am, we are not a couple. We are just friends."

But the old lady didn't seem to hear him. She looked at Lauren and then at Faizan and said, "You both make such a lovely couple." And then, without warning, she took Faizan's hand and then Lauren's wrist and joined them together. She put her own hand over their touching fingers and smiled up at them. "I hope you stay together forever like my Charlie and I did, before he passed on."

Faizan sighed loudly. Why couldn't this lady understand that he and Lauren were not a couple? He had said it several times, but she just didn't get it. He looked at her eyes, how bright they were, how animated her smile was, and then he scolded himself. She was old and believed in love. Of course she would want to see couples in love the way her and her late husband had been. He needed to work on his patience, but at the same time, he had to find a gentle way of getting it through to her that he and Lauren were not together.

He smiled at her and gently removed his hand from Lauren's. "I am sorry, ma'am. I…" he turned when he heard the door open. But he saw no one there. He turned back to the old lady while avoiding Lauren's eyes. "We are not a couple," he said to her. "In fact, I am getting married to the love of my life in a few days. Her name is Zainah and she is a great woman. I will bring her here to see you sometime. You will like her."

The old lady seemed to finally get it as her eyes widened. "Oh, my dear, I am so sorry. Because I am old, I tend to imagine things that are not really there."

Faizan smiled softly at her and said, "It's okay. I understand."

They stayed with her for some time, and she told them more stories about her married life with her husband and how much she missed him. After the visit, Faizan prayed for her, and then he and Lauren left the room.

"That was a nice visit," Lauren said to him.

"Yeah, it was, except for the part where she kept mistaking us for sweethearts."

"You have to admit, though, that it is kinda funny," Lauren said, laughing.

Faizan said, "It's really not," and then laughed along with her. "Okay, it is slightly funny."

"So, you are getting married in a few days," Lauren said as they walked down the hallway. "I am happy for you... I guess."

Faizan frowned and looked at her. Even though he had hoped she'd moved on, he'd had his suspicions that she hadn't. She still liked him. He sighed and said softly, "You are beautiful and smart, Lauren. Soon, you will find someone who will love and cherish you. Any man would be lucky to have you."

She said to him, "Any man but the man I really want. However, I like Zainah, so I wish you both nothing but the best."

They both left the old people's home after visiting with two other elderly women. Faizan offered to drive Lauren to her house, but she refused. "Just drop me at the church. I will find my way home."

They drove to church in uncomfortable silence. He parked in front of the church, and immediately she got out of the car. She thanked him briefly and walked away.

He drove away quickly, relieved to finally be able to get away so he could see Zainah. He drove as fast as he could without breaking the traffic laws. He couldn't wait to see Zainah again and continue their wedding planning. She had told him she had a surprise for him the next day. He couldn't wait to see what the surprise was.

When he got to Trisha's, he knocked on the door and then sucked in his breath sharply as Zainah walked out the door. She looked absolutely beautiful. She had changed from the simple gown she'd had on before he went to church into a knee-length floral dress. Her hair was tied back from her pretty face, showing off her exquisite features and high cheekbones that had fascinated him since the first day he saw her.

"You look absolutely beautiful," he said to her.

She smiled and thanked him.

He studied her face. As usual, it was free from makeup. He smiled as he noticed that her lips looked shiny and full. She had put on some lip gloss today and her lips looked even more inviting than they usually did. He couldn't resist kissing her. He pulled her close and gently kissed her. Her lips were soft and full and tasted like strawberries, and he slowly savored them, kissing her much longer than he'd intended to.

He pulled back after a while and then laughed and apologized. "I'm sorry, Zainah. I have wiped off the gloss on your lips, but I just couldn't resist."

"That's okay," she said, smiling widely. "Who cares about the gloss anyway? I wore some because Trisha insisted I did."

"It looks good on you," he said to her. "But you look just as beautiful without it."

"I'll wear it again if you like it," she said, and opened her purse. She brought out a small, shiny tube, and swiped the gloss on her lips. "How do my lips look?" she asked him.

"Kissable," he said, tempted to kiss her again. He resisted so he would not wipe off her gloss again, took her hand, and they both walked to his car together.

As he drove to the venue they had chosen for their wedding, he said, "We haven't talked about how many children we want to have." He turned to wink at her and she smiled, an embarrassed look on her face.

"I remember a friend asking me about that," Zainah said. "I told her I wanted a lot of children since I grew up in a big family. What about you, Faizan? How many children… or as you Americans would say, kids, do you want?"

He turned briefly, just to look at her. She looked so beautiful and she was his. He smiled and then focused on the road again. He answered, "I want as many as you do."

She giggled and then said, "Well, that means we are going to have a house full of children because that is how many I want."

He laughed and then took her hand and kissed it. His heart raced with excitement as he imagined living with her every day and waking up beside her every morning. Lord, please let our wedding day come quickly.

Her hand remained in his as he drove the rest of the way to the venue. When they got there, he parked in front of the white building that looked like a cross between a mansion and a boutique hotel. Before they went in, he said, "One day, we will tell our children about how we met."

Zainah chuckled. "That would be so much fun, telling them about how you actually fell from the sky and landed in my lap."

He laughed. "That I did."

This time, she was the one who leaned in and kissed him. Just as they separated, his phone rang. He plucked it out of his pocket and looked at it. It was Lauren calling. He held back a groan. What does she want now? he asked himself.

He ignored the call and put the phone back in his pocket.

Zainah looked at him with a curious expression on her face. "Who was that?" she asked.

For a second, he considered not telling her who it was. Why give her any cause for concern? However, with her, he wanted to be an open book. He wanted her to know everything about him. After all, she already knew now of his double life as a covert CIA agent.

He said, trying to make his voice as even as possible, "It was just Lauren."

Zainah nodded slowly and asked, "Why didn't you answer it?"

He blinked. Should he tell her that Lauren still had feelings for him, and that, just this afternoon, she had made it clear? He decided not to. He would tell her everything, but telling her another woman still had feelings for him even when said women knew he was engaged would trouble her unnecessarily. "I'm sure she just wants to find out something about the welfare department. I'll call her later."

You are not being truthful. You should tell her, a voice in his head said.

He brushed the voice aside. There was no need to tell her. Why worry her needlessly? He smiled at her, took her hand again, and they walked into the venue. What he didn't need right now was to start worrying about Zainah finding out that Lauren still liked him. Hopefully, Lauren would find someone else soon and forget about him. Right now, he would concentrate on making his bride-to-be happy and giving her the best wedding she could possibly have.

TEN

Zainah shed her simple house dress. She put on the long-fitted dress she had bought at the clothing store near Trisha's bookstore yesterday especially for her outing with Faizan today. She looked at herself in the mirror and then smiled in self-mockery. She looked like Leila did when they'd stayed at Fatima's house. Whenever Leila went out, she had put on these kinds of tight dresses that Zainah had never seen her in before. Zainah had been shocked at the time about how tight the dresses were and at their low necklines. They had quarreled a few times about Leila's appearance.

But now, here I am, dressed in something very similar, about to go out into the world. She shook her head. That just went to show that it wasn't right to judge anyone about their appearance, she thought with amusement.

And then she felt suddenly sad and slightly guilty as her mind focused on Leila. She didn't even know where her best friend was. Since the day she had called Leila and told her about Audrey and Sienna's offer to act as sponsors so she could come to the United States for the wedding and Leila had refused, Zainah hadn't called her.

Fear suddenly gripped her as she remembered what Leila had told her about going to Nira to look for Malik. What if something bad had happened to her? What if she'd been discovered and forced this time to marry that old man, Dauda? That would not be good, Zainah thought. She had been so absorbed with her wedding plans and with Faizan that she had not bothered to try to contact her best friend since the last time they'd spoken.

She made a mental note to call Miriam this evening. Hopefully, she would get through to her and then she could speak with Leila. That is, if Leila was still at the camp.

Lord, please let her not have gone to Nira, Zainah silently prayed.

She combed hair and braided it, and then slipped on a pair of kitten heels. She picked up a tube of pink lip gloss from the dresser and swiped some on her lips. She looked in the mirror and smiled, remembering the funny expression on Faizan's face when, after he'd kissed her yesterday, he'd told her he had wiped off all her lip gloss.

She grabbed her purse from the bed and went to the living room to wait for Faizan. Turning on the TV, she sighed and began to mindlessly flip through the different channels. She had a love-hate relationship with the TV set. Since she hadn't watched TV for years, it had all been very unfamiliar to her when she'd arrived in America and started to watch it again. Some of the things she watched were shocking and many times she knew she shouldn't be watching it. Still, she went on watching.

She shook her head as she went from one channel to the other and asked herself what she was doing. She turned the television off and then glanced at the clock on the wall to see what time it was. It was already noon. Faizan would be here anytime now.

She had told him the day before that she had a surprise for him that she wanted to show him today. He had tried to make her tell him immediately, but she had refused.

The doorbell rang, and she stood up and walked to the door. She opened it and smiled widely.

"Hi," he said. He took her hands and kissed her, and then he gazed at her as he had done yesterday; with admiration in his eyes. Grinning, he said, "You look beautiful, Zainah. You always do, but today, you look especially stunning."

She beamed. "Thank you." She couldn't resist kissing him again, and then she said, "Are you ready for your surprise today?"

He squeezed her hands and told her he was.

She locked the front door and followed him to his car. Trisha had left with Ruby for her bookstore early this morning, while Frank had left for his restaurant about two hours ago. Zainah liked living with Trisha and Frank, and she liked taking care of Ruby when her parents went out together. Ruby was a handful, but she was a cute and beautiful child. However, Zainah couldn't wait to get married to Faizan and finally move into their own house with him.

Faizan turned and grinned at her as she put on her seatbelt. "So, are you going to tell me now what surprise you have for me today?"

"Okay, I will. Do you remember where we were

the day you got the phone call to go on the CIA mission?"

He nodded but said nothing.

She said, "We were looking for the perfect house to start our lives together. Well, I chose the house for us."

He turned to her and for a brief moment, he frowned deeply. And then he broke out laughing.

She smiled and asked him, "What's so funny, Faizan?"

He said in a voice full of mirth, "I completely forgot that we had to get a house before we got married. It's one of the most important things to do, and I totally forgot about it. Maybe I would have moved into Trisha and Frank's house with you after our wedding."

She laughed. "Well, I did not forget. I went to look at the houses again when I found myself worrying way too much about you. Sometimes I went with Audrey when she was in town. It helped keep my mind off my worries and also helped assure me in some way that you would come back and we would finally get married and start a new life together in the house I ended up choosing."

He smiled at her and nodded. "So, which one did you end up choosing?"

"You will see once we get there," she answered. "Let's go. I'll give you the directions to the specific house that I chose."

"Yes, ma'am." He gave her a mock salute and then began to drive.

She giggled and turned to look out the window. She began to give him directions to the modern three-bedroom house he had told her was his favorite out of all the houses they had viewed, and he chuckled when he realized where they were going. When he parked in front of the house and they both got out of the car, he looked up at the building and turned to hug her.

"It was my favorite house out of all the houses we both looked at," he said. "I am glad you picked this one. Thank you."

"I loved all the houses," she said to him. "But I wanted to live in the house that made you smile." She took his hand and when they went to the front door, she opened her purse, brought out the keys to the house, and unlocked the door. They walked into the foyer and he said to her, "How come you already have the keys?"

She turned to take both his hands and then looked into his eyes. "This is the real surprise, Faizan."

He stared quizzically at her. "What is the real surprise?" he asked.

She smiled and said, "This house is fully ours now. Audrey, Sienna, and Trisha bought this house for us. They said it was an early wedding gift."

Faizan's mouth dropped open and he blinked rapidly.

She felt slightly worried by the look on his face. She didn't know if he was just too surprised to speak, or not happy about the fact that his sisters had bought them a house. She said to him, "What's wrong? Aren't you happy, Faizan?"

His face broke into a smile and he hugged her tightly. "I am happy," he said to her. "It's just that I'm really surprised. It's really nice of them, but…" He stopped speaking.

"What is the matter?" she put her hands on his

shoulders.

"I know they have the money and can afford this because of their inheritance, but, it's just that I wanted to buy the house for both of us."

She lifted his chin with her finger and looked into his eyes. "I understand, Faizan. But look at it from your sisters' points of view. They have the money and they wanted to give us a wedding gift that would be memorable. And just like me, they were terribly worried about you. It was their way of assuring themselves that you would come back. You can say that it was like an act of faith. Besides, we can then use the money you would have paid for the house for our future children."

He smiled widely and nodded. "It's a huge wedding present. I'll have to specially thank them for it. That's really generous of them."

"So are you happy about it? Because I want you to be."

"Yes, I'm ecstatic." He hugged her tightly again and then let her go.

She smiled, feeling giddy, but also a little hesitant as they walked into the living room. His sisters had also furnished the whole house. Would he be happy, or would he think it was way too much?

She looked at him and then smiled. His mouth had dropped open again as he looked around the living room. It had been furnished tastefully with cream and gold curtains, a gold Persian rug, and cream leather chairs. The gold accents around the living room gave it an expensive but not overdone look.

"Wow! They also furnished the living room," he said.

"They did," she put her arm around his shoulder. "Actually, they furnished the entire house." She held her breath as she looked at him.

He beamed. "Okay, maybe I need to call them right now and thank them. This is really generous."

She smiled in relief at the look on his face. He looked genuinely pleased; very happy, in fact. "Let's see the entire house," she said.

They went on a tour of the three-bedroom house. It was big, but definitely nowhere as big as Audrey's or even Trisha's. She liked that. They would still both be able to easily find each other if they were in different parts of the house.

They came to a room that was unfurnished, and he turned to her and asked curiously, "How come this room isn't furnished?"

A thread of excitement went through her as she glanced around the room. She answered, "That's because this will be the nursery. Since we don't yet know what our first baby's gender will be, I decided that this room would be left unfurnished until we do."

He looked at her for a long moment and then took her in his arms. Wrapping his arms tightly around her, he said, "I can't wait for that day when we will hold our first baby in our arms. You will be such a great mother."

"And you will be a great father," she said to him.

She stayed in his arms for a long moment, completely content to stay that way forever. They separated reluctantly after a while and then they went to look at the rest of the house.

After they finished the house tour about half an hour later, they left. On the way back to Trisha's,

Zainah said to Faizan, "I can't believe we will be married in just a few days."

"I can't wait," he said. He took her hand in his, and they held hands as they chatted about their future until they got to Trisha's house. Just before Zainah exited the car, Faizan asked if he could pick her up in the evening to see a movie. "Or we can go out to dinner if that is what you prefer."

"Oh, Faizan, I can't. I'm so sorry. I promised my new friend, Carrie, that I would go with her to visit her grandmother who resides at The Fruitful Vines."

"Oh, okay, no problem. You'll be free tomorrow morning, won't you?"

"Definitely," she said.

"Okay then, I'll pick you up in the morning so we can spend the day together."

"I would love that," she said. She chuckled. "Thank God that we've basically finished everything we have to do for the wedding, or I would be so frazzled. We have your sisters to thank for that."

"Yeah, they've been great. Trisha would not be back from the bookstore by now or I would have come in to thank her for the house. I think I will go to the bookstore now to thank her for the generous gift. I will call Audrey and Sienna while I'm there."

She kissed him and then got out of the car. After waving to him, she went into the house. She immediately changed into a comfortable t-shirt and a pair of jeans. Jeans was not something she was used to, not until she'd come to Rosefield. In fact, she couldn't remember ever wearing them. Not back in Nira when she was a teenager, and certainly not in the women's camp. It was another item of clothing she had objected to when Leila had worn them at Fatima's house.

She left her room and went into the kitchen to cook something special for Trisha, Frank, and Ruby. She wanted to use the gesture to say thank you once again for everything they had done for her and Faizan. She decided to cook her special lamb tagine and couscous for them. She had made it a week after they'd come back from their honeymoon and they had loved it. Even Ruby, who was a very picky eater, had enjoyed the couscous.

When she finished cooking the meal, she went into her room, sat on her bed, and began to read her Bible. After a while, she stretched out on the bed, still reading. Soon, she unknowingly fell asleep. She awoke some time later when she felt something or someone scratching her nose. She opened her eyes and beamed at Ruby who was standing beside the bed, smiling mischievously as she scratched Zainah's nose with her little fingers, and then touched her cheeks and her hair.

Trisha came into the room and chuckled, "Ruby, you naughty little thing! There you are! Come, let Aunt Zainah sleep."

Zainah shook her head and smiled. "Don't worry about it, Trisha," she said. "I'm awake now." She stood up from the bed, lifted Ruby into her arms, and went out of the room with Trisha.

Frank came back an hour later and they all had dinner together.

Carrie arrived at about eight o'clock. Zainah quickly grabbed her purse from her room, kissed Ruby's cheeks, and waved goodbye to Frank and Trisha. She went out to Carrie's car with her.

As they drove to the old people's home, Zainah chatted with Carrie for a while, and then looked out the window at the passing cars. She was grateful for Carrie's friendship. When Faizan had been away and Trisha and Frank were still on their honeymoon, Carrie's friendship had kept her from being really lonely.

She remembered the day she met Carrie. It was a few days after she'd arrived in Rosefield and just a day after Faizan had left for his mission. She had been pushing a cart and walking up and down the aisles of the supermarket, totally confused by all the brands of different products on the shelves. She only wanted to buy a few things, but there were so many brands of all the things she had on her list that she didn't know which ones to pick or which was better than the other.

It was the one problem she had encountered in all the stores she had been to since she'd come to America. In Nira, you only had one or two choices of whatever it was you wanted to buy. At the women's camp, only Miriam went to town to shop for all the things they needed. She never had to worry about what type of brand to buy. Here, however, shopping for just the basic things she needed felt like such a huge chore.

Carrie had walked up to her on that day and asked if she needed help. When she'd told her about her dilemma, Carrie had looked through her list and then helped her to pick out each item, advising her on which brands were better. After they finished shopping, they walked out of the store together.

"I like your accent," Carrie told her, smiling.

"Where are you from?"

When Zainah told her and said she had come to the United States to marry her fiancé, Carrie said she had also just moved to Rosefield. When they reached Carrie's car, without thinking, Zainah asked if Carrie would come to her house to visit the next day. She was so happy to have someone friendly to talk to that she didn't consider how weird it might be to invite a virtual stranger to one's house. With Faizan on his mission, wherever that was, Audrey and Ken still in Miami, Sienna and Bryan back in Peru, and Trisha and Frank away on their honeymoon, all she wanted was someone to talk to so she would not feel so lonely. She just wanted a friend.

Carrie looked taken aback, and Zainah worried that she had committed a faux pas. Back at the women's camp and even in Nira, she would have invited someone she liked and wanted to be friends with to her tent or home. But here, maybe the rules were different. When Carrie smiled and said she would love to come and visit, Zainah was relieved.

Carrie came the next day with her cute two-year-old son, James. He was a mischievous boy, and he reminded her a little of Ruby. Ruby had been taken to Frank's parents' house before Trisha and Frank went away on their honeymoon.

While James ran around the living room, Carrie asked Zainah if she could tell her about where she came from. Zainah told her about Nira and then about the women's camp.

Carrie listened with a look of fascination on her face as Zainah talked about the women's camp, how she had come to live there, and the different

Christian women from all over the world who lived there to escape persecution or who were chased out of their communities like Zainah was. She also told her a little about how she met Faizan but left out the violent details like the time a terrorist attacked her at the camp, and parts about Faizan's connection to terrorism.

After she finished, Carrie shook her head. "Wow! That is a fascinating story. Who knew there was such a place? I would love to visit there one day."

She told Zainah that she'd grown up in Rosefield but left when she got married at twenty. She had come back a month ago with her husband mostly to take care of her grandmother, who now resided in the old people's home.

Yesterday, when she and Carrie had gone out for coffee, Carrie had invited her to come with her to see her grandmother today.

Carrie drove into the parking lot of The Fruitful Vines and smiled at her. "We are here," she said. They walked into the old people's home together, and Zainah followed Carrie down a long hallway and into a small room.

An old lady who looked about ninety was in bed, reading a book, her glasses perched on her nose. She looked up at them, removed her glasses, and beamed at Carrie and then at Zainah.

"Carrie, you are here!"

Carrie went and hugged her tightly and introduced Zainah.

The old lady greeted Zainah as though she'd known her all her life. Zainah sat on a chair near the bed, while Carrie sat on the bed beside her grandmother. The old lady began to entertain them with stories from her youth; stories about how she met her husband, about their lives together, and how in love they were. Zainah listened carefully, a little sad that this dear woman's husband, who had been her everything when he was alive, had passed away.

When Carrie's grandmother finished telling her story, she looked at Zainah and said, "My dear, you're so beautiful. Do you have a sweetheart?"

Zainah smiled and told her she did. "We are getting married in a few days," she added.

"That is lovely!" the old lady exclaimed.

Carrie laughed and said to Zainah, "My grandmother is obsessed with love and romance. Yesterday, when I came to see her, there was a lovely couple who had come to visit and they were standing beside her bed. They were holding hands and my grandmother had her hand on top of their joined hands. The moment felt so solemn, as though my grandmother were marrying them. But it was also really funny. I didn't want to disturb them, and so I went away quietly without being seen. I came back after they left and she didn't stop telling me throughout my visit about what a beautiful and wonderful couple they were."

Carrie's grandmother nodded. "That is because they are a wonderful couple." She looked up with a thoughtful expression. "Such an attractive young couple. They've visited me before and I just love them together. I think their names are Faizan and Lauren."

Zainah's eyes widened in fear and her heart began to pound. Did she say Faizan? She couldn't possibly mean her Faizan. Then again, how common was that name in Rosefield? In all of America? Her heart grew cold at the second name. Lauren ... God, no, please.

Hesitantly, she opened her purse and brought out her phone. She found a picture of him and then stood up. She showed the old woman the picture. "Is this the man you're talking about? The one you said came to visit you yesterday with a girl named Lauren?"

Carrie's grandmother's eyes lit up and she nodded. "That is him! Do you know him?"

She sucked in her breath sharply. Maybe this old woman was mistaken. She turned to Carrie, who was gazing at her curiously, and showed her the picture. "Is this the man you saw holding hands with the lady?"

Carrie looked at the picture and then looked up at Zainah. "Yes." She frowned.

Zainah's heart raced wildly and she shook her head. She began to back out of the room, her mind filled with awful images of Faizan and Lauren together, wrapped up in each other's arms. She fled the room and ran down the hallway and out of the building. She could hear Carrie calling out to her, but she did not stop until she was far away from the building.

She flagged down a taxi, entered, and gave the driver directions to Trisha's house. And then she changed her mind. Faizan would come looking for her at Trisha's tomorrow. She could not bear to see him. She swallowed a sob that threatened to escape her lips and told the driver that she had changed her mind and wanted to go to Hattie's Bed & Breakfast. She wasn't sure what she was going to do after she got there, but she was sure of one thing: she couldn't marry Faizan. The thought that she wouldn't marry the only man she'd ever loved felt like a dagger in her heart. But she couldn't bear the thought of getting married to him when she knew he would carry on his affair with Lauren.

All through the short ride to the bed & breakfast, she ran through her mind what Carrie's grandmother had told her. No wonder Faizan had evaded her questions when he had received that call from Lauren yesterday. He'd had a guilty look on his face and she had wondered about it. Now she knew why. He was cheating on her with Lauren.

Her heart began to tear into shreds and she felt pain unlike anything she had ever known before course through her.

When the driver stopped in front of the bed & breakfast, she paid him and got out of the car. Taking a deep breath, she somehow managed to hold herself together while she paid for a room. After she entered her room, however, she sank to her knees on the floor and wept bitterly.

"Lord, how could he do this to me?" she cried out. She stood and collapsed on the bed. Turning and tossing, she wept and muttered to herself over and over again, "Why, Faizan, why?"

Soon, she mercifully fell asleep.

ELEVEN

Faizan parked his car in front of Trisha's house. He walked to the house, rang the doorbell, and waited.

The door opened almost immediately and Trisha came out in her house robe, eyes bleary. She stared at him, a surprised expression on her face. "Hi, Faizan! Where is Zainah?" she asked, looking past him. "I thought she was with you."

He blinked in surprise and shook his head. "She is not with me," he said to her. "Isn't she in the house?"

Trisha shook her head slowly and a look of fear took over her face. "Are you saying she did not spend the night at your place?"

Faizan frowned. "No, she didn't," he said, his head beginning to buzz. "You know we have this rule that she doesn't sleep over at Audrey's or I here, just to avoid any temptation. I'm very sure she's in her room. Where else could she be?"

Trisha shook her head and said, "And I am pretty sure she didn't come back home last night."

Trisha opened the door wide and Faizan stepped

into the house. They both quickly made their way to Zainah's bedroom door. Without knocking, Trisha opened the door and entered the room, and Faizan entered after her. His heart began to pound with fear when he found the bed made and the room empty.

He turned and said to Trisha, "I don't understand. If she didn't spend the night here, then where did she sleep last night? Where can she be?" He brought out his cellphone from his pocket and dialed her number. He put his phone to his ear and pressed his lips together, praying she would answer his call. But her phone didn't even ring.

"Did she tell you where she was going last night?" Trisha asked.

He sat on Zainah's bed, starting to feel sick with worry. "She told me she was going to see her friend, Carrie. They were both supposed to go to see her grandmother in the old people's home. You're telling me she didn't come back?"

"Yeah, she left with Carrie in a hurry yesterday, but she told us she would come back early. Frank and I went to sleep almost immediately after we put Ruby to bed. Zainah has her own key to the house. I just assumed she changed her mind and returned late in the night."

Faizan sprang from the bed and faced Trisha. "Do you know where her friend Carrie lives?"

Trisha looked up thoughtfully and nodded. "Yes, I think I remember one of my friends telling me that Carrie and her husband live near her."

"Okay. Just give me the directions to the house and I will go look for Zainah."

"I'll come with you," Trisha said.

Faizan shook his head. "You're still in your pajamas, Trish. Let me go. I will get back to you when I find her."

"No, Faizan. I won't be able to stay here not knowing where she is. I'll come with you. Please just give me a second to change and I'll be out."

Trisha quickly left before he could say anything more and Faizan began to pace the living room. He shut his eyes as different images, frightful and dismal, went through his mind. He saw Zainah lying somewhere in Rosefield, hurt, and without anyone to help her. He tried to force the thoughts out of his mind, but they remained. He whispered harshly to himself, "Stop it! Rosefield is a safe place. There's no way something has happened to her." But his words could not assuage his fears.

Trisha came into the living room again, wearing an old t-shirt and shorts, her purse slung over her shoulder. Frank was beside her in his robe, a frown on his face. He said to Faizan, "I wasn't worried when I didn't hear her come in last night because I thought she was at Audrey's with you."

Faizan felt like yelling, but held himself together. She was probably at Carrie's. Even though it was a bit strange that she didn't call Trisha or him to say she would not be coming back yesterday, there was still no need or cause for alarm.

They quickly got into his car, he and Trisha, and she began to give him directions to Carrie's once he pulled out of her driveway. They got to Carrie's house in no time, and he rang the doorbell. He tapped his feet impatiently as he waited, mentally fending off fear and worry. A minute later, a short man wearing glasses and holding a newspaper opened the door and stared at him and Trisha.

"Yes, can I help you?" the man asked, gazing quizzically at them.

Trisha said, "Is Carrie home? We would like to speak with her."

"Yes," he said and gazed at Trisha. "You are Trisha Gardner, aren't you?"

"I am," she said.

He let them in and told them he would go get Carrie.

Faizan sat on the loveseat while Trisha sat on the couch. He took a deep breath and prayed silently, Lord, please let her be here.

He looked up as a blonde woman with a pleasant-looking face came into the living room. She rubbed her face with her hand and smiled at him. She looked quizzically at Trisha and said, "Hey, Trisha! Nice to see you again." She looked at Faizan and faced Trisha again. "My husband said you wanted to speak with me."

Trisha nodded. "Yes. Is Zainah here?"

Carrie blinked rapidly and then she said, "No, she isn't here." Slowly lowering herself on the couch beside Trisha, Carrie looked at Faizan and then at Trisha.

Faizan held his head in his hands, his heart racing with worry. He lifted his head again and turned to Carrie. "She told me she was coming to see you yesterday, but she didn't come back home."

Carrie's eyes widened and she said to Faizan, "You are Faizan, her fiancé. Aren't you?"

"Yes," he said. "Do you have any idea where she might be?"

Carrie covered her face with her hands. When

she raised her face to look at Faizan, the expression on her face was one of fear and dismay. "Your fiancée found out about your affair," she said haltingly. "Yesterday, Zainah and I went to visit my grandmother at the old people's home. My grandma asked her if she had a sweetheart and she said she did. After that, my grandmother began to talk about a couple who had visited her the day before. She told Zainah how in love the wonderful couple was."

As Carrie talked, Faizan's heart flooded with dread. He began to put two and two together.

"I told Zainah how my grandmother was obsessed with love and couples. I then told her I came to visit my grandma yesterday and saw her with the couple. I'm so sorry," Carrie said. "I told her the couple looked like they were really in love. Their hands were joined together and my grandmother had her hand on top of theirs like she was marrying them. Zainah showed my grandmother a picture of you on her phone and asked if the guy in the picture was the man she was talking about, the man who had visited her with his sweetheart. When my grandmother confirmed that he was, Zainah immediately ran out of the room and out of the building. I tried calling her back, but she did not answer. I ran out after her, but by the time I got out of the building, she was gone."

Carrie pressed her lips together and sighed heavily.

Trisha looked at Faizan and asked, "Who did you visit Carrie's grandmother with?"

"Lauren. A group of us from the welfare department went to The Fruitful Vines. Lauren and I had promised Carrie's grandmother we would come and see her last time we were there. So we went to her room to visit." He looked at Carrie and continued. "I tried to tell your grandmother that Lauren and I were not a couple, but she didn't seem to get it. I actually removed my hand from Lauren's, and I then told your grandmother again that I already had someone else who I was engaged to and who I loved. But I guess she still didn't get it."

Carrie shook her head again and said, "Once more, I am so sorry. I should not have jumped to conclusions and thought that you and the lady I saw were a couple."

Faizan did not have the time to acknowledge her apology. He got up from the sofa and turned to Trisha. "Let's go, Trish. We have to find her as soon as possible. She thinks I am cheating on her. Who knows what she'll decide to do?"

Carrie said to them, "Should I come along?"

"No need," Faizan said. "You should wait at home. If she calls you, please contact me or Trisha." He gave her his cell phone number and then he and Trisha left the house and got into his car.

Trisha said to him, "Where are we going to look for her now?"

He replied, "I have no idea. I don't think she knows anyone else in Rosefield who she can spend the night with."

"I don't think so, either," Trisha said. "If she did not spend the night with any friend, where could she be? I just hope she hasn't left Rosefield. Since she believes you have been cheating on her with Lauren, she might be so angry that she actually decides to leave the country again."

His stomach twisted in fear, but he brushed aside the feeling so he could focus on the matter at hand. He had to find Zainah. They were getting married in a few days. A firm determination entered his heart. No matter where she was, he would find her and marry her.

"I will search every single house in Rosefield and even Green Valley if I have to. I have to find her, Trisha," he said. "I have to find her now." An idea suddenly came to him and he said, "If she hasn't already left Rosefield, she might be in a hotel." The idea seemed like the only thing that made sense under the circumstances.

"But we have no hotels in Rosefield," Trisha said. And then her eyes widened. "Hattie's Bed & Breakfast!"

"Yes," he said. He started the car and began to drive to the popular Rosefield bed and breakfast. All the way there, he prayed to the Lord, asking that they would find Zainah there. Because if they didn't, he didn't know where else to look for her. That was the one and only place visitors to Rosefield checked into when they had no other place to stay.

When he got to the bed and breakfast, he parked directly in front of the building, quickly exited the car, and walked briskly to the front door. Walking into the lobby, he went straight to the check-in counter and said to the young woman behind, "I'm looking for a lady named Zainah Keita. I think she checked in here yesterday evening. Could you please confirm that she's here? I would like to speak to her."

The young woman told him to hold on for a

second and then looked down at the computer in front of her. Her fingers clicked away on the keyboard while she gazed at the screen. After a few minutes, she looked up at him and said, "A Zainah Keita checked in last night, but she checked out this morning. I'm afraid she isn't here anymore."

He shook his head in astonishment and turned to look at Trisha who was beside him. "Where on Earth could she have gone?" He turned to the receptionist again and asked if she had any idea where Zainah had gone.

"I'm sorry, I don't," The young woman said.

"This cannot be happening!" Faizan raked his fingers through his hair, completely frustrated. As he walked out of the bed and breakfast with Trisha, he said, "Lord, where on Earth is my Zainah?" He called her phone again, but still it didn't ring.

Trisha put her hand on his shoulder and said, "Don't worry, Faizan. We will find her somehow. At least we know she is safe."

He shut his eyes and then opened them again, feeling weary with worry. "I blame myself," he said. "If only I had reassured her even more when she was worried at your wedding that Lauren and I had a thing."

Trisha said, "Stop being so hard on yourself. It was all a mistake." They got into his car again and sat there for a full minute. He turned to Trisha once more and said, "Now, what are we going to do? I am out of options."

Trisha didn't say anything and they both sat in the car in silence. After a few more minutes, Trisha finally said, "We should go to the airport and see if she's there."

"The airport? I don't think she has the money she needs for a trip out of the country."

"Can you think of anything else to do?" Trisha asked.

He thinned his lips and then nodded. "Okay. We will go and look for her at the airport."

"I'll call Audrey and Sienna and find out if either of them knows where she is," Trisha said. "Maybe she called them yesterday and told them where she was going."

"Keep calling Zainah as well," Faizan said. He began to drive to the airport while Trisha called Audrey. She spoke on the phone for a few minutes and then ended the call. Turning to him, she said, "Audrey doesn't know where she is. Let me call Sienna."

She did, but Sienna also didn't know where Zainah had gone.

"When we get to the airport, where exactly are we going to start looking for her?" he asked. "I guess we'll just look around and ask the airport security. I just hope we find her there because I don't know where else to look if we don't."

Inside, Trisha went to one end of the airport terminal while Faizan went to search for Zainah on the other. He searched everywhere, looking for any woman with Zainah's tall, thin figure and stunning dark complexion, but he only found one person, and it was clearly not her. He asked the airport security if they had seen any woman who looked like her. He described Zainah in detail, but none of them had seen anyone like that.

He combed his fingers through his hair, worry coursing through him. When he saw Trisha coming toward him with a frown on her face, his heart sank.

"I didn't see her," Trisha said. "I'm sorry, Faizan, but I think she has already left Rosefield."

She might be heading out of the country if she has gotten to Boise, he thought in dismay. Once again, he felt like crying out in anger. He took a deep breath and held himself together. As he walked out of the airport with Trisha, he said, "We will have to go to the police station and file a missing persons report."

"But she isn't really missing, Faizan. She checked herself out of the bed and breakfast today," Trisha said. "Since she's an adult, I doubt the police would do anything about it, at least for now."

"I wish Audrey were here," he said. "She might open an unofficial case."

Trisha sighed loudly. "You know she's safe, Faizan. The only thing I can think of is that she is planning to leave America."

He put his hand on his head. "I have to go to the airport in Boise and see if I can catch her before she leaves the country. If she leaves America thinking I cheated on her, that will be the end of it, Trish. I might never see her again."

Trisha didn't say anything.

They got into his car, and he took a deep breath and gripped the steering wheel. He had to go home and get his passport and then fly to Boise. He would call Jake if he found out in Boise that she had already left the country and beg his handler to let him fly out, just this once, so he could go and find her in the women's camp. It was very unlikely that Jake would agree to let him do that, but he had to try. He couldn't let Zainah leave thinking he had cheated on her.

He drove to Trisha's, dropped her off, and promised to call her if he found Zainah. And then he headed for Audrey's to get his international passport, determined that he would find the woman he loved, no matter what it took.

*****

Zainah stood in front of Audrey's front door and rang the doorbell. She waited for a few minutes, but when no one answered the door, she rang the bell again. She sighed deeply as she waited. When she was at the bed and breakfast yesterday, she had woken up in the middle of the night with tears running down her cheeks. "I can't do this," she had whispered as she sat up on the bed. "There has to be some kind of explanation for why Faizan and Lauren were holding hands in the old people's home. And why Carrie's grandmother said they were a couple.

But what kind of explanation could there possibly be? She didn't know for sure then, and she still didn't know now, but she felt that Faizan would never cheat on her. He loved her too much.

She had put away her childish decision to leave the United States and go back to the women's camp and decided that when she woke up in the morning, she would go back to Trisha's and wait for Faizan to come and pick her up as he had told her he would the day before. She would talk to him about it and listen to whatever explanation he gave her. Because without a doubt, there was an explanation for all of the confusion, for everything that Carrie's grandmother had told her.

Unfortunately, because she did not sleep for most of the night, she had woken up later than she wanted to. She had checked out of the bed and breakfast as early as she could and then decided to go straight to Audrey's rather than Trisha's to talk to Faizan. When she arrived at Audrey's, she found no one was home. Faizan's car was not in the driveway. She thought then that he had already left for Trisha's to pick her up and headed there. At Trisha's, she also found no one was home. After changing into a fresh outfit, she took another taxi back to Audrey's, sure that he would be there now, but he still wasn't. She was sure that they had missed each other again.

She sat down on the doorstep and decided to wait for him, her mind racing as she waited. If only I had not been so quick to believe the worst about Faizan, she thought to herself. I should have just gone to talk to him yesterday.

Minutes went by, and she began to wonder where he had gone. And then her heart leapt as she saw his car heading toward the house. She stood as the car stopped right in front of her. She smiled uncertainly as he got out of the car.

He ran to her, his eyes full of worry, fear, and relief. And there was something else in them. Was that guilt? She pressed her lips together as she looked at him. What did he have to feel guilty about?

He held out his hands and she quickly went to him and fell into his arms. He held her tightly and rubbed her back. "Where have you been, Zainah?" he asked in a haunted voice. "I've been looking everywhere for you." He kissed her hair, and then held her away from him.

She looked down, feeling guilty. She was the cause of the worry in his eyes, the tremor in his voice that told her he'd been terribly scared because of her. "I am so sorry, Faizan." She looked up at him. "Carrie's grandmother told me something that made me question our relationship. But I was wrong."

"I know what happened," he said, gently caressing her cheek. "You thought I was cheating on you with Lauren."

She looked down again. "I should have trusted you. I went to Hattie's Bed & Breakfast and then I couldn't sleep. I knew in my heart there was no way you would cheat on me. So I came back here to find you, but I didn't see you."

"Trisha and I have been searching everywhere for you. We went to Carrie's house first and then to the airport. I was about to go to Boise now and see if I could catch you at the airport before you flew out of the country. My plan was to call Jake if you had and tell him that I had to fly out to North Africa to see if you were at the women's camp." He took hold of her shoulders and searched her eyes. "Zainah, let me explain what happened."

Even though she had craved an explanation since this morning, she suddenly found she didn't really need one now. She knew deep down in her heart that no matter what she'd heard, she could trust him. She shook her head. "There's no need to. I already know that you wouldn't cheat on me. I was just insecure."

"I blame myself for your insecurity," Faizan said. "I should have told you that Lauren and I went to The Fruitful Vines together after our welfare meeting. We visited Carrie's grandmother months ago and she made me promise to come back with

Lauren. At that time, she kept insisting that we were a couple even though I told her we weren't. When Lauren and I went to visit her two days ago, she kept calling us a lovely couple and then joined our hands together. I removed mine and told her firmly that Lauren and I were not a couple and that I was in love with someone else. I even told her I was about to marry the girl I loved. I thought she got it then, but apparently she didn't."

Zainah smiled sadly.

Faizan continued. "Not telling you that Lauren and I had gone to the old people's home together was a mistake." He ran his hands down her arms and took her hands. "I have to tell you something, Zainah. I don't want to hide anything from you anymore." He threaded their fingers together and said, "Lauren still likes me. She told me so. But I have never given her any reason to. Are you angry with me?"

Zainah chuckled and said to him, "Why would I be angry with you? Just like I told you when I first came to Rosefield, I understand that you are an attractive man. Women will want you and I have to live with that if I'm going to be with you." She laughed. "I'm ok with that, I guess. I mean, it's not a bad thing for my man to be desirable to other women. I trust you fully, Faizan. I trust you with all my heart. I'm sorry for my childish behavior. It will never happen again."

He folded her in his arms and kissed the top of her head. "I'm just glad you're here with me. I was so scared when I couldn't find you."

They stood hugging in front of the house for long while and then Faizan took her hand and pulled her into the house. They both sat on the loveseat and soon began kissing. She pressed her body closer and closer to his, and then knew she needed to pull back immediately.

But she didn't.

Thankfully, he pulled away from her, stood up, and looked down at her with a rueful smile on his face. "Three days more, Zainah. In three days, we can kiss as long as we want and do whatever we want without feeling guilty. For now, though, I think we've had enough kisses."

She smiled ruefully and took a deep breath to still her racing heart.

He held out his hand to her and she took it. "Let's go to the park or to a restaurant. Or maybe to the movies or something. We shouldn't stay here alone."

She smiled as he pulled her up from the sofa. "You're right."

As they drove away from the house in his car, she kept counting the days in her heart. Today was a Wednesday, tomorrow, Thursday... There were only three days left until their wedding, but it felt so far away, like there were still three more weeks before she could finally marry Faizan. She turned to look longingly at him as he drove, and then she gave a long, wistful sigh. In three days' time, she would finally be married to him. And then he would be fully hers, and she his.

TWELVE

As Leila boarded the bus that would take her to Kazi and from there to Nira, her emotions churned with a confusing mix of excitement and fear. She had found a job as a dishwasher in a small restaurant near Fatima's house. The advantage of the job was that it paid whenever she could come to work. When she couldn't, someone else did the dishes and was paid for the job. She had worked for a full week and had earned enough money to go back to Nira and see Malik. Once she was back from Nira, she would continue to work so she could earn enough money to repay Fatima.

She had jumped at the chance to get the job, even if it was as a dishwasher, as she was desperate. After her first day at the job, she had smiled in self-mockery as she remembered how she had quarreled with Zainah when Zainah got a job as a maid. At that time, she had wondered how Zainah could work as a lowly maid and had told her it was beneath her. Now, she was the one working while Zainah was in America, probably living in a big house and about to marry the love of her life.

She now understood why Zainah had taken the job as a maid. Zainah had been desperate to find Faizan then, just as she was desperate to find Malik now. She would do anything, including scrubbing toilets if she had to, in order to be with Malik again.

The bus quickly filled with passengers, and half an hour later their driver drove out of the station. Leila bowed her head and silently prayed that this journey would not be full of problems, the way the last one, and even the one before that, had been. She prayed that they would not encounter robbers on the way this time and that Malik would be home. There was a niggling doubt at the back of her mind that Malik might still not be in Nira when she got there. Even though Khadija had assured her that he would be back in a week, Khadija had also told her that the number of days Malik stayed in Nira varied. Sometimes, he stayed for two days, other times for three. It was the one thing that Leila worried about the most. What if he stayed for only a day? What if, by the time she reached Nira, he was gone?

After she finished praying for the trip, she felt slightly better. By God's grace, everything would go well.

But what if it doesn't? a voice in her head said. It's not like you are sure this is what God wants you to do. In fact, it's almost certain that this is not His will for you.

She brushed away the anxious feeling the voice in her head had caused and focused on how she would feel when she saw Malik. She could just imagine his big brown eyes sparkling when he saw her. She was sure he would be ecstatic, and so would she.

As night approached, the serenity that had settled over her since after her prayer for the trip began to dissipate. Fear gripped her as she remembered the incident with the robbers. She remembered how she had been thrown to the ground and how her back and her legs had hurt for a long time after that. She couldn't afford for that to happen on this trip. She couldn't afford for anything to slow her down. If she didn't get to Nira fast enough, she could end up discovering that Malik had left by the time she got there.

As the driver sped down the road where the robbery had happened, she began to pray earnestly. Even after they passed the spot where it had taken place, her fear did not cease. It was completely dark outside now. Who knew what lurked behind the huge trees that lined both sides of the road?

The women who sat on her left and right sides were asleep, and many of the other passengers in front of her were also sleeping. But she couldn't sleep. She kept her eyes wide open, as though by doing that she could keep any danger lurking behind the trees or on the road away.

She continued to pray, asking for protection. She stayed awake until just before daybreak when she finally dozed off. She woke up about two hours later and pressed her lips tightly together when her stomach rumbled with hunger.

The aroma of grilled meat filled the air, and she noticed that many of the passengers were eating and drinking. No wonder she felt so hungry. The driver had probably stopped at a spot on the road where hawkers sold food to travelers so that passengers could buy food for themselves. Unfortunately, she had been asleep and hadn't gotten a chance to buy food for herself. She would have to endure the hunger until the driver stopped at another place where she could buy food. Who knew when that would be?

They drove by small towns and villages, some with inhabitants of no more than fifty people. Sometimes, there was traffic. Other times, they drove down winding roads and did not see any other cars for an hour or two. At one of the towns they went through, there was traffic. She bought a loaf of bread and two hardboiled eggs. She also bought two small bottles of water. She ate quickly and washed the food down with one of the bottles.

She slept better that night and woke up early in the morning. A few hours later, the driver drove into the bus station at Kazi. She came down from the bus and quickly got into a bus going to Nira.

It was only after she boarded the bus that she really began to worry about her journey to Nira and the dangers she might encounter once there. This time, just like the last, she was going to reach Nira in the daytime. The risk of being seen by someone from Malik's father's house was great.

Her stomach twisted and turned with fear as the driver sped toward Nira. She told herself to stop worrying, but she couldn't. Her fears, after all, were justified.

They began to approach the Nira market and her heart began to drum. She would be clearly seen by everyone once she came down from this bus. She had not even made a plan for how she would get to Malik's house without being seen by anyone connected with his father. Consumed by the thought of finally getting to see him again, she had not thought to make a plan.

The bus stopped directly opposite the market and she came down with the other passengers. For a short moment, she stood at the back of the bus, contemplating what to do. And then she made a quick decision to take the path Khadija had told her to take on the day she'd left Nira a week ago.

Unlike the path that she had taken when she'd arrived at that time, which had led her to the front of Malik's house, this path would lead her to the back. Following the path that led to the front meant that she would have to walk past his father's house. There were almost no buildings on the path that led to the back of his house. She would sneak inside through the window she had escaped through the last time. Hopefully, that window would be open now. But if it wasn't, she would have to knock on it until Malik opened up for her. There were holes in her plan, she knew, but the plan would have to do.

She followed the narrow path, walking slowly until she got to the back of Malik's house. A few people walked by, but none of them paid any attention to her. The window wasn't open. Her heart plummeted in disappointment. She had pictured the window open when she'd begun to make her way here.

She put away her disappointment quickly and peered through the window into Malik's room. She couldn't see clearly, and she wasn't sure that anyone was inside.

Her pulse quickened with excitement and dread as she tapped on the window twice. She waited for some seconds. When no one came to the window, she slowly knocked on it again. Once more, she waited, but still no one came.

What if Malik can't hear me from inside the house? What if he's not even at home?

For a minute, she pondered on what she could do, and then she decided to go to the hut she had stayed in to wait the last time she came here. Like then, she would wait in the hut until it was night-time.

She turned around, and then her eyes widened in horror and her heart began to pound as two brawny men began coming towards her. She recognized them. They were two of the men who had captured her and Zainah that night they were about to escape from Nira, after Malik had let them out of the shack Mr. Keita had locked them up in.

She looked back, trying to find a way to escape, but she knew she would never be able to outrun the men. Still, she made a run for it. They quickly caught her and began to drag her along with them, while she screamed at the top of her voice. She screamed and screamed, but nobody came to her aid. She fought the men with all her might, but she couldn't escape their grasp. They kept dragging her along with them until they stopped in front of Malik's father's house.

She kept shouting and tried to escape again as one of them left her to open the gate of the house. But the other man's hold was too strong for her to break.

The men dragged her into the house, and her muscles tensed when she saw Mr. Keita sitting alone in the living room, a wicked grin on his face.

The brutes let go of her and went to stand at the door.

Fear consumed her as she looked into the cruel eyes of the man who was Malik, Khadija and Zainah's father. How could such a wicked man be the father of three of the nicest people she knew? She could not understand it.

"So," he jeered at her, "you are even more stupid then I thought. You actually came back here, just for Malik." He laughed out loud and then abruptly stopped laughing. "You fool. You actually thought I wouldn't find out that you were the one who was living in my son's house for a full week. You actually thought that my daughter would choose you over me."

Leila trembled at the evil look in his eyes, but she had to know where Malik was, no matter how afraid she was. She asked in a voice she hoped was free from fear, "Where is Malik?"

Karim Keita laughed again and shook his head. "Khadija told me all your plans after I threatened her. She told me you were coming back here again in a week, and so when Malik came back, I immediately sent him to work again. I actually did not believe that you would come back when Khadija told me of your plans. Not after I nearly caught you the last time. But here you are. Such a foolish, foolish girl. But I am so glad you came back. I have plans for you. Since you are so determined to come back here, you will stay here forever. Unless, of course, your husband chooses to go back to Saudi Arabia."

Leila glared at him. What was he talking about? She shook her head and said, "I have no husband."

"But you do! You are already married to my

friend, Dauda. You will go to him and spend the rest of your life in purdah. And you will have to convert to Islam, of course."

Leila stared at him in horror. Her body began to tremble and she said in a small voice, "I will not marry your friend or convert to Islam."

"Yes, you will, and did you not just hear what I said? You are already married to Dauda. The marriage rites were said before you and Zainah managed to skip town." He narrowed his eyes and looked at her with a thoughtful expression. "You will also help bring my daughter, Zainah, to Nira."

Leila sank to her knees and began to weep, asking the Lord to deliver her.

Karim Keita glowered at her and yelled, "Stop that now!" He stood on his feet and stared at her in disdain. "Nobody is going to come to your aid. Understand that now!"

She continued to pray as the men hurled her up from her knees.

"Lock her up in the shack!" Mr. Keita ordered. The men began to take her away but Karim Keita held up his hand and told them to wait. He looked at her and said, "This evening, you will call Zainah and tell her she needs to come to your rescue or you will be killed. Do you hear me?"

In spite of her fear, Leila shook her head. "I will do no such thing!"

He pursed his lips, and for a minute, he said nothing. Finally, he said to her, "If you do as I say and call Zainah, I will let you go. I will even let you see Malik. Maybe you two can be together."

Her eyes widened in surprise and confusion. With all her heart she wanted to see Malik, wanted to be with him. Her heart began to pound as she thought of the offer, and then she sighed. There was no way she would betray her best friend. Zainah would be forced into purdah, married to a stranger. She couldn't live with herself if she let that happen. Besides, there was no assurance that Karim Keita was actually telling the truth and would let her see Malik if she did what he wanted her to.

He said to her, "I will even let you go now and tell you exactly where Malik is so both of you can be together. Just call Zainah and tell her what I told you earlier. Let her know she has to come to your rescue right now."

Leila stared at the man. *Lord, please help me to stand strong.* Everything in her screamed for her to agree to what Karim was saying. If she called Zainah, she could see the love of her life today and finally get to be with him.

But she ignored the voice in her head screaming at her, and said, "I will not call Zainah. Not even if my life is in danger. Not even if I don't ever get to see Ma . . ." she choked on the words. She would never see Malik again; never ever get the chance to marry him. If Karim Keita let her live, she would be given away to someone else to marry and live out the rest of her life in bondage, with regret as her daily companion.

Mr. Keita stared at her and then snapped his fingers and beckoned to one of the men near the door. "Give me that cell phone." He turned to Leila. "So, my girl, are you ready to call Zainah now?"

Leila shut her eyes briefly and then opened them again. She said to Karim, "I won't call her." And then every hope, dream, and desire she'd had for the future died as she said, "Do whatever you will with me."

Karim Keita glared at her with blazing eyes and then nodded. "Have it your way, then. I'll find another way to get Zainah here. You will be locked up and tomorrow or the day after, you will be brought out to prepare to meet your husband. This time, it will be a private affair so that no one will know or be able to interfere. You won't be able to escape this time. No one will come to 'rescue' you." He looked up at his men and ordered again, "Take her away!"

The men took her to the shack where she and Zainah had been locked up months earlier and locked her in. After they left, she sat on the cold floor and closed her eyes. Overwhelming bitterness engulfed her soul. Bitterness against God for not answering her prayers and for letting this happen to her, against Khadija for betraying her trust, and bitterness against that evil man, Karim Keita.

She lifted up her eyes and cried out, "What have I done? Why did I come here?" She had come because she was urged on by love. Now, she would never get to have the love she had craved so much. She would never get to see the man she loved again.

Her heart grew heavy until the pain became unbearable. She threw up everything she had eaten that morning and then curled up on the ground and prayed to die.

*****

Leila slowly stood up from the ground as the door of the shack opened. Someone had come to bring her food yesterday evening, and another person in the morning. Apparently, Karim Keita's plan to break her and get her to divulge Zainah's number did not include starving her. It was probably because he planned to marry her off to his friend and didn't want her to look gaunt when he did. She felt sick to her stomach just thinking about it. Well, this time, she would not eat the food they brought her.

Her muscles tensed as Karim Keita himself stepped into the shack, a smirk on his face.

"So, are you ready to do what I asked you? Or do you prefer to spend the rest of your life in purdah?"

Leila shifted away from him as he approached. Her back was to the wall as he stepped close to her. His eyes looked her over.

She shook her head and said slowly, "I've already told you. I am not giving you Zainah's number or calling her for you. No matter how many times you ask me to, I will not change my mind."

"Not even if I tell you that Malik is in Nira now, and that you can see him if you give me Zainah's number?"

Leila's mouth dropped open and her heart began to race. "Malik is here?"

"Yes," Karim said.

Tears filled Leila's eyes. Her heart felt jumbled with emotions ranging from total confusion to anticipation. She had to see Malik now. But that would mean giving this evil man Zainah's number. But she was safe in America. She looked at him and asked, "How do I know you are telling the truth? Malik might not be around at all."

"You have to trust me. I meant it before, and I mean it now. If you give me Zainah's number, you will not only get to see Malik, but you will be free to have the relationship with him that you've been dreaming of. I'll even give you my blessing." He held up a finger, "As long as you talk to Zainah on the phone and tell her that you will be killed unless she agrees to come to Nira."

Leila stared at the man. Malik's face stayed firmly in her mind and the urge to see him was overwhelming. Lord, what am I going to do? She prayed silently. She said to Karim, "I know you still want to force Zainah and I to marry your friends. I'm not going to do that to Zainah. Besides, she will soon be marrying the man she loves in America."

"I know she will soon be getting married," Karim said. "Khadija told me you told her about Zainah's upcoming wedding. That's partly why I want her to come. I certainly do not want to force her to marry my friend. She is already married to him. Both of you are married to my friends. Like I told you before, the rites had already been said before both of you were taken away."

Leila looked away from Karim Keita. She hadn't wanted to believe him when he told her before that she was married to some old man she didn't know. She felt sick.

Karim continued. "After everything that happened, my friends and everyone in this village will never want to have anything to do with you or Zainah. My friends were thoroughly disgraced. No one wants to marry you or Zainah anymore. But I care about her. She can't get married to someone else until she dissolves this present marriage. It's an abomination that will bring a curse to her, her present husband, and whoever she is joined to in the future. My friends are eager for her to return so the marriage can be dissolved. You will also have to dissolve yours before you can marry Malik."

Leila's heart raced at the thought of marrying Malik, but she said, "What about what you told me earlier? That I would be taken to my husband's house in a day or two and stay in purdah forever?"

"I said that because I was desperate," he said to her. "I just want to see my daughter. I want to know she is safe now, but I don't want her to come under a curse. Besides, after so many years of not seeing her and then finally getting to see her months ago, I don't want to lose her again. I need to see her now." He looked deep into Leila's eyes and pleaded, "Please, do this for a father."

She took a deep breath, and then said as firmly as she could, "Okay, I will call Zainah for you as long as you bring Malik here, first of all, and then promise me that you will not harm Zainah in any way."

Karim Keita did not say anything for a full minute, and then he sighed loudly and said, "Okay, then. I will do as you ask. I will bring Malik to you, but he'll remain just outside the door and speak to you there. However, you'll be able to see his face clearly and make sure he's the one. I also promise that I will not harm Zainah in any way."

Leila searched his face to see if he was lying to her or telling her the truth. His expression revealed nothing and she knew she had no choice but to trust him. "Okay, I'll call Zainah after I speak to Malik."

Karim Keita grinned and then nodded his head. "Good. I'll bring Malik to you in the morning. Remember, you will have to keep your word, or you will suffer greatly."

"I will keep my word as long as we keep yours," she said.

He turned around and walked out of the shack. Leila heard the door firmly lock from the other side and then sat on the ground once again. It felt as though two weeks had passed, but at the same time like she had only been here for a few hours. All she spent her time doing here was praying and weeping simultaneously.

Her heart drummed with excitement and nervousness. At last, she would get to see and talk to Malik again. He would probably be angry at his father for locking her up, but she would tell him to let it go. All that mattered was that they had been united and were finally together.

She couldn't sleep a wink that night as her body trembled with excitement and anticipation. And a bit of dread. There was a slight chance that Mr. Keita was lying to her. But then, she trusted that he truly wanted to talk to Zainah. That he truly wanted to see his daughter again. She also had to trust that the Lord was in control and that she was not being played by Karim Keita.

Rays of sunlight began to stream into the shack through the small window, and she stood as her excitement reached its peak. She suddenly looked down at herself and groaned. She has been wearing the same outfit since she was locked in here.

She ran a hand across her hair and then tried to pat it down as best as she could. She was sure she looked a complete mess. If only she had remembered to ask Karim Keita to get Khadija to bring a change of clothes for her and some water to freshen up. She quickly braided her hair, rubbed her face with her hands, and straightened her midi dress as best as she could.

Any time now, Malik would come. She couldn't hold in her excitement.

Leila blinked as the door opened. Karim Keita walked into the shack, two bodyguards behind him. She looked past him and the bodyguards to the door, but Malik was not there. She shot Karim an angry look and said, "Where is Malik? You said he would be here this morning."

Karim laughed and waved over one of his bodyguards. The man brought out a phone from his pocket and walked up to her.

Leila glared at Karim. "The promise you made me was not to speak to Malik on the phone but in person. You told me he would come here this morning." She suddenly couldn't control her anger anymore and screamed, "Where is he?"

Karim glowered at her. "You have no right to be making any demands." He looked at his bodyguard and said, "Show her."

Leila's eyes widened as the man clicked on the phone and then held it out to her. She took it hesitantly and then stared in horror at the picture on it. "What are you doing to him?" She cried. She gaped at the picture, totally horrified. Malik was tied to a chair, gagged, his hands and feet bound up.

"You have to call Zainah right now and tell her what exactly I want you say or Malik will not live to see the end of today."

"You monster!" she cried out. "How can you do this to your own son?"

He waved his hand as though he were waving away a fly and said to her, "You really thought I would give in to your demands?" He laughed and then said, "Are you ready to do what I asked you to?"

She cried out and sank to the floor, the phone still in her hand.

"Call her with that phone!" Karim ordered.

Leila bit her lip as spots danced in front of her eyes.

"Call her right now!"

Leila's hands trembled as she slowly dialed Zainah's number. Tears flowed down her cheeks and sorrow filled her heart. She was sure now that Karim Keita wanted her to call Zainah and get her back here not because he wanted to see his daughter, but in order to forcefully give her away to his friend. She was also sure that the same fate awaited her. But there was nothing she could do. Malik's life was in danger. Never had she imagined that Karim Keita would hurt his own son just to get Zainah here.

Zainah's phone began to ring and Karim said, "Put it on speaker."

Leila did as he asked and then looked down at the floor, her chest tightening painfully. Her heart somersaulted as Zainah's voice came on the line. "Hello, who is this?"

Karim Keita pointed at the phone and said to Leila, "Speak!"

"Hello, Zainah, it's Leila."

"Oh, my Lord, Leila! I'm so happy to hear your voice! How are you? Where are you? Are you finally going to come to my wedding?"

Leila trembled as she said haltingly, "I'm . . . in Nira. I've been captured by your father." She looked up at Karim Keita and then said, "My life and Malik's life are in danger. He said we are married to those men already, Zainah." It became too much for her to bear and she broke down.

Karim grabbed the phone from her and said, "Zainah, you have only two days to come back here. If you don't, whatever happens to your friend and your brother will be on you."

Zainah yelled, "You animal! Don't you dare touch Leila or I will kill you!"

Karim laughed. "Listen, you are to come back here alone. I have my men posted around the village. They will tell me if you come with anyone. Your friend and your brother will pay for it if you do." Zainah began to say something, but he cut her off. "You better not try to send anyone here to rescue Leila like the last time. Malik is not here in Nira. If you try to send anyone to rescue her, you are to blame for whatever I do to him." Karim clicked the phone off and then grinned at Leila. "See, that wasn't that hard to do, was it?"

Leila felt like throwing up again. Everything felt just like a terrible nightmare. She was to blame for all this. If only she had not come back here.

Karim said to her, "Now we will wait. Everything will depend on Zainah coming back." He began to leave the shack, and then the phone rang again. He clicked on it and said "Hello, Zainah?"

"How do I know you will keep your word and release Leila and Malik if I come?"

"You will have to trust me," he said.

Leila wanted to scream and tell Zainah not to come. She wanted to tell her that the man was untrustworthy and would not keep his word, but

Malik's life was in danger. She could not afford to do anything that would put his life at risk. Even though she couldn't trust Karim Keita, the only chance Malik had to stay alive was if she kept her mouth shut.

The phone call ended and Karim stared at Leila for a long moment. Finally, he turned around and left the shack. Again, his bodyguards followed him out and locked the door.

Leila knelt on the floor, bowed her head, and began to pray earnestly about the nightmarish situation that she and the people she loved were in right now. For a long time, she prayed, groaning and asking the lord for a miracle. But when she finally sat up, she felt just as hopeless as when she started to pray.

Lord, what have I gotten myself into? she thought. If only she had listened to Zainah and Fatima. Now, she had gotten her best friend in trouble. And she had put the man she loved in danger. She'd always had good self-esteem, but now, she hated herself so much she felt like ending her life.

And maybe I should end my life right now. It's not like I have anything to live for.

She looked around the empty shack. How would she end her life in a place like this?

There was a broken shard of glass lying on the floor at the other end of the shack. She stood and went to pick it up. She wept as she held it to her stomach, ready to plunge it in.

"Do it now," she said to herself. She shut her eyes, willing herself to end it all, and then suddenly let go of the shard. It smashed on the floor into tiny bits and she backed away, crying. She could not bring herself to do it. She sat down on the floor again, hating herself even more for not having the courage to end her life. She suddenly couldn't hold back anymore and screamed, "Lord, why won't you help me?"

She heard and felt nothing. She knew there would be no deliverance for her. The only thing she was certain about was that she would soon be handed over like a birthday present to a man old enough to be her father. She would be forced into a life of captivity and basically become a sex slave. And because of her, Zainah would end up the same way. The worst part was, neither of them would get to be with the men they loved. That, more than anything else, would haunt her for the rest of her life.

THIRTEEN

For what seemed like ages, Zainah sat on her bed, staring at the wall in front of her. She could not stand, could not talk or even do anything. Only waves of terror went through her body. Leila had been kidnapped by her father, and Malik was also in danger. And if her father was telling the truth, she was married already to her father's friend, a man she didn't even know.

Everything she had heard on the phone, Leila's fear-filled words and her father's threats, seemed unfathomable. How could all this happen on the eve of the happiest day of her life? She wanted to fall to the floor and scream and tear out her hair, but somehow she knew the tears would not come. She was too shocked to even cry.

Finally, she opened her mouth and said, "Lord, what am I going to do?" She tried to rise from the bed, but she felt too weak. The phone call seemed like a bad dream, and she prayed that she would somehow wake up, safe and calm, in her bed on her wedding day. But it was useless; of course this wasn't a dream.

What would she tell Faizan? How could she leave him and go back to Nira? But, how could she not? Leila needed her help, and so did Malik. She covered her face with her hands and then cried out, "Lord, I can't leave Faizan, I can't!"

She gathered herself together and then stood up from her bed. She had to tell Faizan about the phone call. She quickly grabbed her purse from the bedside table and went out of the room. As she hurried to the living room, she bumped into Trisha.

Trisha smiled at her and said, "Where are you going in such a hurry?" And then she gasped. "You look awful," she said in alarm. "What is wrong, Zainah? Is it something about the wedding?"

Zainah shook her head and said, "I'll tell you when I come back. I have to see Faizan right now." She hurried past Trisha to the living room and opened the front door. She heard Trisha yell her name and then turned.

Trisha held up her car keys and dangled them. "I'll drive you to see Faizan," Trisha said. She hurried up to Zainah and took her hand.

Zainah said, "Are you sure? What about Ruby?"

"Ruby is with Frank. Come, let's get into the car," Trisha said. "I can't let you go out alone in the state you are right now."

Zainah got into Trisha's car and they drove away from the house. All the way to Audrey's to see Faizan, Zainah's heart raced. All she could think of was that her life was about to come to an end unless Faizan's secret agent friend could somehow get her and Leila and Malik out of this quagmire, the way they had rescued her and Leila months ago.

They got to Audrey's house and Zainah rushed to the front door. Audrey and Ken had already arrived in Rosefield yesterday for the wedding. Sienna and Bryan also arrived this evening. If something wasn't done now, this wedding would not happen.

"Oh, my Lord, please let it not be. There's nothing more I want than to marry Faizan right now." She rang the doorbell and tapped her foot impatiently. Seconds later, Audrey appeared at the door and smiled widely when she saw Zainah and Trisha.

And then the smile melted off her face. "What's wrong?" she asked Zainah as she let her and Trisha into the house. She hugged Zainah briefly and kissed Trisha's cheek.

"Where is Faizan?" Zainah asked.

"He's on the upstairs patio with Ken. Let me go get him now." She left quickly, clearly sensing that something was terribly wrong.

Trisha said, "What is it, Zainah? Please tell me what is wrong. I'm freaking out right now."

She opened her mouth to speak just as Faizan walked into the room, a frown on his face. He asked in alarm, "What's wrong, Zainah?"

Zainah quickly stood and rushed up to him. She fell into his arms and cried as he held her and rubbed her back. Ken also came into the living room. After a while, Zainah pulled back from Faizan and looked into his eyes. They were full of worry, but still his features held restrained patience and concern. Even though he was clearly worried about her, he still waited patiently for her to tell him what was on her mind. She said to him, "We have a huge problem, Faizan."

He took her hand before she continued speaking

and went to sit on the loveseat. He pulled her down with him and put his arm around her. Trisha, Audrey and Ken sat down on the couch facing them. All eyes were on her as she said, "I just got a call from Leila and my father."

She told them everything that Leila and her father had told her, and then she broke down crying. "If I don't go back, my father said he would kill Leila and Malik."

She jumped when Faizan suddenly shot up from the sofa and roared in outrage. Nobody spoke as everybody watched him. Finally, he looked down at Zainah and said, "You're not going anywhere. I doubt he will kill his own son. And that first marriage did not take place at all. I'm sure your father is lying."

Zainah looked down at the floor and then looked up at him. "I wish he was, but actually, now that I think about it, I believe he is telling the truth. I remember that imam saying the wedding rites before those men rescued Leila and I. But that is not the main thing right now. My best friend's life and my brother's life are in danger. That's the main thing. If I don't return to Nira, my father will kill them… at least Leila." She shuddered. "I can't let that happen. Maybe your friends in the government can help."

Faizan raked his fingers through his hair and began to pace the living room. He finally came and stood in the middle. He folded his arms on his chest and looked down at her again. "I'll call Jake."

Ken tentatively glanced at Trisha and Zainah, and then shook his head. "Let's talk upstairs," he said.

"Zainah already knows I am a federal agent,

Ken. And Trisha is family," Faizan said impatiently.

Trisha frowned and asked, "What are you both talking about?"

Nobody answered her question.

Ken shrugged and Faizan brought out his phone from his pocket. "I'm calling him now," he said. "Ken, will you come with me so you can speak to him as well?"

Ken nodded and stood. They both left the living room with Faizan holding his phone to his ear.

Zainah sighed wearily while Audrey and Trisha stood beside her, rubbing her back and telling her everything would be alright. She knew they were only trying to help, but the reality was that her only hope was Jake, Faizan's friend. If he did not or could not help, everything would be lost. She waited, holding her breath, praying that Jake would come through for them now.

Faizan and Ken did not return to the living room until twenty minutes later. When they did, the expression on Faizan's face was one of rage and fear. Ken avoided looking at Zainah.

Faizan went straight to Zainah, lifted her out of her seat, and hugged her tightly. When she pulled back, she saw there were tears in his eyes. "What did Jake say?" she asked him.

He dabbed at the tears in his eyes and said angrily, "He completely refused to help. He said he couldn't help again because it would be an abuse of his power and if it was found out he would be in trouble. Nothing I or Ken said made any difference. He flatly refused to help. Worst of all, he warned me not to try to leave the United States. He said if I was caught leaving, I would spend the rest of my life in jail."

Zainah's heart stopped as she listened to him. She slowly sat down, her legs shaky and unable to carry her any longer. She cried out, "What are we going to do, Faizan? Oh Lord, please help me!"

Faizan sat beside her and said with grim determination on his face, "I don't care what Jake says. There's no way I will let you go back to Nira on your own. I'm going back with you. We will find a way to rescue Leila and your friend and also force your father to dissolve that marriage. Then we can finally get married."

Zainah looked up at him with tears in her eyes and shook her head. "You can't come with me, Faizan! You heard what Jake said. If you are caught, you will spend the rest of your life in jail. Besides, my father warned me to come alone."

Ken leaned forward on his seat and said, "That's true, Faizan. Even if you're not caught leaving the country, which is very unlikely, you will never be able to come back to the United States again."

Faizan's jaw tightened and he said, "I don't care! I am not letting Zainah leave this country and go to Nira on her own. Do you know what that man who calls himself 'her father' will do to her?"

Zainah caught his face with her hands and turned his face to hers. She searched his eyes and said to him with her heart breaking, "I know how much you care about me, Faizan, and that's why you want to go with me. But also remember that I care for you as well. I love you with all my heart. If you are caught and taken to jail to spend the rest of your life there because of me, I will never forgive myself. And there will never be a chance of us being together. At least if I go alone, I might have a chance to convince my father to dissolve the marriage and also let Leila and Malik go."

Faizan started to shake his head, but Zainah kissed him fiercely on the lips to stop him from speaking. "Please, Faizan," she said exasperatedly. "Please think about it. Nothing good will come out of your coming with me. It will anger my father and put Leila and Malik's lives at risk. And it will also get you into trouble here. Please just let me go alone."

He said in a voice filled the pain, "But how can I do that? You're my life, Zainah! How can I let you go? And on the eve of our wedding? It's too painful to even think about."

Zainah pulled him into her arms, and Ken put his hand on his shoulder. "Zainah is right, Faizan," Ken said. "For now, it's better she goes on her own. But we will stay here and keep trying to convince Jake to help. If we can do that, it will work out better than trying to go with her."

Zainah said, "Besides, you know my father has bodyguards with him all the time. You can't fight all of them on your own, Faizan. You know you can't."

The grim look on Faizan's face finally melted and his shoulders sagged. He took her in his arms again and held her tightly. He squeezed her and rocked her back and forth. She put her arms around him and cried silently on his shoulders.

Ken, Trisha, and Audrey left the living room, leaving them alone to have their privacy. Zainah kissed him. She began to pull back, but he held her to himself and kissed her again and again. "Promise you'll come back to me," he said, as he kissed her hair and her chin.

Her heart felt like it was breaking into tiny pieces as she gazed at his face. He looked so miserable. She knew she couldn't promise anything and yet she did. "I promise I'll be back, Faizan. I'll do everything in my power to try to convince my father to dissolve that marriage so I can come back and finally marry you."

She thought about the wedding as they remained in each other's arms. They would have to postpone it. They still had sixty days left to get married before she had to leave the country, but she was leaving now, and didn't know when she would return. They would probably have to start the visa process again.

Or cancel it, a mocking voice in her head said.

She shuddered and tried to press away the voice in her head, but it remained. It continued to mock her, telling her that she was already married to another and would never marry Faizan, never know what it would mean to be his wife. Even though there was nothing she wanted more than that, she would never get to have it.

She held him even tighter, trying to get comfort from him, and committing to memory his handsome face and the feel of his arms around her. She felt like curling up on the floor and sobbing loudly, but she had to be strong, at least at this time.

After a long moment, she finally pulled back from him. He took her hand and threaded his fingers through hers. Looking into her eyes, he asked, "When do you leave?"

The sorrow in his eyes broke her heart all over again, but she could not look away. She answered,

"My father said I have just two days to be in Nira so I'll have to leave as soon as possible. First thing in the morning."

He sucked in his breath sharply and then nodded. He squeezed her hands and then said in a voice that chilled her and reminded her of the way he used to speak before he gave his life to Christ. "If you are not back in a month's time, I don't care what anybody says. I will come to Nira and get you out, and if anyone tries to stop me, I will kill that person. And if I find out your father harmed you in any way, so help me God..." He thankfully didn't finish his sentence.

She looked into his eyes and caressed his cheeks. "Faizan, please promise me you will not do anything rash. Remember what the Lord would want you to do."

He gazed at her for a few seconds and then he sighed loudly and relented. "All right, I will not do anything rash, but you have to come back to me quickly, Zainah. Remember we are supposed to get married in less than sixty days."

"I will," she said.

They hugged again as she continued to cry, wetting his shirt with her tears. She might never come back, and there was nothing she could do about it.

*****

The sun burned brightly in the sky when Zainah stepped out of Bamako–Sénou International Airport, holding a small traveling bag. By God's grace, she would not stay in Mali for long.

You will probably stay here forever, the voice in

her head, which had been mocking her since the day her father called, screamed at her.

Her pulse raced as she took a taxi to the bus station where she would get a bus that would take her to Nira. She had considered staying at a hotel before she got here, but now she couldn't wait to get to Nira and get it all over with. The earlier she got her best friend and brother out of trouble and also dissolved her marriage, the quicker she could go back and marry Faizan.

Her taxi got to the bus station quickly and after she had paid the driver, she went into the bus terminal. She stood in line and waited for her turn to pay for her bus ticket to Kazi and from there to Nira.

When it was finally her turn, she bought her ticket and then went outside to wait for the other passengers to board the bus. She sat on a bench in front of the terminal and looked around her. People where hawking their wares on their heads while passengers roamed around. Some buses were being boarded by passengers, while some, already full, were leaving the bus station. The place was rowdy, but all the noise could not shut out the voice in her head that kept telling her she would never see Faizan again.

She clenched and unclenched her fists and tried to push away the fear threatening to take over her mind. But she could not shake it. She took deep breaths to keep from hyperventilating. Ten minutes later, she entered her bus with the other passengers.

Throughout the trip, she stared out the window, deliberately playing a game in her mind where she tried to spot how many changes she could see in the landscape, all the while trying to keep her mind from dwelling on her predicament. However, she did not succeed in distracting herself from her problems. She could hardly focus, as her mind continually revolved around Faizan and the wedding. She wanted to sob loudly, right there on the bus, but she held herself together.

After hours of wrestling with her emotions, she finally fell asleep.

When she woke up again, her stomach twisted in dread as she noticed that they had already passed Kazi. The bus was now speeding toward Nira. She had not even known when the bus stopped at Kazi. That meant she had been sleeping for hours, dead to the world around her. But she wasn't surprised. She'd hardly slept at all the night before, and she hadn't slept during the flight to Bamako, either.

The closer they got to Nira, the more frightened she became. Who knew what exactly she would encounter when she got to her hometown? She'd come to realize that her father was an unpredictable and very cruel man. She had always somehow excused him in her mind during her years in exile at the women's camp. He had chased her out of her community and away from her family because he didn't know better, she had told herself. But now that she understood the depths of his wickedness, she wondered how he could ever be her father.

She began to pray earnestly as the bus drove into the bus station in Nira. Getting off the bus, she walked out of the station and quickly made her way down the road so she could avoid being seen by anyone in the market opposite the station. Even though her father's house was not far from the station, she found a taxi that was empty and got in, telling the man to take her to Karim Keita's house.

The taxi stopped in front of her father's house and Zainah took a deep breath. She let out her breath slowly, trying to let go of her nervousness. Paying the driver, she sat in the taxi for a few seconds, and then got out slowly with her traveling bag. Not wanting anyone around to see her, she went straight to the gate and tried to push it open. It was locked.

She moaned and then knocked on the door. Seconds later, the doors opened and Khadija peered out at her. Her eyes grew as big as saucers and an expression of shock took over her face. She came out of the house, pulled Zainah into a tight hug, and then said, "Oh Zainah, you shouldn't have come!"

Zainah rubbed Khadija's back and said to her, "I had no choice. I had to come. Leila is being held captive by Papa. And Malik also, I think."

Khadija began to weep silently and took Zainah's hand in hers. She looked into Zainah's eyes.

Zainah frowned. "What is the matter, Khadija? Did Papa hurt you in any way?"

"I did a very bad thing," Khadija said. "I betrayed Leila. She and I had become friends, but I sold her out because I was afraid of what Papa would do to me." Khadija shook her head and began to cry harder.

Zainah opened her mouth to ask her what really happened, but their father suddenly appeared at the door. She glared at him, loathing him. The man had made the lives of everyone around him miserable. How could he be her father?

"Zainah, you are here!" her father said, grinning at her.

Khadija quickly left, and Zainah narrowed her eyes at him. "You wicked man! How can you be so heartless?"

He opened the doors wide and said, "Enter, my daughter. I've been waiting for you. You will soon find out that everything I do, I do for your own good."

Zainah shook her head. "No, everything you do, you do for yourself, only for your own selfish reasons." She entered the house, climbed up the stairs, and walked into the living room. Her father entered after her and shut the door behind him.

"Where is Mama?" she asked her father. She couldn't believe that her mother had stood by and watched him do everything he'd done to her, to Khadija. What kind of woman let anyone treat her children that way?

Her father was staring intently at her. He finally said, "Your mother is traveling. Sit down, Zainah, and let's talk about why I asked you to come here."

She sat on the sofa facing him and leaned forward to look him in the eye. Her heart was beating with fear, but she would not give him the pleasure of knowing that she was afraid. She wanted to give an impression that she was confident and would not be bullied by him. She said, "Yes, about that, the earlier that farce of a marriage can be dissolved, the earlier I can leave this place and go back to the love of my life. But first, where is Leila? I'm here now, so release her right away."

He laughed and shook his head at her. "I don't know why you think that you are here to bargain with me. A marriage cannot be dissolved unless both parties want it dissolved. Your husband . . ."

She cut him off. "I don't have a husband!" She stared at him and said firmly, "I have a fiancé, and he isn't here. He is in America."

Her father narrowed his eyes and went on as if she had not spoken. "Your husband does not want your marriage dissolved. In spite of everything that happened, he still wants to remain married to you. You should count yourself lucky, Zainah. He is a very wealthy man. You and Leila will be given to your husbands tomorrow."

Zainah's mouth fell open, and for a brief moment, she could not speak. She finally found her voice and said, "I knew you could not be trusted." She decided to lie to him. "Listen, my husband-to-be has friends in the government. They were the ones who rescued us the last time and they are here in Nira now. I told them to step in and get us if Leila and I are not out of here by tomorrow."

Papa chuckled. "Zainah, you have never been a good liar. My men are all over this town looking out for any strangers and strange activity. They saw you when you came into Nira. They would have informed me a long time ago if any of those armed men you are talking about were in Nira now. Besides, I told you not to bring anyone with you. I know you would not risk the life of your friend and brother and defy me."

Zainah sighed. "Okay, but I want to see Leila right now. You promised to let her go if I came back here. And you also promised to free Malik. So wherever you have him tied and locked up, please let him go."

"I'm not going to let Leila or your brother go," her father said. "I have to make sure you do as you say and go back to your husband's house without any problems tomorrow."

Zainah's mouth dropped open, and she shook her head. "I never agreed to go back to my so-called husband. Besides, I have a fiancé that I love very much and I am going to marry him as soon as I get back to America. Why would I promise such a thing?"

"Why can't you get it in your head that you are already married and that your husband isn't going to ever dissolve the marriage? You are going to your husband's house tomorrow and that's that."

She glowered at him and said, "How can you be so wicked?"

He looked at her and chuckled, "Wicked? I am doing all this for you."

She yelled, "No, you are not! You are doing this for yourself!"

His mouth turned up in a crooked smile. "I guess you are right, Zainah. Your marriage to Jibril, and your friend's to Dauda, will ensure that my business continues to thrive."

Her loathing for her father increased as she stared at him. She suddenly couldn't see or think straight and lunged at him. Immediately, two of her father's bodyguards appeared from nowhere, grabbed her, and moved her far away from him.

Her father's smile melted from his face. He stared at her as though he had never seen her before. Turning to his bodyguards, he said, "Take her and lock her up in the shack."

They began to drag her away and she yelled, "You are an evil man! May God repay you for all the evil you have done."

They dragged her out of the house and carried her kicking and screaming until they came to the shack. They unlocked it, pushed her in, and locked it up again. She turned around. The shack was dark and she could see nothing. She began to feel the wall for the light switch and then swung around as she heard Leila's voice say, "Is that you, Zainah?"

Zainah found the switch and immediately switched the light on. The room flooded with light and she gasped. Leila was huddled in a corner of the shack, disheveled. Immediately, Zainah went to her and they fell into each other's arms.

"Why are you in the dark, Leila?" Zainah cried. "What has my father done to you?"

"I'm so sorry, Zainah," Leila said, tears streaming down her face. "It's all my fault."

Zainah rubbed her back, trying to comfort her. "Stop apologizing, Leila. It's not your fault."

Leila sniffed and said, "If I had not given your father your phone number, if I did not even come here in the first place, all this would not have happened."

"Stop it!" Zainah sighed. "Stop blaming yourself. It's my fault. If I had not brought you here in the first place, we would not be where we are today."

They clung to each other and wept in each other's arms until they were exhausted. They both sat on the bare floor and clung to each other.

At last, Leila said, "We are in deep trouble, Zainah. What are we going to do? Is there any chance that your Faizan's friends will save us again this time?"

Zainah shook her head. "I don't think so. Faizan called the man who sent those men to rescue us the last time to see if he could help again, but he said he can't. Nobody is coming to save us this time, Leila. We are on our own now."

Leila began to weep again. "Your father told me that we were going to be put in purdah. He said those men are planning to move to Saudi Arabia where we will remain forever in bondage." She cried louder. "I will never get to see Malik again."

Zainah thought about what Leila had said and then about Faizan. Suddenly, the full reality of her situation came crashing down on her, and a terrible feeling of utter hopelessness enveloped her. She lay on the ground and prayed that God would take her life, because she could not imagine being married to someone other than Faizan. She couldn't imagine living without him. She would virtually be a slave. Even worse than that, a sex slave. She and Leila both would.

Leila lay down next to her and looked her in the eyes. "I tried to take my life." She looked away. "With a shard of glass I found right there."

Zainah's jaw dropped, and she sat up. She looked down at Leila and said, "Tell me you did not. You are only joking, right?"

"I did. Death looked better than the future for me."

Zainah shuddered. What would she have done if she'd come in here and found her best friend lying on the floor dead? There had to be a way out of here. She said to Leila, "Let's pray and ask the Lord to work a miracle for us. 'Cause he's our only hope."

Leila shut her eyes and leaned back on the wall. She shook her head and said, "I can't pray anymore. I've been praying since they brought me here, Zainah. I've prayed and prayed and prayed, and still, there is no deliverance. Now you're here, suffering with me."

Zainah leaned back against the wall beside Leila and dashed at the tears in her eyes. "We have to keep praying, Leila. We have no other hope or choice. We need to pray that the Lord will work a miracle and rescue us somehow."

She took Leila's hand and began to pray. She prayed and cried at the same time. She cried out to God from her heart, but somehow her prayer seemed like it held very little hope and faith. But it was all she had in her—tiny faith, and even less hope.

After she had prayed, she hugged Leila again. "We need to trust that the Lord will work a miracle for us, and quickly too."

Leila said nothing and Zainah added, "My father said we will be given away to those men tomorrow. That cannot happen. Somehow, the Lord will deliver us before then."

She stood up, unable to remain seated anymore. Pacing the shack, she started to pray again. Faizan's face stayed on her mind as she prayed. Tears flowed freely down her face as she wept and asked the Lord to save them so she would see Faizan again.

For what seemed like hours, she paced the floor, weeping and praying. When she finally got tired, she went to sit down near Leila and found that her friend was asleep.

Zainah's heart grew heavy as she looked at Leila. *If only I had not returned here with her months ago. We are both in this awful situation because of me.*

She leaned her back against the wall, feeling exhausted, and then lay beside Leila to try to sleep. But she couldn't. Her father's words kept echoing in her mind. Tomorrow, you'll be given away to your husbands, he had said. The thought of that happening made her sick to her stomach.

She stayed awake throughout the night into the next day. And even though she felt exhausted and sleepy, she stood up once again and began to pray earnestly. Amongst all she prayed about, she asked that the Lord would quickly send a miracle for them, or take her life now, because death would be better than the fate that awaited her and Leila.

FOURTEEN

Faizan tossed and turned on his bed, but he could not sleep. He stood up finally and switched on the lights. What am I doing here? he asked himself. The woman he loved was thousands of miles away and he didn't know what was going on with her even now. For all he knew, she could have been misled by her father. Maybe the man had insisted that she could not dissolve her marriage and would stay married to one of those men that he had forced her to marry the last time. I have to go to her.

He couldn't stay here doing nothing. But Jake's warning rang in his mind over and over again. If he left the United States and was caught, he would spend the rest of his life in jail. More than that, even if he succeeded in evading being caught, he would not be able to return to the United States again. He would not get to see his sisters again. He was between the devil and the deep blue sea.

He ran his fingers through his hair, his emotions in disarray. "Lord, please give me wisdom," he prayed. "Show me what to do."

But in his heart, he already knew what he wanted to do. He couldn't let Zainah handle her problems all alone in Mali. He had to go get her. He would risk everything for her, including spending the rest of his life in jail. He knew once he left the United States, the likelihood of coming back would be nil. He would miss his sisters terribly. After spending a lifetime without a real family, finally finding them and being a part of their family had been everything to him. But, Zainah was his life now. Even if it meant not ever seeing his sisters again, he would give it all up to be with her.

He stood and began to pace the room. Already, his mind was made up. He would find a way to sneak out of the country and go to Mali to find Zainah. If she was in trouble, he would help her, even without Jake's help. If there was a way to leave the country without being seen, he had to find that way.

He glanced at the clock on the wall and his heart twisted. It was one a.m. Today was supposed to be his and Zainah's wedding day. Now it would not be held because of her wicked father.

He went out of the room and walked to Ken and Audrey's room. He felt hesitant to wake them up in the middle of the night, but there was nothing he could do. He knocked on their bedroom door and waited. When no one answered, he knocked once more.

Ken opened the door and stared at him. "What is it, Faizan?"

"I need to speak to you, Ken." Audrey appeared at the door and stood behind Ken. She stared curiously and asked, "What's the problem, Faizan?" She hit her forehead and then she shook her head. "I'm sorry for asking. Zainah has just left the country and might be in a dangerous situation, and I'm asking what's wrong. You are worried about her, aren't you?"

Ken shook his head at Audrey. "He's distraught, Audrey. You shouldn't have just spelled everything out like that."

"It's okay," Faizan said, smiling sadly at his sister. "I am terribly worried about Zainah." He turned to look at Ken again and said once more, "I need to speak to you," He faced Audrey and added, "And you too, Audrey."

Audrey held up a finger and said to him, "Give me a second. Let me put on my robe."

He nodded and went to the living room with Ken. He sat on the sofa near the door while Ken sat on the couch facing him. Audrey came out a minute later and sat beside Ken. They both looked quizzically at him.

Faizan looked at Audrey and Ken and then cleared his throat. He began, "I can't do this. I can't sit here and do nothing. I have to go find Zainah. I don't trust her father. Who knows what is happening to her right now?"

Ken leaned forward and his eyes searched Faizan's face. "I know how hard this is, but you know what will happen if you try to leave the United States. The government has eyes everywhere. They will find you. You will never be able to successfully leave this country without being seen."

Faizan nodded and then said, "I need your help, Ken. As Jake's friend, you can help . . ."

Ken shook his head. "You and I called Jake together and he told both of us that he would not be able to help this time."

"We need to try again."

"No, Faizan. You're asking way too much of me. Jake said that if he tried to help one more time, he would be in trouble with the powers that be. He is my friend, but I can't ask him to put his job on the line in order to do me a favor."

"Please, Ken," Faizan said, leaning forward in his seat. "You know very well that I am right about Zainah's father. Zainah might be in trouble right now. You know the story of how he tried to force her to convert to Islam and get married to a stranger. Come on, Ken. Please help me. Zainah is part of this family. I know you care for her as well. You don't want her to get hurt, do you?"

Faizan ran his fingers through his hair and said, "Besides, I'm not asking you to ask Jake to do the same thing he did last time. He doesn't have to send any men to the area to rescue Zainah again. I just need his help to get out of the country without being caught. After all, when I left on that covert mission, he was completely in charge of getting me out of the country."

Audrey put a hand on Ken's shoulder and said, "Ken, you need to try to speak to Jake again."

Ken didn't say anything for a long moment, and then he sighed and said, "Okay, I will call him." He frowned. "But you will have to manage your expectations."

"Will you call him now?" Faizan asked eagerly.

Ken frowned again and pointed at the clock on the wall. "Look at the time, Faizan. If I wake Jake up now, all I will get is a grumpy, angry man who will refuse any and every request I make. Please let's wait until morning."

Faizan groaned in frustration and pressed his lips tightly together. He finally sighed loudly and nodded. "Okay, we will wait until morning."

Ken stood and Audrey stood up with him. "Ok, it's all settled now. I will call Jake in the morning." He smiled at Faizan and then took Audrey's hand. "Let's go."

After Audrey and Ken left the living room, Faizan sat back on the sofa and shut his eyes. He felt better, but only a little. Jake might refuse to even hear them out. All he could do now was wait.

He picked up the remote control from the coffee table, knowing he couldn't go back to sleep now. He switched the TV set on to distract himself from his morbid thoughts and began to flip through the channels. Finally, not finding anything that could sufficiently distract him, he switched off the TV again.

He closed his eyes and began to pray that the Lord would grant him favor and that Jake would somehow agree to their request. Because if Jake refused to help him, he would have to resort to finding a way to help himself. And that would mean trying to sneak out of the country on his own without being caught and getting thrown in jail for the rest of his life.

Faizan's eyes flew open as someone tapped him on the shoulder. He looked up and saw it was Ken. "Is it morning already?" he asked, rubbing his eyes. He had dropped off to sleep in the living room while still praying.

"Yes, it is," Ken said. He sat down beside Faizan and looked at him. "I called Jake early in the morning, Faizan."

Faizan sat up and nodded. "What did he say?" he asked, as his heart pounded with hope and dread.

"I told him to help you unofficially, as a friend. It took a lot of pleading, but he agreed to help."

Faizan's eyes widened in shocked joy, and then he raised his fist in triumph and roared, "Yes."

Ken lifted a finger and added, "But you will have only twenty-four hours to get Zainah out of there. A private plane will be waiting for you at the same place it was the last time you left the country. It will take you to Bamako and you will find your way to Zainah's hometown. You have to retrieve her quickly and then be at the spot in Bamako where you were dropped off by the plane, as soon as possible. If you are not there when your twenty-four hours expire, the plane will leave without you and Jake will wash his hands of you. You will then not be able to get back into the country." Ken searched his eyes. "Can you do that, Faizan?"

Faizan nodded, his heart soaring.

"You are sure about that, Faizan? You will be considered a fugitive if you are not back in the time Jake set for you."

"I understand that," Faizan said.

"Okay," Ken nodded. "You leave for Mali this evening, at six o'clock on the dot."

Faizan smiled. "Thank you so much, Ken. Thank you!"

Ken sighed. "Please try to come back. And be very careful back there. Audrey will kill me if anything happens to you," he sighed, "even though she was the one who encouraged me to call Jake and ask him to help you."

"I'll be careful and try my best to come back."

Ken smiled again and then stood up. "Well, I have delivered the message I was given. Your sister is waiting for me in bed. For, you know…" He winked at Faizan.

Faizan shook his head quickly and pretended to shudder. "No, I don't!" He chuckled. "I certainly don't want to know what goes on in private between you and my sister."

Ken laughed as he walked away. He turned back before he left the living room. The expression on his face was sober again. "I mean it, Faizan. Please come back."

Faizan sighed and then said, "You know, Ken, that there might be a chance I don't come back, either because I am not able to get Zainah out of her town fast enough, or because I get hurt. There are really no guarantees."

Ken pressed his lips together and then sighed loudly. "I know." He smiled sadly at Faizan and then turned around and walked out of the living room.

Faizan stared at the wall for some minutes. His sisters would be devastated if he didn't come back to Rosefield. They had gone to so much trouble to look for him. He wondered whether to tell Trisha and Sienna, who had arrived with Bryan from Peru yesterday, about his quest to rescue Zainah.

Almost immediately, he decided not to. Knowing his sisters, especially Trisha, they might try to talk him out of it because it would be dangerous and there was a chance he might not ever come back to the US. Not that anyone could talk him out of it, but he didn't want them to try. And he especially did not want them worrying about him needlessly. Audrey was a police officer. In situations like this, she was less emotional. He would trust her to make up something to explain his absence for the next two or so days. But if he couldn't come back for whatever reason, she would have to tell them the truth. Poor Sienna was pregnant. Hopefully, it would not affect her or the baby in any way.

He stood up and went into his room to prepare for his trip to Mali.

FIFTEEN

Zainah opened her eyes as the door of the shack flew open. Her father's bodyguards walked in and made for her. She backed away from them, but they pulled her up on her feet. They also pulled up Leila who was asleep beside her. Zainah shielded her eyes from the sun as they led her and Leila out of the shack. She walked with unsteady steps as they took her to her father's house. Leila stumbled slightly and was steadied by one of the bodyguards.

Zainah glowered at her father as they entered the living room. He was sitting on the sofa with his legs crossed, drinking a bottle of beer. He looked up at her and ordered his bodyguards to let go of her and Leila. He said, "Both of you, sit down."

Leila sat down on the couch, but Zainah refused to sit. She stood, glaring at him.

He shrugged and said, "Well, have it your way." He looked at Leila and then faced Zainah again. Dropping his bottle of beer on the table, he said, "Any moment now, your husbands will be here to take you away. You're both to get ready so that when they come, you will both look presentable."

Zainah's heart filled with such hatred for him that she felt like putting her hands around his neck and strangling him for all he had done and was doing to her and to Leila. She shut her eyes briefly and confessed her violent thoughts silently to the Lord. She opened her eyes and said to her father, "And what if we refuse to go with those men?"

He laughed and said to her, "Then you will both die. It will not be at my hands, but at your husbands' hands. They will have the right to kill you."

Leila whimpered beside her, while Zainah continued to glower at her father. She said, "What kind of law or tradition allows such a thing to be done?"

He said, "That has always been how it is in Nira. And there is nothing you can do about it."

Leila began to wail.

Zainah felt like doing the same herself, but she knew it would accomplish nothing. She also knew that life as it was and had been for her would end today. Or maybe it had ended on the day she'd come back here.

Once again, Faizan's face filled her mind. It was what caused the greatest pain. That she would never see him again.

Her father snapped at one of his bodyguards, "Go and call Rabia and Khadija."

Zainah raised her brows. So her stepmother was back from her long stay at her mother's. Her own mother wasn't back yet, but it wouldn't make a difference if she were. She had not protected Zainah when her father had chased her out of Nira years ago or married her off to one of his friends. Instead, she had totally supported him.

A minute later, Zainah's stepmother walked into the living room. Khadija walked in after her. Zainah noted how they totally ignored her and Leila as they stood before her father. She kept staring at Khadija, trying to catch her eye, but her younger sister completely ignored her. She wasn't surprised by her stepmother's refusal to look at her, but Khadija ignoring her was another thing.

Their father said to Khadija and Zainah's stepmother, "Both of you, you're in charge of making sure that Zainah and her friend here look as beautiful as possible. Their husbands are going to come and take them to their matrimonial homes today, so they have to look their very best."

Zainah shifted close to Leila, who was still crying, and put her arm around her. She would not let go of Leila willingly. And she would not go with the man who her father insisted was her husband willingly. They would have to drag her away.

Her stepmother stood before her and Leila. Khadija finally looked at her and said in a small voice, "Let's go, Zainah." She looked at Leila and then averted her eyes quickly.

Zainah looked up at her and said, "Khadija, you know what is happening here. We are being forced into a situation that we don't want to be in. How can any woman be forced to marry a man she doesn't love or even really know? You know it's not right."

Khadija looked away, and then looked back at her with pleading eyes. "Please, Leila, Zainah, please let's just go."

Zainah looked away from her and sat where she was, her hand still around Leila's waist. Her stepmother said in a more commanding voice than

Khadija's, "Get up, Zainah." She looked at Leila, "And you, too. Let's go now."

Zainah ignored her.

Her father snapped his fingers, and two of the bodyguards came and hauled Zainah and Leila up. Zainah winced in pain as one of the bodyguards dug his fingers into her arms. Khadija and her stepmother led the way while the bodyguards forcefully pulled her and Leila along with them behind.

They got close to the bathroom and the guards stepped back. Zainah's stepmother led her and Leila to the door of the bathroom while Khadija followed behind. "Go into the bathroom and wash up," Zainah's stepmother said to her and Leila. "And be fast about it."

Zainah glared at her and refused to move. She knew her resistance was futile, but she didn't feel like being pushed around by anyone, especially by the people who were supposed to be her family but acted more like her enemies.

Khadija came and looked her in the eye. "Please, Zainah. Please do as she says." She looked at Leila with tears in her eyes and then quickly looked away again. She said to Zainah, "Please."

Zainah searched her sister's eyes. There was something in them that caused her to finally give in. She took Leila's hand and then went into the bathroom. Shutting the door behind her, she turned to Leila. "We have to find a way to get out of here," she said.

Leila wiped the tears from my eyes and laughed without humor. She said, "Look around you, Zainah. Your father's men are everywhere. There is no way out of this place. There's nothing we can do.

God has abandoned us."

"Don't say that, Leila. God has not abandoned us."

"Yes. Yes, he has. Our fate now is worse than death."

Zainah's heart was heavy, but she tried her best to inject hope into her voice as she said, "God has a plan for our lives. You have to believe that, Leila."

Her words were spoken out of a lifetime of continuous trust in God. But at this time, she spoke them with very little faith. She looked up at the bathroom window. It was small, like the window in the shack, and it had iron bars.

She bit her lip. Outside, her father's bodyguards were all around the house. His men lurked in every corner of the community. Maybe Leila was right. Maybe God had truly abandoned them.

Somebody suddenly knocked loudly and Zainah jumped. Her stepmother yelled, "Zainah, I can't hear the water running. What are you both doing in there?"

Zainah looked at Leila and said, "We better start showering now. Knowing my father, he would not hesitate to get his men to stand watch while my stepmother bathes us."

Leila quickly shed her clothes and got into the shower. Zainah walked to the mirror beside the bathtub and gazed at her face. Her eyes looked glazed and hopeless. It was just the way she felt. For the umpteenth time since she woke up, she prayed, "Lord, please do something! Please deliver us!"

Leila said over the sound of the running shower, "Is that woman out there Malik's mother?"

Zainah lifted her brows, wondering why Leila

was asking her about that. She reluctantly answered, "Yes, she is. Why do you ask?"

"Umm... maybe she can tell me where Malik is... or maybe if we tell her what your father did to Malik, she might get angry and help us escape."

"Leila, forget about that," Zainah said. "It's not going to work. Everyone in this house, including my own mother, bows constantly to my father's wishes. My stepmother is not going to do anything if we tell her about Malik. I doubt she will even believe us if we did."

Leila didn't say anything more about it. She stepped out of the shower minutes later and began to dry her body with the towel hanging near the shower curtain. Zainah shed her own clothes and got into the shower. She showered quickly and then stepped out and wrapped herself with the towel folded on the shower rack.

Leila, a pink towel wrapped around her body, said, "So this is actually going to happen. We are going to be wives to those men who are old enough to be our fathers. And then we will spend the rest of our lives in purdah."

Zainah had no words. She began to take deep breaths as she felt herself starting to panic. She still held onto a shred of hope that the Lord would come through for them. But doubts had mostly polluted her heart, and she couldn't see a way out of their predicament.

Someone pounded on the door again, and Zainah's stepmother said angrily from behind the door, "You two... are you both giving birth in there? Come out right now!"

"We better come out now," Zainah said to Leila

bleakly.

They both left the bathroom together and followed Zainah's stepmother to her bedroom. Khadija was there, waiting beside the bed. Zainah felt like throwing up. Colorful beaded kaftans were laid out on the bed, clearly for her and Leila. They had washed and were going to now be stuffed and dressed like holiday turkeys in preparation to be feasted upon.

Leila grabbed her elbow and looked away from the clothes.

Zainah's stepmother looked at her and Leila and ordered, "Put those on."

Zainah didn't move. Neither did Leila, and Zainah's stepmother said again, "Put the clothes on, both of you, or I will have to call the men to force you to do so. You would not want that, would you?"

Zainah drilled her with an angry stare and then whispered to Leila, "Let's put them on." She said loudly so her stepmother would hear, "The same way you treat other people's daughters is the same way others will treat yours." After she had said the words, she wished she hadn't. Not that the woman didn't deserve them, but it was completely useless and she didn't want to be this sort of person who said words like this when she was hurt.

She felt like laughing in self-mockery at her thoughts. She was about to face a situation which she considered a living death, and she was thinking about what was appropriate to say to her stepmother or not.

Her stepmother sneered, "My daughters will not have to be forced to do anything they are supposed to, Zainah. Neither will they neglect the faith with which they were raised for a strange one."

Zainah turned her back to the woman and picked up one of the kaftans. It was a blue, intricately embroidered outfit. In ordinary times, she would have loved to put this on. Today, all she wanted to do was rip the kaftan into tiny pieces.

Leila picked up the other one. Hers was red, with a different pattern of embroidery, but equally elaborate. She examined it carefully and then turned to Zainah and whispered, "I'm not putting it on."

"I don't want to put it on either, Leila, but we don't have a choice. Just like my stepmother said, you don't want any of those men to come in here and supervise us while we dress up."

Zainah put hers on and then watched as Leila did as well. She refused to look at herself in the mirror and then stood unmoving as Khadija began to comb and then braid her hair. Her stepmother braided Leila's.

Somebody knocked on the door and Zainah's stepmother went to see who it was.

"He wants them to come out now," a male voice said. "Their husbands are here."

Zainah shuddered. She prayed in her heart, Lord, if you will ever help me, I need your help now.

The door shut again and her stepmother walked up to her and Leila. "Your husbands are here," she said in a matter-of-fact way. "You better hurry up, Khadija, and finish Zainah's hair."

Khadija finished with Zainah's hair quickly and then stepped away. Zainah's stepmother also finished Leila's hair and stuck a shiny pin in it.

"Let's go," Zainah's stepmother said. She put

her hands on Zainah and Leila's shoulders and led them to the door and out into the living room.

Zainah pursed her lips. Her father was sitting on the couch, drinking a glass of liquor. Across from him were the two men who her father had given her and Leila to in marriage. Zainah's father looked up at her and Leila as they slowly walked into the living room.

The men her father had called Dauda and Jibril gazed at them. and Zainah cringed. The men were looking at her and Leila like cows being closely examined in order to determine how best they could be slaughtered for consumption. One of the men, the one she had been given to, who she remembered her father called Jibril, finally turned to her father. He nodded and said, "She is very beautiful. Just like I remembered."

The other one said the same thing about Leila, and Leila grasped her hand.

The men and her father continued to talk for a while about her and Leila, but Zainah tuned their words out. She looked around her, looking for a way of escape, but there was none. Her father's men stood around the living room.

An overwhelming sense of hopelessness settled on her as the men stood up. They shook her father's hand and then went out of the house. Zainah pursed her lips as her father nodded at two of his bodyguards, and they came to stand behind her and Leila.

She walked out of the house, clutching Leila's hand, her father's men behind her. Her father walked in front of her and Leila. She wondered if this would be her life from now on. Would she always be under watch, constantly surrounded by bodyguards so she would not be able to escape?

She squeezed Leila's hand as they walked to two cars parked in front of the house. One of the cars was a white luxury SUV and the other was an identical black one. Her father said to her, "Zainah, come this way." He pointed at the black car, and said, "That is your husband, Jibril's car."

Leila's hand immediately tightened around hers and she refused to let go. Zainah did not want to the separated from Leila either. Two burly men, clearly bodyguards, but not her father's, came and pulled her away from Leila. She guessed they were her so-called husband's and Leila's. They virtually bundled her into the black car while Leila cried out. Zainah looked out of the window as they forced Leila into the white car. Leila's cries pierced her heart.

The car door was firmly shut and then Zainah turned sharply as someone took her hand. The man called Jibril, supposedly her husband, held her hand and gave her a smile that sent an awful chill down her spine. She scowled at him and wrenched her hand away.

He narrowed his eyes and said coldly, "You will learn soon enough to be obedient."

One of his bodyguards got into the front seat beside the driver, and Jibril said to his driver, "Go!"

Zainah shuddered at the ice in his voice and at his words.

The driver immediately drove away. As the car wove through Nira, Zainah's heart pounded. She looked out of the window, wishing she could jump out of it. All the while, she felt Jibril's eyes on her.

Every person on the street whose eye she could catch, she looked at directly in the eye. None of them seemed interested in her plight. She knew that crying out for help would be a waste of time. None of these people in her community cared about her or any young woman in this kind of situation. It was their way of life, their custom; they were all in support of this forced marriage, which was, in truth, nothing but kidnapping and imprisonment.

The driver finally pulled up to a house so big and beautiful she thought she was no longer in Nira. She looked up at the house and trembled in fear. It looked like a place where one could be locked up and never ever found again. Tears swam in her eyes as she thought about Faizan, but she blinked them back.

The driver opened the door for her and she reluctantly came out of the car. Jibril walked beside her as she slowly made her way to the house. He put his hand around her waist, but she stepped away from him. When he laughed out loud, she cringed.

She entered the house and found it exorbitantly and garishly furnished. She looked around her. It was all too much.

Jibril said, "Welcome to your new home. I hope you like it."

She refused to look at him or acknowledge him. All she wanted was to lock herself up somewhere and cry for a whole month. She thought about Leila and wondered how she was coping. Without a doubt, Leila's emotions would be in tatters, just like hers were.

Jibril kept staring at her as if he wanted to devour her and she could not stand it anymore. She said to him, "Can I go to my room now? It has been a long day and I need to rest."

He stared at her for a long time, clearly considering whether to give in to her request or not. Finally, he said, "All right, you may go. Barika will show you to your room." He grinned at her and she noticed a wicked glint in his eye.

He turned to one of the men standing near the door and said, "Go and get me Barika."

The man nodded and left. A minute later, he came back with a woman who looked about forty and elegantly dressed in a silk cream boubou. The woman gazed at her with a curious expression on her face.

Jibril said, "Barika, this is my new wife, Zainah. The one I told you about."

Barika nodded and her features closed up so that Zainah could not read the expression on her face.

"She's now one of you," Jibril said. "Take her to my room and make sure she is ready for me tonight."

Zainah's heart skipped a beat. Waves of panic ran through her as she followed Barika out of the living room. They walked down a long marble tiled hallway. On both sides of the hallway were doors, probably rooms for Jibril's other wives. Barika turned to her and said with a voice laden with animosity, "These rooms belong to the other wives in the house. All the children stay upstairs."

Zainah's heart pounded violently as they finally stopped in front of a large, ornate door. Barika opened the door and Zainah entered a room that was as large and elaborately furnished as the Rahmanis', the rich people she had worked for months ago. She had fled the house after her boss had tried to get her to sleep with him. Now she had run into something worse.

Barika confirmed her fears. "This is Jibril's private room," she said, scowling at Zainah. "As the first wife, I am supposed to prepare you for your night with him." She sneered as she regarded Zainah and added, "But I am sure you will manage without me."

Zainah's stomach lurched and she thought she would lose the breakfast that had been brought to her in the shack that morning. She said to Barika, "What will happen if I don't want to stay here?"

Barika laughed. "You can choose to stay of your own free will and play your role as a new wife, or be forced. And trust me, staying of your own free will is better." She turned around and left Zainah in the room.

At first, Zainah stood frozen, unable to move, and then she turned around and tried to open the door. As she guessed, it was locked. She shook the doorknob, but the door did not budge. She banged repeatedly on the door until she was exhausted. Finally, she sank to the floor and shut her eyes. She couldn't cry anymore. She had exhausted her tears. She curled up on the floor and let Faizan's face fill her mind. She had been trying to push his face away from her mind for hours now, because thinking about him had been too painful. Now, she felt numb with pain. She embraced the agony as she thought about him, his smile, the way she felt when they kissed. She would never feel that again, never be warmed by his smile.

The pain felt physical. She let it take over for

a long moment and then she finally stood. She couldn't just sit here like this and let that wicked man come and have his way with her. She had to do something.

But what could she do? This house was a fortress. There was no way of escape. She looked at the ensuite bathroom. Maybe she could lock herself in there when he came. It might not solve the problem, but it could buy her some time.

Buy you time for what, exactly? she thought in self-mockery. She wouldn't be able to stay in the bathroom forever. Even if she could manage to stay locked up in the bathroom that night, she would have to come out at some point. This was that wretched man's bathroom. She was married to him and trapped in this house. The inevitable would happen eventually. And like Barika said, it was better for it to happen willingly than forcefully. She might be a virgin, but she knew what that meant.

The thought of what would soon happen to her felt unbearable. She stood and went into the bathroom. She locked herself in and began to pray for a miracle. That was the only thing that would save her now.

SIXTEEN

Faizan leaned forward as his driver approached a signboard on the road that read, WELCOME TO NIRA. His watch told him it was a few minutes to seven p.m. Soon, darkness would fall, and he would not be able to see properly. It was unlikely that this small community had electricity. He still had to trace Zainah's father's house. After that, though, darkness would be his friend. It would enable him to get Zainah without anyone seeing him, except the people he needed to carry out his plan.

He had disembarked from the plane that Jake had sent to take him to Bamako and immediately hired a taxi to drive him to Nira. The driver had quoted a very high price, but Faizan had not argued with him. He had very little time to get Zainah out of Nira and back to Bamako where they would take the plane back to the United States. If he missed the twenty-four-hour window set by Jake, he would be stuck in Mali. So would Zainah.

They began to drive through a small market and he told the driver to slow down. He stuck his head out of the car window and called out to a man who was walking by. "Please, can you tell me the way to Karim Keita's house?" he asked the man in French.

The man stared curiously at him, probably because it was clear he was a stranger. "It's not far from here," the man answered. "Just keep going and then turn left. When you see a tailor's shop called Tailleur Africain, drive down the road and you will see a big house. That is Karim Keita's house."

Faizan thanked the man and told the driver to move on. They followed the directions that the man had given them, and as they began to approach the only house that could be Karim Keita's, Faizan told the driver to turn left and park on the opposite side of the house, a few feet away.

"But we haven't reached the house yet," the driver complained.

"Just do as I say," Faizan told him.

The driver grunted and shrugged. He turned left and drove to the other side of the road. When he stopped the car, he turned around and said to Faizan, "Now what?"

"Now, we wait," Faizan replied.

The driver blinked rapidly, and then shrugged once more. He turned around again and began to whistle.

A few people passing by turned to stare at the car, but none seemed overly curious. Faizan fixed his gaze on Zainah's father's house. Contrary to what the man who had given him directions here told him, it was not very big. However, compared to the other tiny houses and huts around, it was huge. His eyes settled on the front gate of the house, watching to see who would come in or go out. It would be great if Zainah came out, but he was sure that would not happen.

His emotions roiled as he watched the house. Hopefully, Zainah's father had not hurt her in any way or locked her up somewhere. Faizan prayed she was free and safe. He put his hand on his belt and felt for the handgun which he had hung on a holster around his waist. There was another gun in his backpack. The guns were two of the things Jake had left for him on the plane at his request. His plan was to force Karim Keita and the man Zainah had been forced to marry to dissolve the marriage. After that, he would get her out of Nira. He planned to do all that without having to resort to any type of violence. But the gun was just a safety measure.

For about fifteen minutes, he waited in the car. When it was sufficiently dark outside, he exited the car with his backpack. He began to make his way slowly to the house, looking this way and that as he walked to the front gate. But just as he got to the front of the house, the building suddenly lit up like a Christmas tree. The sound of a powered generator disrupted the quiet evening.

Faizan slowly retreated, and then walked to the back of the house. He was grateful that it was dark there. The security light at the back of the house had not yet been switched on. He quickly hid behind a huge tree near the back door and waited to see if anyone would come out of the house. After some time, he went and tried the doorknob to see if it would open. It did not.

He went to wait behind the tree again while he pondered on what his next move would be. He didn't know how many people were in the house.

If he somehow found a way inside, he had to be careful so no one would see him until he could get to Zainah and her father. It was a tricky situation. Zainah had told him that she had a large family. If one of the children or one of the wives saw him and raised the alarm, it would disrupt his plans. He couldn't enter the house just like that, but he had to enter now. He had very little time. He looked at the house again. How would he get to Zainah and then her father without being seen by anyone else in the house?

A man, young and strongly built, suddenly came out of the back door. He stood near the tree Faizan was hiding behind and lit a cigarette. Faizan surreptitiously studied him. From his bearing, he was most likely one of Karim Keita's bodyguards. Faizan wasn't sure if the man had a weapon, but it didn't really matter if he did. He wasn't holding one at the moment.

The man dropped the cigarette on the ground and crushed it with his foot. Faizan drew his gun and slowly walked out from behind the tree. The man began to turn toward his direction and Faizan quickly walked behind him and then pressed the gun to the man's back. "Move an inch and you die," Faizan said coldly. He hoped the man would not do anything funny because he did not want to harm him. Thankfully, the young man did not move.

Faizan whispered in his ear, "Now, unlock the back door."

The man hesitated and Faizan pressed the gun harder to his back. "Move," Faizan ordered.

The man moved. He unlocked the door quickly. Faizan kept the gun pointed at him while he unzipped his backpack with his left hand. He brought out a pair of handcuffs, cuffed the man to the railing surrounding the porch, and then duct-taped the man's mouth so he would not be able to call out for help.

Faizan looked around him one more time and then entered the house. His eyes widened as he stared into the eyes of a frightened teenage girl. In a flash, he reached her and covered her mouth with his hand before she could scream.

"Shhh," he whispered. "I am not going to hurt you. Are you Zainah's sister? I'm her friend. My name is Faizan. Maybe you have heard of me. If you have, please nod."

The girl nodded and Faizan breathed a sigh of relief. "I am here to rescue her and take her back to America. Where is she?"

The girl mumbled something, and Faizan sighed. "Don't scream when I remove my hand," he warned.

She nodded and he slowly removed his hand from her mouth. He held his breath, waiting for her to scream, but she did not. He blinked in surprise when she grabbed his hand and dragged him with her into the bathroom connected to her room. She locked the door of the bathroom and then said to him, "At any minute, one of my father's men will find you here." Her voice was laden with fear as she stared at him. "You are my sister's fiancé, aren't you? She has told me so much about you and so has her friend, Leila. I know you love my sister very much and I love her, too. I will tell you where she is, but you have to promise me that you will truly take her out of there and also rescue Leila."

The girl began to cry and Faizan awkwardly

pulled her in a hug in order to comfort her. He let her go again and asked, "Where is Zainah?"

The girl said to him, "Her husband and Leila's came to take them away."

Faizan's mind flooded with rage. "I knew her father could not be trusted," he said. He looked at Zainah's sister and asked angrily, "And what about your father? Where is he?"

"He is not at home. I heard him saying he was going to Jibril's house. That is the man Zainah is married to."

Faizan nodded slowly. Zainah, her father, and the man who had married Zainah by force would be in the same house. He could rescue her after he had forced both men to dissolve the marriage. He couldn't believe his luck.

But he immediately chided himself. Hadn't he asked God to help him rescue Zainah easily before he came here? This was not luck. This was an answer to his prayer.

Zainah's teenage sister began to cry again. "It is my fault. I was the one who told Papa that Leila was going to come back to Nira. Papa got Zainah's number from Leila by threatening and lying to her."

As much as Faizan felt sorry for the girl, all he wanted to know now was where the woman he loved was. "Can you give me directions to the house Zainah is in now?" he couldn't bring himself to say "her husband's house."

The girl nodded vigorously. "I can take you there myself."

Faizan shook his head. "No. It will be too dangerous for you. Just give me directions to the house."

"I want to go with you and Zainah to America."

Faizan shook his head again. "That won't be possible either."

She bowed her head for a few seconds and then said, "Okay. I will give you directions to Jibril's house, but promise me that whenever you can, you'll find a way to get me out of here."

For some seconds, he stared at her. And then, even though he knew he should not promise her anything, he did.

She smiled through her tears, and then gave him detailed directions to not only the house where Zainah was, but also where Leila was.

He started to open the bathroom door, but she shook her head. She opened the door herself, looked this way and that, and then said, "No one is coming. Quickly, you have to go now before anyone comes here and sees you."

She went ahead of him and opened the back door. When she saw the handcuffed bodyguard, her eyes grew wide.

Faizan shrugged and stepped out the back door. Just before she closed the door, he turned around and asked, "What is your name?"

She whispered, "Khadija. My name is Khadija."

"Thank you, Khadija," he said.

He quickly hurried to the car and then said to the driver, "We are going to pay someone a visit." He gave the driver directions to the house where Zainah was. He had promised Khadija to also rescue Leila, but he would not think about that right now.

They began to approach a house that was bigger than Audrey and Ken's back in Rosefield. The house was a mansion and was brightly lit, like Zainah's father's house. Faizan groaned. From the little information he had gathered from Khajida, the man who owned the house had many other wives. How would he find Zainah in such a huge house? The house was probably filled with women and children. God had given him a miracle in Zainah's father's house. However, he wasn't sure the Lord would perform another one for him here.

He told the driver to drive a little farther away from the house. They stopped near what looked like a farm. It was a land covered with vegetation, the perfect place for the car to be hidden. It was totally dark here, but he could see the mansion clearly.

"Are you sure all this hiding in the night is not dangerous?" the driver said to him. "You will have to pay me more."

Faizan ignored him. This time, he sat in the car and studied the big house. There were about four men standing in front of the house, all armed with guns. Bodyguards.

He saw another bodyguard come out from behind the house and groaned again. Five. The only thing he could do now was to wait in the car until Zainah's father came out. Hopefully, the man Khadija had said was called Jibril would come out with him. He would use the element of surprise once both men came out and maybe kidnap both of them.

He smiled at the rush of adrenaline he felt. It was familiar and exciting and he had missed the feeling. And then he told himself to calm down. He was enjoying this more than he should. This was what he did in his past life. He had vowed not to return to this life again, but unfortunately, his hand had been forced.

The driver began to grumble again and Faizan promised to double what he had agreed to pay him. The man stopped grumbling, seemingly happy with the new price.

Twenty minutes later, two middle-aged men walked out of the house and Faizan sat up. He immediately knew it was Karim Keita and his friend, Jibril, the man who had forcefully married Zainah.

Both men began to walk towards a black SUV near the house, and Faizan sprang into action. Quickly exiting the car, he ran to the men with both guns raised, one pointed at the middle-aged men, the other in the direction of the bodyguards. If any of these bodyguards tried to prevent him from his mission, he would have to shoot, even though he didn't want to. He prayed silently that the Lord would prevent that from happening.

He was just a few inches from both men and had his gun trained on them before the bodyguards in front of the house saw him. Suddenly, they surrounded him, their guns pointed at him. This is it, then, he thought to himself. His training at the terrorist group began to take over. "Put down your weapons or your bosses die," he shouted at the bodyguards.

Fear was etched on the faces of Karim Keita and his friend. Faizan said to them, "Tell your men to put their guns down. I will not harm either of you if you cooperate. I just want to talk. If any of your men tries anything, however, I will shoot both of you."

The one called Jibril told his men to put their guns down. Once they did, he looked again at Faizan and said, "You won't be able to escape. You know that, right?"

Faizan said, "I'll take my chances."

"What do you want?" the man asked.

Faizan looked at Zainah's father and said, "I am Faizan, Zainah's fiancé. I came all the way from America to rescue the woman I love. All I want is for both of you to dissolve the marriage and I will take Zainah away peacefully."

From the corner of his eye, he saw one of the guards slowly raise his gun. Without turning to directly look at him, he shot the ground beside the man's feet. The guard jumped and Faizan focused once more on the middle-aged men. "I told you to control your goons. Next time, you will catch a bullet," he pointed his gun directly at Jibril, "If any of them move."

Jibril said to his bodyguards in a shaky voice, "I told you all to stand down."

Faizan said, "Now, are you going to do what I asked, or do you want me to carry out my threat?"

He noticed again another bodyguard slowly raising his gun, and he sighed heavily. This time he had to shoot someone. Should he first shoot Jibril in the leg, or the bodyguard?

He swung around and shot the guard in the knee. The man screamed and dropped to the ground, moaning in pain.

He decided not to shoot Jibril. "You and you, bind his wound up now," he said to the bodyguards on his left. "He'll live." It was a shame that he'd had to shoot the man, but he'd had no choice.

The guards carried the wounded man away while Faizan kept his gun pointed at the older men in front of him. At the same time, he watched the remaining guards from the corner of his eye. Unfortunately, judging from the looks in the guards' eyes when he had turned to them, the man he had shot might not be the last one he would have to shoot.

"Maybe I should just shoot you now," he said to Jibril.

The man stepped back slightly, turned to Zainah's father, and said in a shaky voice, "I don't think your daughter is worth my life. Maybe we should dissolve the marriage now," he looked at Faizan, "just like he wants."

Faizan blinked. He hadn't thought it would be so easy. There was probably something amiss. He said to Jibril, "Send one of your bodyguards to get Zainah."

Jibril nodded at one of his bodyguards and the man hurried away. A few minutes later, the guard came out of the house, pulling Zainah along with him.

Faizan's mind flooded with rage. "Stop holding her roughly!" he barked. "You are hurting her. Let her go right now!"

Her eyes grew round in clear surprise as she looked at him, and then she tore away from the guard and began to run toward him. He held out his hands to her and then realized he had made a fatal mistake. The bodyguard behind him had taken his brief absentmindedness to raise his gun and pull the trigger. The sound of a gunshot pierced the air and he knew he'd been shot.

He blinked just as Zainah screamed and wrapped her arms around him. And then he realized he felt no pain. Terror gripped him as he looked at Zainah's face, and then he screamed. Her eyes were shut and her body felt lifeless in his arms. He gnashed his teeth at the bloody gaping hole in her back. The idiot guard had shot Zainah instead of him. He collapsed on the ground still holding her body and gave a deep guttural roar. "You killed her!"

Her father and Jibril rushed up and crouched down beside him. Her father looked up at the bodyguard and barked, "You idiot! What have you done!" He put his hands on his head. "They killed my daughter." He whispered, "I killed my daughter."

Faizan placed his fingers on her neck and felt a faint pulse. He shook his head and then barked, "We have to take her to the hospital now! She is still alive, but barely."

Jibril said to his men, "Carry her into the car now! You... get my driver!"

Faizan's body trembled with rage. He felt like shooting all the men here, including Zainah's father, but he controlled himself. Instead, he prayed urgently, "Lord, please heal her. Let her live." He stood up, lifting her with him, and elbowed away one of the guards that tried to take her away from him. Jibril's driver opened the car for him and he gently placed her in the back seat. He sat next to her, cradling her body, his heart pounding.

Her father sat in front of the car with the driver, groaning and muttering something about never knowing it would end like this.

Faizan tried to stay calm as they headed to the

hospital, but his heart was full of dread. If she died, he would blame himself forever. She would not have been shot if he hadn't come here to rescue her.

He couldn't hold his grief in any longer and said, roared, "Lord, please let her live!" He would not be able to continue to live if she died. He kept checking her pulse as they drove, praying she was still alive.

They finally got to the hospital, or rather, clinic, and Faizan carried her into the small place. From the look of the place, it didn't seem like they would have everything needed to treat her. He groaned and committed her to God's hands again.

A stretcher was brought and she was quickly rolled away to the theatre to try to save her life. Faizan sat on a bench overseeing the reception area and Karim Keita sat beside him. Faizan turned and glared at the man. There were few people he hated as much as he did this man who had virtually sold his daughter into a marriage she didn't want to be in. He said with angry loathing, "If she dies, I will kill you!"

The man looked away from Faizan and put his hand on his head. "I should never have given her away to the goat called Jibril, but I felt I had no choice."

Faizan looked at him in disdain. This wasn't a father. This was a monster. He did not deserve Zainah. He wanted to tell the man what he felt about him, but he held his tongue. He had said enough to him already.

The hours went by slowly. Faizan intermittently paced the hospital floor while Zainah's father dozed on and off. Faizan continued to pray silently for Zainah to recover. He held on tightly to the hope that God would answer his prayer and refused to entertain the thoughts of death trying to flood his mind.

Faizan was at the other end of the reception area when a woman, about Karim Keita's age, entered the clinic and walked up to Zainah's father. She wore an angry expression on her face. Faizan blinked as Khadija came in after her and went to her father as well. From where he stood, he saw them quarrelling, but he couldn't quite hear what they were saying.

Khadija saw him and headed his way. There were tears in her eyes. When she reached him, she said in a tortured voice, "What happened? A messenger from Jibril's house came to tell us that Zainah had been seriously injured."

Faizan told her everything. When he finished, he said, "I've been praying for her. The Lord will heal her."

Khadija stared angrily at her father. "That wicked man. I will never forgive him if…" she broke down without finishing her sentence.

"She won't die!" Faizan said, more for his sake than Khadija's. "She is strong. Most of all, she loves Jesus. He will heal her." He said it with as much conviction as he could muster, but in the depths of his heart, he was afraid. Very afraid.

Khadija said with a voice full of despair, "Your Jesus did not stop her from being forced into a marriage to a stranger or from being shot. Why would he heal her now?"

Faizan did not know what to say to her. He changed the subject and asked, "Is that your mother?" If it was Zainah's mother, he wanted to go and greet her and apologize for what had happened.

"My stepmother," Khadija said.

Faizan felt emotionally exhausted. He sank down to the floor and then shot back up when the doctor came into the reception area.

"Is she okay?" Faizan cried out, walking over to the doctor. Khadija and Zainah's father also walked over.

The white-haired doctor looked at Faizan and asked, "Are you her husband?"

Faizan nodded before he could think about the question.

"He's not!" the woman who was Zainah's stepmother said. "This is her father and I'm her stepmother. How is she? Can we see her now?"

The doctor looked down and Faizan's eyes widened in terror. No, Lord! Please! She cannot be dead.

"Doctor!" Khadija screamed, "Where is my sister? Is she dead?"

The doctor shook his head. "She isn't… but she is in a coma. She might not make it to tomorrow morning."

Faizan did not know what came over him. He rushed the man and grabbed him by the collar. "That is untrue! She will be fine!" The doctor stared at him sympathetically and Faizan sighed. He let go of the doctor and put his hand on his head. "There has to be something you can do to help her," he said to the doctor. He briefly glanced at Khadija who was weeping loudly and at Karim whose head was bowed, and then faced the doctor again. "She can't die. We are supposed to get married soon. Please tell me you can do something for her."

"I'm sorry," the doctor said. "We've done everything we can do for her. We can only pray." He looked at Zainah's father and stepmother, and then at Khadija. "I suggest you all go and see her now. It might be your last chance to see her alive." He smiled sadly at them and then beckoned for them to follow him.

Faizan wanted to grab the man by the collar again and let him know that Zainah would live, but he held himself in check. As he followed the man, fear threatened to suffocate him. Zainah's family followed. They walked slowly, as if their unhurried steps could delay the inevitable—seeing her, as the doctor said, for the last time.

SEVENTEEN

Faizan's heart flipped violently as he stepped into the room where Zainah lay. There were so many tubes stuck in her nose and mouth. He went to stand by her bedside and took her hand. She looked so peaceful and yet it felt as though she was not here. He felt like falling to the floor and weeping, but instead he lowered his head and kissed her forehead.

Her father came into the room with her step-mother and Khadija. He stood on the other side of her bed and looked down at her. "If only I had not given Zainah to Jibril."

Faizan felt like yelling at him and telling him to leave Zainah's bedside, but he had no right to. The man was her father, after all. Still, he could not resist saying, "You and that man did this to her. If she dies, I will hold you both responsible."

He glared at her father, but the man did not say anything. His eyes looked haunted and he looked broken.

Khadija came and stood beside Faizan. She

sighed and then looked down at Zainah. "We cannot lose her, Faizan. If your god answers prayers, he needs to answer yours right now. We cannot afford to lose her."

Faizan looked down at Zainah and then prayed again for a miracle.

Zainah's father and stepmother soon began to argue about something, and Faizan tuned their voices out. He touched Zainah's hair, and then couldn't hold back his tears. They fell like torrents down his cheeks. He touched his forehead to hers and then once again asked the Lord to give Zainah a miracle and heal her. He raised his head and looked at her. She looked as lifeless as she had before he prayed. Every hope he'd had that God would have mercy and heal her began to evaporate. He gave a deep sigh of pain. Suddenly, fear gripped him and he couldn't bear to be in the room anymore. He turned around and fled the room.

Racing out of the hospital, he went to the parking lot, lifted his face to the sky, and screamed. "Lord, help me. I can't do this."

It was already morning. Anytime now, the doctor would come to tell him that she was dead. He didn't have the strength to stay in the same room when she passed. By now, the plane that was supposed to take him and Zainah back to the U.S would have left. His heart felt sick with pain. He was stuck here, yet he would be without the woman he loved. He couldn't go back to his sisters in Rosefield for comfort. His life was simply over.

He held his head with his hands and felt like tearing his hair out. For a long time, he walked up and down the parking lot, and then he chided himself for staying away from her room. He had to go back into the hospital; to her.

But he remained where he was. Staying here in the parking lot was a way to postpone the inevitable. If he went back now and was told that she had passed, he would fall to pieces. At least staying here, he could pretend that she was just in the hospital, alive and well.

He began to pace the parking lot again, his face lifted to the sky. And then he took a deep breath and told himself that he needed to have courage. He strode into the hospital, his heart in his throat. The closer he got to the hospital building, the more afraid he became. He forced himself to enter the building and then ran into Khadija.

"Faizan!" Khadija exclaimed. "Where have you been? I have been looking for you!"

His heart began to thud. Shaking his head slowly, he said to her, "Please, Khadija, don't tell me she's gone! I don't want to hear it."

Khadija stared at him and then laughed. She suddenly grabbed him and hugged him tightly. "Zainah has woken up. That was why I was looking for you; to tell you that she is awake and she is asking for you." Khadija hugged him again.

Faizan's mouth dropped open and he raced to Zainah's room. He stopped in front of her door and hesitated, almost afraid that between the time Khadija came to find him and now, her condition would have changed for the worse again. He slowly opened the door and saw Zainah sitting up in her bed, talking to her father.

Never in his life had he felt happier and more grateful to the Lord than he did right now. He lifted up a quick prayer of thanksgiving and hurried into the room. Her eyes lit up when she saw him and he fell into her arms. He kissed her hair, her cheeks, and her lips. "I am so glad you are alive, Zainah," he said. He hugged her fiercely, his tears mingling with hers.

"You came for me, Faizan," she said, smiling through her tears.

Zainah's father touched his arm and Faizan looked up at the man. "I was just asking for Zainah's forgiveness before you came in," her father said. "My love of money nearly cost me my daughter's life." He looked down at Zainah and said, "When you were shot and I saw you lying on the ground, I knew it was all my fault. I knew I would blame myself for the rest of my life if you died. I'm so sorry, Zainah. Please forgive me."

Zainah smiled and nodded. "Because of Christ, I forgive you." She held out her hand and her father's eyes widened. He went to her and hugged her tightly.

Faizan watched them, joy flooding his heart and soul. Her stepmother also went and asked for her forgiveness. They stood talking with her for a few minutes, and then Zainah said, "Can I speak with Faizan alone?"

Her father and stepmother nodded and told her they would be outside the room. They left and Khadija came and kissed her. "I love you, sister," she said, running her fingers through Zainah's hair.

"I love you too, Khadija."

Khadija smiled and then left the room.

Faizan sat by her on the bed. "How do you feel?" he asked, gently brushing back her hair from her face.

"My back and chest feel sore, but I am not in too much pain." She chuckled. "I guess the pain medication the doctors have been pumping into me is working. Before you came, the doctor came here and declared that my being alive was a miracle. He also said that my wound is healing rapidly, and that he doesn't understand why." She grinned at Faizan. "Someone has been praying for me."

Faizan smiled back at her. "I've been begging and bargaining with the Lord since yesterday. I was blaming myself for putting your life in danger. If I had not come, you would not have been shot."

She reached out and caressed his cheeks. "I am glad you came to rescue me, Faizan. And there are worse things than being shot. I had started to pray that I would die in that man's house."

Faizan burned with rage. "Did he touch you?" he asked, trying to control his anger. "Because if he did…"

She shook her head. "No, but if you had not come when you did, he would have." She took his face in her hands, lowered his head, and hungrily kissed him.

He kissed her back, relishing the softness and taste of her lips.

And then she gasped and pulled away from him. She said, "I'm still a married woman, Faizan. Until we get my marriage dissolved, I don't think we should be kissing."

He wanted to argue and say the marriage was a farce, but he thought better of it. He gave a long sigh and looked longingly at her lips. She chuckled and then the expression on her face became somber. She fingered the spot on his shirt that was stained with her blood and said, "I'm glad you were able to leave America without being caught, Faizan, but it means you will not be allowed back."

He nodded and said, "I don't care. All that matters is that you are alive and we can be together."

Her brows knit together and she said worriedly, "But what about your sisters? You won't get to see them again. I know how much you love them. Oh, Faizan, I am…"

He put his finger on her lips and stopped her words. "Shh, all that doesn't matter right now. All you need to focus on is getting better. And then we can get married."

She frowned, "Talking about getting married, from my father's apology, I am sure he won't be against dissolving my marriage, but what about Jibril? He might not agree. I think he has something on my father. If we can't dissolve the marriage, we can't get married, Faizan."

"Stop worrying about all that, Zainah," Faizan said. "Let me do the worrying for both of us." He bent down and planted a kiss on her cheek and then he sighed. "I forgot you said we can't kiss until your marriage is dissolved." He searched her eyes. "I'll make Jibril agree to dissolve the marriage. In fact, he already said he wasn't interested anymore."

"Yes, but that was when you were holding a gun to his head, wasn't it?"

Talking about his gun, he had almost forgotten about the weapons. Somehow, in all the confusion yesterday, he'd still had the presence of mind to carry his backpack with him to the hospital. It was sitting on the chair beside the bed. He reached for it, unzipped it, and found the weapons inside.

She suddenly gasped again, and his heart jumped in fear. "What is it?" he asked her. "Are you in pain?"

"Leila! Faizan, you have to go get her!" Zainah covered her mouth with her hand. "Oh my God! I hope that Dauda hasn't touched her."

"I was going to get her after I got you, but the shooting changed my plans," Faizan said. "By now, her husband would have heard what happened and beefed up security at his house. The element of surprise is gone. I don't know if I can successfully get her out of the house on my own."

Zainah nodded. "That's true. It would be too dangerous for you. I think the only solution would be my father talking with Leila's husband and mine and convincing them to get end the marriages. But like I said before, I think they have something on my father. He won't be able to convince them easily, even if he pays back all the money they paid for my dowry."

"Perhaps he owes them money."

She nodded. "I have been suspecting that he does owe them money. He loves money, my father. That is probably why he has been acting so crazy."

"Plus, he doesn't know the Lord," Faizan said to her.

"Yes. That is the main thing." She winced and then shifted. When he asked if she was in pain, she smiled, but didn't answer. Instead, she said, "Getting my father to convince his friends to dissolve the marriages now is the only option we have. And it has to be done as soon as possible. Who knows what Leila is going through now?"

He stood and said, "Let me go talk to your father about it. You need to rest for now."

"No, I want to speak to him myself."

"Zainah, you just survived a harrowing experience. You shouldn't stress yourself in any way. Please, rest. I'll speak to your father."

"No, Faizan. He might not take you as seriously as he'll take me. He regrets what he did and the fact that I nearly died. He will listen to me. I need the marriage dissolved as soon as possible, especially because of Leila. I am so worried about her."

"I can threaten him again with my gun," he said, partly teasing and partly serious.

She shook her head and rolled her eyes. "I'm serious, Faizan."

Faizan looked at her for a full minute and saw she wasn't going to back down. He nodded and said, "Okay. I will go and get your father. But promise me that after you speak with him, you will rest."

She smiled. "I will. I promise."

He bent to kiss her and then straightened immediately. "Oh, Lord. I am not supposed to kiss you. I forgot again. I'm sorry."

"Go, Faizan," she said, smiling.

He nodded and walked to the door. He turned once more to look at her, overwhelmed with gratitude to God that she was alive. And then he walked out of the door to find her father.

EIGHTEEN

Leila's heart skipped a beat as someone barged into her room. She lifted her head from the pillow and then gave a huge sigh of relief when she saw it was Rekiya, Dauda's first wife.

Yesterday, he had told her without mincing words that she was going to spend the night with him. As she walked down the hallway of the big house, completely horrified at what was now her fate, some women, who she guessed were the other wives, had stared at her with looks of bitterness and hostility on their faces. Only Rekiya had been nice to her. The first wife had smiled sympathetically at her as they entered her new room together and said, "Dauda isn't a bad man. Don't worry about it. Everything will work out somehow."

As much as Leila appreciated her kind words, she knew they were empty. Nothing was going to work out. All she could look forward to from today was hell on earth.

She had stayed curled up on her bed, asking God to somehow perform a miracle and rescue her.

And it seemed he had done so. At least, partly. Dauda had not come into her room the night before, or this morning. Still, she knew she wasn't yet out of danger. She frowned at the frightened look on Rekiya's face, which only buttressed her fear. Sitting up on the bed, she asked, "What is it, Rekiya?"

The middle-aged woman answered, "Our husband had to rush out of the house yesterday when he got a message from his brother. None of the wives know where exactly he had gone. But he has just returned, and he told me why he left the house in a hurry yesterday."

Leila's heart raced wildly with fear. She didn't care why he had rushed out yesterday; only that Dauda was back, and that meant she would soon be summoned to his room.

". . . brother's new wife was shot . . ."

"What did you say?" Leila gasped. She looked intently at Rekiya, and said, "Did you just say that his brother's new wife was shot?"

Rekiya nodded. "A man claiming to be her fiancé came to Jibril's house yesterday wielding a gun. Apparently, there was some kind of shootout or something, and his new wife was shot by mistake."

Leila shot out of the bed and looked at Rekiya, fear wrapping itself around her. Her voice trembled as she asked, "Do you know if the new wife's name is Zainah?"

Rekiya's eyes grew round and then she covered her mouth. "I just remembered that both of you are friends. I should not have told you like this. I am so sorry."

Leila began to shake her head slowly. "No, no, Lord. Please, it can't be Zainah!" She searched Rekiya's eyes and asked, "Please tell me the truth. Is my friend alive?"

"I don't know. Dauda didn't say. The only thing he said was that we have to start packing."

"Why?" Leila asked.

"He said we will be leaving for Saudi Arabia soon. He seemed very frightened. I think he said something like the man who claimed to be your friend's fiancé was working for the American government. Dauda is afraid that the Americans will send men to come and raid the house, and that they may hurt him and us as well."

Leila sank to the floor and began to weep. It was all too much. First, she had been married off to a stranger, and now Zainah had been shot. And then, to add to it, her so-called husband wanted to pack and ship them all off to Saudi Arabia. If she went with him, she would never ever see Malik or Zainah again.

She cried out, "That is if Zainah is still alive. Oh, Lord Jesus! Please let her be alive!"

Rekiya stooped down and put her arm around Leila. "I'm really sorry."

Through her tears, Leila looked up at Rekiya and asked, "Can you find out from Dauda if my friend is still alive?"

"I will. Please try to be hopeful." She smiled sadly at Leila. "Dauda instructed me to tell all the wives to pack up their things now. We will probably leave tonight or tomorrow morning." She rubbed Leila's back comfortingly and then stood up and left the room.

Leila stood up and wiped the tears from her eyes.

I have to find a way out of here. I have to find a

way to get to the hospital to see Zainah.

She couldn't bear the thought of leaving without ever seeing her again.

Maybe if she asked Dauda, he might let her go and visit Zainah. Rekiya had told her several times that he was not a bad man. Even though she didn't want to see him, there was no other way to leave the house except with his permission.

With grim determination, she left her room to look for Dauda.

Lord, please make him agree to let me go and see Zainah, she prayed quietly as she made her way down the long hallway. She wasn't sure exactly where Dauda's room was, but she would open all the doors in the house and accept any abuse that came her way if she opened the wrong door, until she found him.

She reached a door that was slightly separate from the other rooms. Without knocking, she opened the door, praying this was his room. She walked in, her stomach churning. If he refused her request to go see Zainah, she didn't know what she would do.

His back was to her as she came into the room, but he swung around and his eyes widened in surprise when he saw her. He stared at her as she approached him, seemingly lost for words.

"Please," she began, "I heard my friend, Zainah, was shot yesterday. I would like to go and see her." Tears flooded her eyes. "I need to know that she is alive." Leila became frantic as she spoke. "She is my best friend. I have to see her!"

Dauda frowned deeply and Zainah knew he wasn't going to let her go. She sank to her knees.

She would crawl on the floor and plead with him if she had to. But she needed to see Zainah.

He looked down at her and then lifted her from the floor. He shook his head and said with surprising kindness, "I am sorry, Leila. But I can't let you leave the house as I think it's not totally safe for you to do so. However, I heard your friend is alive and on the way to recovery."

Leila suddenly felt like a huge weight had been lifted off her shoulders. At least Zainah was alive and well. She took a deep breath and gave God thanks silently. She looked up at Dauda and found him staring intently at her. His eyes looked kind. Maybe he would let her go to Zainah if she begged him again.

She said, "Thank you for telling me that. Still, I need to see my friend. She has always been there for me and I need to be there for her now."

She held her breath as he looked at her for a long moment. She could not read his thoughts, as he had an even expression on his face. Finally, he shook his head again. "If I let you go, you might try to run away. Besides, that man who claims to be your friend's fiancé is still in Nira. Who knows if he has an army somewhere?" He turned away from Leila and said in a firm voice. "I told Rekiya to instruct all the wives to pack up. That includes you, Leila. We will all leave the country tonight. Now, please leave me. I need to start packing my things and so do you."

Leila stared at his back in anger. She wanted to scream at him, to attack him, and tear out his beard, but she knew that would not go well for her. She pressed her lips together tightly, turned around, and walked out of the room. She strode back to her room and collapsed on the bed. After a while, she knelt on her bed and looked out of her window. Some guards were patrolling the house while some stood at the gate. It was as though Dauda had hired more men to watch the house overnight. There has to be a way out of this house, she said to herself.

But whatever that way was, she had to find it before nightfall.

*****

Leila watched as her suitcase, containing the clothes and toiletries that Rekiya had gotten for her on the day she moved into Dauda's house, was hauled into the trunk of the bus that would transport all the wives to the airport.

She had tried to find a way out of the house by checking all the windows to see if there was one she could climb out of. But all the windows had iron bars and the house was surrounded by guards. She had been forced to pack her things when Rekiya came to check on her and told her they would be leaving in a few hours. "In a few minutes, Dauda will be checking to see that each wife has all her things packed. You need to pack your things now," Rekiya had said.

Leila straightened her abaya, the one that Rekiya had given to her just this morning. It felt very unfamiliar and uncomfortable to have her entire body covered, but she had said nothing when it was given to her. She was not planning to wear it after today. Since she didn't find a way out of the house, she'd decided that the best place to make her escape was at the airport. With all the wives and the children traveling together, she hoped there would be enough commotion at the airport so she could easily sneak away without being seen.

One of the bodyguards watched closely as she entered the bus. She took an empty seat near the window and prayed silently to the Lord, asking that he would help her escape easily at the airport.

She looked around the bus. The other wives had already boarded. They were all dressed in abayas. She had not spoken to any of them yet and had only seen them when she'd arrived yesterday. She looked out the window at the white bus beside theirs and smiled at the children on the bus. There were about twelve or thirteen of them, as far as she could see. Their ages ranged between three and about seventeen years, and the older ones were in charge of taking care of the younger ones.

The bodyguard shut the door of the bus and an unsmiling driver entered the driver's seat and started the vehicle.

Leila looked out of the window again and then turned when someone came to sit beside her. She smiled at Rekiya, a genuine smile for the woman who had been so kind to her since she arrived at the house.

"You still look so worried," Rekiya said. "I heard that your friend is doing well so why are you still so upset?" She nodded. "You are worried about leaving this country for another, aren't you?"

Leila sighed and said, "I am worried about a lot of things. Even though my friend is doing well, I wish I could be with her now. I'm worried that I will never get to see her again. And also . . ."

"What?" Rekiya stared quizzically at her.

She pressed her lips tightly together. She had nearly blurted out that she was worried about Malik, the only man she'd ever loved. Thankfully, she'd managed to keep that piece of information to herself. Once she escaped at the airport, the first thing she planned to do was to go see Zainah. After that, she would do everything in her power to find Malik.

As the bus began to move, Rekiya regaled her with stories about Dauda and the other wives, and especially about the children's antics. Leila listened half-heartedly while she pictured herself making her escape.

"...the private plane."

Leila blinked as she focused once again on what Rekiya was saying. "Did you just say private plane?" she asked Rekiya.

The older woman tilted her head and her eyes studied Leila's. "You have not been listening to what I've been saying, have you? You also weren't listening when I was speaking with you in the morning. Are you always this absent-minded?"

Leila's heart raced with dread. She was afraid to ask Rekiya to clarify what she had said earlier. However, she went ahead and asked, "You said something about a private plane. Are you saying we are not going through customs or checking into our flight at the airport?"

"We usually don't when we travel with Dauda. He holds all our travel documents and all the checks are usually done before we travel." She stared curiously at Leila. "Why do you ask?"

Despair settled on her. She bit her lip, shook her

head, and said, "No reason. I was just curious." She looked away from Rekiya as tears flooded her eyes.

Oh Lord, Jesus, what am I going to do?

Without the commotion that going through customs and fully checking in a huge family would cause, she had little hope of ever escaping.

She felt Rekiya's hand on her shoulder but did not turn around this time. The tears poured down her cheeks, and she quickly wiped them away.

Rekiya said, "I know how you feel, Leila. You'll miss your loved ones here. I will, too. But Dauda is our husband and we have to follow him wherever he goes."

Leila wanted to scream at Rekiya and tell her she had no idea how she felt. She wanted to shout at the top of her voice that Dauda was not her husband, and that she did not have to go wherever he went. But she didn't. Doing that would only get her into trouble. The last thing she needed at this time was to attract undue attention to herself.

She kept staring out the window, praying that the Lord would show her another way for her to escape. She couldn't go with Dauda and all these women to Saudi Arabia. It would be the end of her life.

Rekiya droned on about their duties as wives in the house, but all Leila could think about was Malik. His face remained in her heart. If she couldn't find a way to escape, without a doubt she would never see him again. And she would never see her best friend again, either.

The pain and injustice of it all was too much to bear. Her emotions churned and roiled. Her head began to ache and she felt a panic attack coming on.

She shut her eyes and began to pray for peace. She also prayed for wisdom.

A minute later, she began to feel some sense of peace settle over her. She took a deep breath, and then opened her eyes. Rekiya had given up trying to have a conversation with her and was talking to one of the other wives in front of them.

Leila was grateful for that. She was tired of listening to Rekiya tell her that Dauda was a good man. For her, a good man loved and married only one woman. She could not, no, would not share any man she married with other women. She couldn't stay in this marriage. The Lord would not allow it. He would make a way for her to escape.

As they began to approach the small airport, her heart beat faster and faster.

They all got down from the bus when they reached the airport and Leila looked around her. The children walked in front of the wives, Dauda behind them. Three bodyguards surrounded the wives. One stood directly behind Leila.

They all entered the airport building together. Leila was dismayed when they went straight to the terminal, and then began to make their way to a small plane a short distance away.

She kept looking around, trying to see if there was a way of escape. But there wasn't. Even if she made a run for it now, she would be caught in seconds.

She continued to pray, holding on to a shred of hope that the Lord would rescue her soon. Lord, please, you have to help me. I can't go to Saudi Arabia as one of the many wives of this man.

It felt like an out-of-body experience as she

moved closer to the plane when the wife in front of her started to board. She hesitated for a minute and turned around. Rekiya was behind her. She smiled encouragingly and said, "Go on, Leila."

Leila could not move. She stood frozen, contemplating her fate. One of the bodyguards walked up to her and stared at her. He turned to Rekiya and asked, "Is there a problem?"

Rekiya quickly shook her head and said, "No, there is no problem." She looked pointedly at Leila. "Is there a problem, Leila?"

Leila looked at her and realized that Rekiya was blinking rapidly, clearly trying to tell her with her eyes that she should enter the plane or something unpleasant would happen. Leila considered screaming at the top of her lungs and letting anyone around know that she was being taken out of the country unwillingly, but there was really no one around who would listen to her. She knew without a doubt that no one would help her. She would enter this plane on her own accord or be bundled in. In this place, and with this man, she had no will of her own. She was her husband's prisoner now.

"Enter," the bodyguard said firmly to her. "You are holding others up from entering the plane."

She felt sick to her stomach as she turned around and began to board the plane. And then she knew she couldn't do it. She turned around again and screamed, "They are taking me on the plane by force! I don't want to go!"

She looked at Rekiya. Her eyes had grown as wide as saucers. The bodyguard was staring at her as though she was nothing but a child throwing a tantrum. She looked around as she screamed again.

Perhaps the airport security would come and help her. It was unlikely, she knew, but not impossible.

Her heart soared with hope as a man in uniform headed their way. Dauda also walked up to her and narrowed his eyes. "What is the meaning of this, Leila? You are preventing everyone behind you from entering the plane."

She scowled at him and then looked at the man in uniform. He reached them and asked Dauda what was wrong. She frowned, totally indignant. He hadn't even looked at her once. She was the one who had been screaming, but he acted as though she was not even present.

"Is everything okay around here?" The airport security guy asked.

"No, no it is not!" Leila shouted. She was surprised at herself. She had never done something like this, but she was desperate.

The security guy glanced at her and then back at Dauda. He asked again if there was a problem.

"There is no problem," Dauda said. "It's just a personal thing. My wife is angry with me and that is why she is screaming. I'll handle it."

Leila watched in anger and frustration as Dauda handed the man some money and he nodded. The man smiled at Dauda and then left. She should have known better than to bother. Now, from the way Dauda stared at her, she knew she would pay for what she had done somehow.

Dauda went to the back of the line again and the bodyguard said to Leila once more, "Enter the plane."

Leila felt completely numb and hopeless as she boarded the plane. Inside, she found an empty seat and sat on it. She bit her lip as Dauda came and sat beside her. He didn't look at her, but she could guess what he was thinking. He was letting her know that she now belonged to him forever and that there was no way of escape.

She turned from him and prayed loud enough for him to hear, "Lord, Jesus, please help me!" She didn't care what trouble she got into by praying loudly in the Lord's name. For all purposes, she was already in the deepest trouble she could ever be.

"You might want to say your prayers silently, especially as we are headed to Saudi. It will not go well for you there if you pray like that."

She turned away from him and kept praying, silently this time. As long as the plane had not taken off, there was still hope for a miraculous rescue.

The plane soon began to glide on the runway, and Leila's heart thudded. And then it took off.

For some minutes, she sat in disbelief. She was leaving behind everything and everyone she loved for a future that was bound to not end well. Not when she was a Christian heading for a Muslim country. Not when she was a woman who would fight the marriage that had been forcefully imposed on her. She would either end up dead soon or be a prisoner.

She thought about the women's camp, the daily prayers she had taken for granted, the women as they went about singing praise songs loudly as they did their chores. She would never get to do that again. Not until she got to heaven, which might be very soon. Zainah's face appeared in her mind. And then the tears poured down as Malik's did. She bent down her head and wept silently for the love she had lost forever.

NINETEEN

Zainah took Faizan's hand and smiled as she looked into his eyes. They were in the prayer tent, at the women's camp. Their guests were all the inhabitants of the camp. After her marriage had been dissolved, she and Faizan had mourned—she for Leila, and he for his sisters who he'd left behind in Rosefield. Since they couldn't get married in Rosefield where his beloved sisters were, they had decided to go to the other place where there were people who truly loved them. They had chosen to come to the women's camp to get married.

Faizan smiled back at her and then turned to look at Miriam, who was officiating their marriage. An overwhelming joy flooded her heart as she watched Faizan and then she grew slightly glum. She would finally be married to the man she loved more than life, but her best friend was not here to witness this happy day with her.

She had been shocked when she heard that Dauda had moved his entire family to Saudi Arabia three weeks ago, taking Leila along with him.

Since then, she had prayed constantly for her best friend, asking the Lord to comfort and be with her, and that somehow, He would help Leila find a way out of Saudi Arabia again.

Tears filled Zainah's eyes as she repeated her marriage vows after Miriam. As she did, she looked into Faizan's glowing eyes and her heart soared with joy once more, and her despair fled. She continued to speak her vows, her eyes planted solely on Faizan's, a huge smile on her face. After she finished saying her vows, Faizan began to say his. Halfway through, his voice choked with emotion and he paused.

Zainah squeezed his hand and smiled encouragingly at him.

"I love you," he whispered to her. He continued to repeat the vows after Miriam. When he finished, the women and children behind them cheered.

"And now, by the powers vested in me by God, before these witnesses, I now declare you husband and wife." Miriam turned to Faizan and smiled, "You may kiss your bride."

Zainah heart pounded with excitement and ecstasy as Faizan lifted her veil and kissed her. He drew back again, and Miriam said, "Everyone, I now present to you the newest couple in town, "Mr. and Mrs. Gardener."

Zainah held Faizan's hand as they both turned to face the crowd in the tent. She smiled at the familiar faces of the women she'd lived with for years. She saw, on many of their faces, hope and happiness, and she knew they were not only happy for her, but also hopeful that if she had found love and an opportunity to start a family of her own right in this place where there were no men to marry, they could too one day.

Zainah gasped as Faizan swept her off her feet and began to carry her down the aisle of the prayer tent. All the women began to clap and cheer for them. The children laughed and danced around the tent.

Outside, Zainah posed for photographs with Faizan. After the photograph with just her and her groom, they took another one with her close friends at the camp. She began to feel slightly gloomy again, recalling that Leila wasn't here, and then she pushed the gloom away.

She and Faizan took another round of photographs with more women in the camp and then Fatima came and stood beside her and Faizan for a photograph with them. Zainah smiled at her. She was the one who had helped Zainah get the photographer and a few other things for the wedding, including the simple white dress she wore as her wedding gown.

Fatima whispered to her, "When you were searching for your Faizan months ago, I told you everything would work out eventually."

Zainah smiled in appreciation. "Yes, you did."

After the photographer finished taking the pictures, Fatima said to Zainah and Faizan, "You two are so in love with each other. You will both have a great wedding night."

"Fatima!" Zainah exclaimed and chuckled with embarrassment.

Faizan laughed. He held Zainah tightly to himself and said, "Oh, we definitely will. There is no doubt about it."

Zainah felt a warm sensation in her belly and stared into Faizan's eyes. She felt overwhelmed with love for him and leaned in to kiss him. The camera flashed just then, and she turned.

"I had to capture that," the photographer said. "The moment was just too beautiful to pass up."

She and Faizan took more photographs, some with only the children. After the photographs, they went back into the prayer tent for the reception. The women had already moved around some of the rug and pillows. Zainah sat on the richly embroidered pillow that the women had kept for her and Faizan on top of a delicately woven red rug.

The wedding was so different and much simpler than the one she and Faizan's sisters had planned in Rosefield. But somehow, this seemed a little more special. Maybe because all the women she loved were here. Except for her best friend. The familiar sadness settled on her, and she sighed.

Faizan sat beside her on an identical pillow and took her hand. He kissed it and said, "It will work out somehow, Zainah. The Lord is with Leila no matter where she is."

Binta, talkative as usual, had been chosen to be the MC of the occasion and as she came out to the front, she began to talk about Zainah and Faizan. How he had fallen from the sky and now was Zainah's husband. Everyone laughed when she said, "Who says good husbands don't fall from the sky?"

Zainah smiled at Faizan and shifted closer to him. "I can't believe I am finally your wife," she said.

"And I can't believe that I am now your husband," he said softly.

The wedding went on with the women and children providing the music. They ate the food that all the women in the camp had cooked, simple but hearty dishes. After they ate, Faizan took Zainah's hand and went to the middle of the tent. Someone raised a song of praise, and he and Zainah held each other tightly and danced. After that, the children sang while everyone came out and danced round the tent.

The wedding went late into the night with everyone dancing and singing. They all provided the music for the wedding. The songs were sometimes sung off-key, but Zainah thought it was funny.

At about two in the morning, Faizan took Zainah's hand and led her out of the tent. Zainah smiled as they walked away, hearing the joyful singing and laughter of the women still celebrating her wedding.

They both entered the tent that Zainah had shared with Leila and a few other women, but which would now be where she and Faizan would begin their lives together as husband and wife. The women had kindly decorated it with an abundance of bright colored rugs and mats, and embroidered pillows with gold tassels.

Faizan said, "Our new home, Zainah. It's nowhere like the one we were supposed to live in Rosefield, but it's warm and cozy, and we have great neighbors." Her heart drummed with excitement as he pulled her into his arms and kissed her passionately. He finally drew back and said, "I love you so much, Mrs. Gardner." He kissed her again.

When he drew back this time, she felt slightly sad. Because of her, he would never be able to go back to the United States and see his sisters. "I'm so sorry that your sisters aren't here for our wedding, Faizan. I know you will miss them, but I will try my best to make up for it." She kissed him slowly and then pulled back again.

He smiled at her and his eyes swept over her, causing her to tremble. "I like where this is going," he said. And then he sobered. He cupped her face with his hands and said, "I will miss my sisters and the life I had in Rosefield, but nothing can trade the joy I feel now that I am finally married to you. You bring me so much joy, Zainah. I love my sisters, but you are my family now. You are enough."

She had silently feared he would soon come to resent her for taking him away from his family and the life he had in the United States. But now, his words melted away her guilt. "And you are enough for me, too," she said to him.

He hugged her tightly and then twirled her around. She squealed in delight when he dipped her and then held her close. They began to dance to the music floating in from the wedding tent, and Zainah knew that her life with Faizan would always be like this: it would be a wonderful dance.

A LOOK AT: LOVE WILL PREVAIL

When Audrey decides she's ready to have a child, she expects husband Ken to be thrilled by the news. What comes next is more of a slap to the face. Audrey hopes that a trip to visit Sienna and Brian's orphanage, along with their newborn Ethan, might offer some much-needed inspiration.

Across the sea, Leila struggles through harrowing circumstances to return to her beloved, Malik. But even if God rewards her with the deepest desire of her heart, she could be chasing an impossible dream.

Faizan has embraced married life with wife Zainiah, and holds onto his dream of one day returning them to the US. Faizan's ex, Lauren, has had less fortune in love. After a string of bad dates, Lauren resorts to a dating app to find a good man who's ready to take a wife. God answers her prayers, but her online love interest is far from the virtuous soulmate she expected.

COMING APRIL 2020

ABOUT THE AUTHOR

Like the characters in her stories, Emma Easter juggles a range of identities.

In the low-income community where she works, Easter is known as a family medicine physician who treats patients of all ages and backgrounds.

College friends see her as an accomplished musician, having studied and mastered five classical instruments—but behind closed doors, she's just as comfortable rocking an air guitar to Creed. And when she isn't giving her heart, soul, and sanity to her three young children she's indulging in her most secret identity of all: meeting new characters, crafting fresh plots, and exploring every corner of her imagination.

Across all these different roles, one cohesive thread has tied everything together: her faith and love of Jesus Christ.

Find more great titles by Emma Easter and Christian Kindle News at https://christiankindle-news.com/our-authors/emma-easter/

www.ingramcontent.com/pod-product-compliance
Lightning Source LLC
Chambersburg PA
CBHW030652260626
47157CB00007B/2617